STRANGER AT SUNSET

ALSO BY EDEN BAYLEE

Anthologies
Fall into Winter
Spring into Summer
Hot Flash

Novellas and Short Stories
Seduced by the Blues
Act Three
The Norwegian
The Austrian and the Asian
A Season for Everything
Unlocking the Mystery
Summer Solstice
The Lottery
Seeking Sexy Sadie

STRANGER AT SUNSET

a novel

EDEN BAYLEE

lowercase publishing

Stranger at Sunset

Copyright 2014 Eden Baylee

All rights reserved. No part of this book may be used or reproduced by any means, graphic, electronic, or mechanical without the written permission of the author except in the case of brief quotations embodied in critical articles and reviews.

This book is a work of fiction. Names, characters, businesses, organizations, places, events, and incidents are either the product of the author's imagination or are used fictitiously. Any resemblance to actual persons, living or dead, is entirely coincidental.

For more information, contact eden.baylee@rogers.com

Cover design and interior by JB Graphics
www.john-beadle.com

Edited by Annetta Ribken
www.annettaribken.com

ISBN-13: 978-1500927288
ISBN-10: 1500927287
eISBN: 978-0991785728

For John

FROM THE AUTHOR

Stranger at Sunset is a departure from a genre I've become known for—literary erotica. It's also my first novel. Those who have read my novellas and flash fiction know that characters drive my stories. As much as I enjoy telling a good tale, I love writing about the motivations and actions of people. For me, a story exists because people make it happen. People do not exist because of a story.

A trip to Jamaica in 2013 following Hurricane Sandy inspired *Stranger at Sunset*. It is the first in a series I envision will include at least three books, if not more. It all depends on how much the characters have to say. Lucky for me, my protagonist, Kate Hampton has a lot to say. As with all my female characters, she is a strong, intelligent woman. But she is much more than that. She is complicated and passionate, and she is unpredictable. It has been a pleasure to discover her, and her story is just beginning.

With a natural curiosity for people and a fondness for psychology, penning a mystery with a psychological bent seemed the ideal choice for me. I invite you to take a trip with me to Jamaica in *Stranger at Sunset*. It'll be a vacation like you've never experienced.

CONTENTS

PROLOGUE 1

BEFORE THE TRIP 5

DAY ONE
Arrival 20
The Owners 29
Friends 33

DAY TWO
At the Airport 38
Affinity for Water 46
Lunch 51
Zen Garden 66
For Men Only 72
Alpha Beta 80

DAY THREE
Meditation 84
Bitten 92
Dinner Guests 95
Nightcap 106

DAY FOUR
Incompatible 114
The Review 121
At the Beach 126
Linked Destinies 135
A Friendly Game 140
All Work and No Play 145
Temperature Check 151

DAY FIVE
Morning Swim   158
Early Wake-Up Call   160
Scented Resentment   164
Consequences   169
Bar Banter   176
Cleanup   184
Playing Doctor   189

DAY SIX
A Brand New Day   194
The Visitor   198
Taking Care of Business   204
Something's Cooking   216
Vacation Cut Short   220
Missing   227
Disposal   235
Calling the Police   238

DAY SEVEN
In Deep Trouble   241
Found   248
Identification   253
Interrogation   260
Cooked   272
Levity and Fiction   278
Secrets   286

DAY EIGHT
Karma   298
The General   303

DAY NINE
Good-bye   308

EPILOGUE   310

NEXT BOOK   325

ABOUT THE AUTHOR   333

"Unexpressed emotions will never die. They are buried alive and will come forth later in uglier ways."

— *Sigmund Freud*

PROLOGUE

The body plummeted two and a half stories into the sea. It bobbed between crests before foamy waves swept in and yanked it under the surface. The tide rushed out dragging its new possession deep into the ocean's dark belly. Swells curled and collapsed against the shore. The evening breeze whistled an eerie tune.

Despite how tightly his fingers gripped the large barrels, the binoculars trembled in the man's hands. He now wished he had bought the more powerful Porro-prism model. This less expensive design darkened the image, especially against a pale orange sky reflecting the chopped glass of the water. While adjusting the diopter ring behind his right eyepiece, he bit down on his lower lip.

A silhouette met his lens, haloed by the glow of the setting sun. With his breath thickening the atmosphere, he pressed the eyepiece harder against his face to stop from shaking.

The woman stood naked with her hair pinned up, loose strands trailing down the nape of her slender neck. Her palms rested on the metal railing of the balcony. As she stared out at the churning sea, he zoomed in on her face, then moved his binoculars downward to her breasts, lingering there longer than he should have. Slowly, he lowered his gaze to her flat stomach. Firm thighs extended off the arc of round buttocks. A dancer's body—willowy and muscular, but not too muscular, she was beauty and grace, and yet, what she just did …

A hint of dark pubic hair blurred past his lens. While he re-calibrated the magnification, she drifted out of focus. When he brought her back in view, her contemplative mood had changed. She moved a chair to the corner of the terrace. Gathering up a pile of bed sheets, she crossed the threshold into the room and scurried out of view.

He dared not avert his eyes. The light was fading fast, and night would soon fall upon the villa like a magician's cape. With his elbows pressed to his sides, he loosened his grip on the binoculars and tried to flex his aching fingers.

She had to come back, right?

The doors leading to the patio were still wide open. Secluded in his dark corner of the island, he spied the room as if ogling a dollhouse with its front wall sheared off, scaled down to about the same size too.

The naked woman strolled back into his field of vision as a cramp sneaked up on him. A painful twitch stabbed his wrist, reminded him of old wounds. He dropped the binoculars secured by a strap around his neck to shake out both his hands. By the time he brought the lens to his face again, she had disappeared, no … wait, she popped up from behind the bed carrying two pillows. With an unhurried pace, she stepped out on the balcony and propped the cushions on the chair, even fluffed them before re-entering the suite. She closed the wooden French doors behind her.

The light in her room replaced the sun's blush, a poor substitute given a set of floor-to-ceiling jalousies bracketed his view. He waited to see what she would do next. His breathing deafened his ears as if he were wheezing through a mask; adrenaline pumped in his veins. She moved in front of the window facing him. With hands on her hips, legs spread apart, she stood full frontal and stared straight at him. He shrank back and jostled her image.

Could she see him?

With his naked eye, he peeked in her direction. Nothing had changed. Motionless, she continued to stand in position. Unable to resist, he gathered his wits and raised the binoculars once again, adjusted the focus ring on her legs—those legs that seemed to go on forever.

Horizontal louvers interrupted his view of her body as he slanted the lens upward, advancing an inch at a time. He paused at her navel, swallowed hard, paused again when his lens reached her breasts.

Blood pumped in his ears as he moved up the curves of her collarbone to her long neck. When he met her eyes, he expelled a bellyful of relief. She wasn't looking at him; she was looking through him. Her almond-shaped eyes trapped him in irrational fear of discovery.

Like a leech, he clung to her to draw out her secrets, imagined the pulse at her neck racing, wondered how it would feel to pull the pins from her hair, to touch her porcelain skin. Only a tiny squint betrayed her otherwise stoic expression.

As if she could read his mind, she turned away and broke the spell. When she faced him again, the mischief in her eyes had disappeared. She cranked the window handle, tilting the slats in unison against one another, narrowing his view with each turn of her wrist. He held his breath with one last image of her—a lowering of her chin before the light vanished from the room.

A shiver crawled up his spine despite the warm night. He lifted the strap of the binoculars from his neck and placed the heavy lens on a table beside him. The glowing numbers on his Luminox watch showed it was not yet half past six. The dusky sky would fade to purple and then to black within minutes. Without thinking, he lit up a cigarette, watched the smoke curl around itself as it rose into the air. A chorus of crickets joined an orchestra of noisy night critters. From some deep crevice of his mind, he recalled a myth about crickets, their nocturnal mating call a foreshadowing of death. He knew the details of the lore once but was in no mood to scrape his numbed memory for it now. The irony, however, was not lost on him.

As he listened to the sounds of the night, he took another puff and butted out. He needed to quit; smoking no longer calmed his nerves. From his back pocket, he pulled out a device and tapped one of several pre-programmed numbers.

With the cell phone pressed to his ear, he waited for an answer.

BEFORE THE TRIP

The ding of an incoming e-mail diverted Kate Hampton's attention away from her reading. The clock in the upper right corner of her laptop's screen read 11:09 p.m. She massaged her temples and bookmarked the page of the online medical journal.

Outside, powdery flecks flew by the window of her apartment in the Lower East Side, confirming a forecast that called for cooler temperatures by tomorrow morning. Another storm was on its way to blanket New York City in six more inches of snow.

Kate loosened the hair from her bun and shook it out. Long, dark tresses fell below her shoulders in a tousle. Almost time to call it a night.

With a few clicks, she toggled to her e-mail program where several unread messages filled her inbox. A quick note sent to her colleague, Jack, confirmed a lunch date for next week. She trashed the remainder picked up by her spam filter. Kate stifled a yawn and was about to close down when a new message popped on screen.

The subject line read: Look forward to seeing you/

Advice needed

Kate opened a greeting from Anna Pearson, who co-owned Sunset Villa Estate in Jamaica with her husband, Nolan. The note was a nice touch before Kate's trip in less than a month's time, only … this was more than a *Happy Holidays* wish.

Anna wrote:

> Kate, I need your professional opinion.
>
> As you may know, the resort was hit by Hurricane Sandy, and we had to cancel year-end reservations to repair damages. We should be fine by the time you arrive in January. The bigger issue concerns a bad review we received from Matthew Kane of *Travel in Style* magazine. His critical remarks in the summer issue precipitated a landslide of cancelations.
>
> Nolan and I were not here when he stayed at the villa, but the staff swore he never brought his issues to them. A month later, his scathing review hit the newsstands. Given its negative impact on the resort, we invited Mr. Kane back at no expense to him or his magazine for a week's stay. We are hoping he will retract his review or re-evaluate his complaints and write a second,

more favorable review. He hasn't accepted our invitation as yet. If he comes, it will be during the same week you are here.

Did we make a mistake by inviting him back?

Kate stumbled upon Sunset Villa two years before she ever met Anna and Nolan. At the time, the estate belonged to an elderly British couple who lived on the property. In a serendipitous twist of fate, the Pearsons acquired the resort. Their management of the villa impressed Kate enough to return every year since they bought it.

Now her favorite travel destination was at the mercy of one man's review? How bad could it be?

She opened the attached link in the e-mail, which took her to the online version of the magazine and Matthew Kane's review.

Kate took deep breaths. As she moused down the page, the nasty words limped off the screen and exploded like landmines in her head. She had read similar words before. Unpleasant … hurtful … but when? Where? An eerie sense of déjà vu crawled over her skin.

"No," she heard herself say. "No!" Why was this happening to her again?

A tingling sensation at the top of her scalp traveled downward, like cockroaches inching their way toward her feet. Unable to prevent fragments of memories from bubbling to the surface, she dug her nails into her temples.

The associated feelings of despair flooded back as well. She scratched her scalp hard to stop the prickling on her body. Her gasps caught in her throat, echoed in her ears. Dropping to the floor, Kate fought for calm.

She folded her legs in a lotus position and relaxed her arms, resting her hands near the soles of her feet. With eyes tightly shut, tears squeezed down her cheeks. An episode such as this had not happened in months. "Relax," she consoled herself. "Just relax."

Kate visualized compartmentalizing the memory in its own maximum-security cell. The solid, steel door banged shut. Once locked, she flung the only key into open waters. It floated for a short time until gravity pulled it under, twisting, spiraling, turning end over end, finally resting on the murky ocean floor.

The creepiness on her skin subsided as the unwanted memory slithered back into a dark corner of her brain. Her breathing slowed. Kate remained on the floor, her mind a dizzying swirl of thoughts transporting her back in time.

* * *

Kate was seventeen when Dr. Sidney Boyd, a renowned neurobiologist from the University of California informed her of her "gift."

"You have what is called eidetic memory, young lady." He beamed with excitement when he told her. "It's commonly referred to as total recall or photographic memory. Less than three percent of the world's population is known to have it."

Dr. Boyd led a team of scientists to find subjects who considered themselves with above-average memories. Kate always knew she had a quirky brain, a freakish memory for facts, so she enrolled in the yearlong study to earn extra money while putting herself through school. A sample of thirty-five participants whittled to seven after preliminary tests. In less than a month, Kate became their star subject.

"How your brain works is truly remarkable, Kate. You're not just limited to visual cues. You have an incredible memory for all the senses. We can't possibly grasp the implications of our findings in such a short time," Dr. Boyd said.

A year in the study may have been a short time for him, but it dragged for Kate. She tired of each test successfully completed, which only spurred the ambitious researchers to come up with more challenging experiments for her.

Oftentimes, painful memories arose, which drained her energy for days. It was Dr. Boyd who taught her to file away these memories by visualizing them as prisoners. Throwing away the key was an essential part of locking up the memory. Early on, when Kate had one of her episodes, she imagined dropping the key down a sewer or burning it in a fire pit. For reasons unknown to her, the memories returned. Only after she envisioned tossing the key into the ocean did they stay away. For good, she hoped.

In time, she learned to segregate bad memories but

had no control over what could spark them to resurface. Comparable to dark family secrets, they sat in her brain, hiding. For Kate, her gift was a curse.

Near the end of her term, Dr. Boyd pleaded with her to continue in the study for another year. "There is more to learn from you, Kate, much more. The clues you've provided to what the brain is capable of is nothing short of staggering. I want to continue the study with you and no one else. Let me see what I can negotiate to make it worth your while."

"It's not the money," she said.

"What is it then?"

Over the year, headaches and nightmares had wreaked havoc on her life. Kate was confident they would disappear once she left the study, so she chose not to disclose the details to Dr. Boyd. He would only put her through more tests. "The experiments have opened doors to memories I'd sooner forget," she said, expecting him to offer sympathy.

"Do you know the odds of finding someone like you again in this lifetime?" With his hands on her shoulders, he looked at her in a fatherly manner. "Do it for science, Kate."

Her thoughts crystallized at that moment. She was merely a lab rat to him. "I'm sorry, Dr. Boyd, but science is not my responsibility."

* * *

Dark brown eyes clicked open. Kate rose from the cold

floor and brushed the wetness from her face. Matthew Kane's article stared back at her from the computer screen, just long enough for her to hit the delete button.

Although his was the only one-star review for Sunset Villa on a popular online travel forum, he'd received numerous votes for it. These votes stuck his review to the top of the site, which meant it was the first one seen by a potential vacationer.

Based on what he wrote, Kate attributed several traits to him, a brain exercise she did for almost everyone she met. The simple game of word association drew on the first few letters of the person's name, matching them with her first impressions of their character. Her intuition was seldom wrong.

In Matthew's case, she chose the words: M: maladjusted; A: awkward; TT: tantrum-thrower.

Kate reached for the phone and grimaced at the sight of several nails tinged crimson with blood and ripped-out hair.

Damn it.

She had to stop mutilating herself every time she had an episode. Balling both hands, she held them against her lips and took deep breaths. Her head throbbed where she had torn into her scalp.

Matthew Kane, a maladjusted, awkward, tantrum-thrower created such rage inside her.

But why?

* * *

A week later

An incoming message from Dr. Jack Campbell read: *I'm running late, see you in fifteen.*

Kate caught the eye of the waiter who promptly sashayed his way to the table.

"I'd like two glasses of your 2010 Caymus Cabernet," she said.

"Of course."

"Would you send some bread too, please?"

"Right away." The young man zigzagged between tables toward the bar.

Seated at the corner table of their favorite lunch haunt, Kate texted back her date. Not yet noon, and the popular SoHo eatery was already packed. Out of the corner of her eye, Kate saw a female server approach the table with a basket and a steel jug.

As the young woman set the bread on the table, Kate said, "You're Samantha Chapman, aren't you?"

The petite twenty-something cocked her head. "That's right. I'm sorry, and you are …?"

"Kate Hampton. I attended your mother's birthday party at your home last year."

Recognition lit up the girl's face. "Oh yes … Of course, Dr. Hampton, isn't it? How are you?"

"I'm well, thank you." Kate smiled. "When did you start working here?"

"Just last week." She filled Kate's water glass.

"Are you still studying Art History at NYU?"

The server's cheeks colored. "You have a great memory."

Kate dismissed the compliment. "How is your mom?"

Samantha scanned the tables near her and dropped her eyes. "Not well, I'm afraid. It's been a rough couple of months since Dad left."

"I'm so sorry to hear." Kate stroked her chin. "I had no idea."

As if afraid to be overheard, Samantha hunched lower. "Mom found out he was having an affair with one of his TAs. I'm so angry with him."

"Oh no." Kate feigned an expression of surprise.

"It might be good for her to talk to you. She's depressed, and …" Her eyes drifted upward.

Footsteps drew near as someone brushed the back of Kate's chair. "Sorry, I'm late." A man swaggered by her as if he had just stepped off the cover of a romance novel.

Kate offered him a slow nod as he took a seat across from her. "I ordered a glass of wine for you," she said.

"Good. I need it." He placed his bag on the floor and scraped his chair out from under the table, settling his tall frame into the seat.

Samantha poured water in the man's glass and ogled him as if she were appraising a rare painting.

"Have your mother call me if she wants to talk." Kate handed a business card to the server. "I'm here over the holidays and my home number's on the back."

"I'll tell her to call you … and thank you." Samantha nodded and walked off with her water pitcher.

Jack arched an eyebrow. "Friend of yours?"

Kate sighed, shook her head. "An acquaintance more than a friend. Her mother, Melanie Chapman, is a professor at Columbia—Genetics, brilliant woman. Unfortunately, she married someone less than stellar."

"You know the guy?" Jack loosened his tie and unbuttoned the top shirt button.

"No, I met him at Melanie's fiftieth birthday party, disliked him immediately." Her voice shifted from lighthearted to grim.

Jack picked a roll from the basket and broke it in half. "Uh oh ... what three words did you attribute to him?"

"*Lecherous, egotistical*, and *shortsighted*," Kate said with a hard edge.

"Hmm ... lecherous, egotistical, shortsighted." Jack squinted, his pupils moved up to the left. "His name was Les?"

"Lester, actually." Kate flattened her lips. "He had his eyes on my cleavage the entire time we spoke, which was less than a minute. I'm not sure he grasped that I didn't approve of his wandering eye at his own wife's party."

"Men. Not everyone can be perfect like me." Jack exposed straight rows of teeth against tanned skin.

"Perfect ..." Kate tilted her head and fidgeted with her knife, "... but tardy." With a twisted smile, she looked back at him.

"My apologies." He folded his hands over his heart and gave his best *please forgive me* look. "Another crying patient, happens a lot this time of year, hard to ask her to leave when she's sobbing."

Kate exhaled a loud breath and picked up her water glass. "You need to cut them off before it gets to that point. You're too soft, Jack."

"Logical but not always realistic." The corners of Jack's full lips drooped and deepened the lines in his forehead. "This one needs a strong woman's voice, something I don't have, obviously." When the waiter brought their wine, Jack leaned back in his chair.

Kate waited for the server to leave before grinning at Jack. "Are you afraid another female patient will fall in love with you?"

"Very funny, Kate." Jack parodied frustration with a twisted mouth.

Of course, she was joking. She met Jack for lunch at least once a month. A few months ago, he had confided that several of his female patients displayed flirtatious behavior toward him. Suspecting erotic transference, she tried to help him limit his risk. Kate trusted Jack as an ethical therapist, but beyond that, she knew he didn't care for women, not in the biblical sense anyway.

"Sorry Jack, I couldn't resist." She offered a sweet smile.

"I only let you tease me because I love you Kate. Here's to another blizzard headed our way ... and to Christmas too." He raised his wine glass and toasted her.

"To a White Christmas, and I can't wait to get the hell away from it." Kate puckered her lips and took a drink—blackberry with a hint of dark chocolate. *Perfect.*

"Good choice." Jack nodded his approval and took

another sip. "Back to my patient, you do realize emotions can't be turned on and off like a faucet."

"Of course," she said, her tone serious. "Build in a buffer of fifteen minutes before the session ends if you suspect crying to happen."

A muscle clenched in Jack's well-defined jaw. "Not so easy, you know psychiatry isn't filtered through a prism of pure logic."

"Works for me."

He picked up his glass and tipped it toward her. "You don't fool me, Kate. You have a soft spot too."

A tinge of humor lifted her lips. "Yes, but my soft spot closed up thirty-four years ago." She tapped the top of her head and gave him a toothy smile. "Nice tan, by the way. Was it hot in Vegas?"

Jack pointed his chin. "All right, keep your ice queen status if you like." He swallowed more wine. "Yes, damn hot in Vegas, though nothing like the summer months. Still, anywhere warmer than here is great. Even Chris had a good time, and he's not much for the heat."

"Sounds like you both enjoyed yourselves." With menu in hand, Kate scanned the day's lunch specials.

"I'll bet you can't wait for Jamaica." Jack waved over the waiter. "You go to the same place every year, right?"

"Yes, though this year will be intriguing." She raised an eyebrow at him from behind her menu.

"Oh?"

The waiter came by and took their orders before Kate proceeded to tell Jack about Anna's e-mail.

"So this Matthew Kane has accepted the trip?"

"Yes, he'll be there during my week."

"Hmm …" Jack rolled his eyes. "And you tagged him as a maladjusted, awkward, tantrum-thrower, bet you can't wait to meet him."

Kate pursed her lips. "The Pearsons always have an interesting mix of people, but I have a bad feeling about this guy."

Jack took another piece of bread. "But how can you help?"

"I was thinking about that." Kate rested her forearms on the table. "Let me run this by you, and tell me if I'm out to lunch … no pun intended of course."

Jack snorted and spread butter on his roll. "Shoot."

"It has to do with the age old debate of psychopath or sociopath? I don't know which one Matthew Kane is yet, but I'm certain he falls into one of the buckets."

Jack indulged in a mouthful of wine. "That's as old as the nature or nurture debate. You can't know until you meet him. Is he able to attach to others? Can he feel guilt or shame? Is he capable of empathy?"

"Based on what he wrote in his review, no."

Raising his nearly empty wine glass, he flagged down the waiter. "That points him toward psychopathy, although … You want another glass of wine?" He lifted his eyebrows at her.

She shook her head.

Jack held up a finger and indicated one refill to the server. "Don't you think you're taking this a little too personally, Kate? He may just have strong views. He's a writer out to attract readers and sell a magazine. So he stretches the truth, it doesn't mean he has a mental disorder."

"Perhaps, but he is a narcissist." Her forceful manner seemed to surprise Jack.

"How do you figure?" He tugged his collar and thanked the waiter who set another glass in front of him.

Kate tented her fingers under her chin. "Despite predicating his reviews by saying his destinations are never notified of his arrival beforehand, he expects to be treated differently. His contempt toward other vacationers is evident in his words."

"So the man has an inflated ego, so do I at times."

Kate clicked her tongue at him. "Jack, you're playing devil's advocate, and this is purely theoretical, but there is something not right about this man. Either he's greatly embellished the inconveniences, or he has fabricated them altogether. It points to callous, grandiose traits typical of psychopathic behavior."

"So what do you plan to do?"

"I need to see how he behaves in person. Is he manipulative and charming like a psychopath?" Kate dipped her chin. "Or is he easily agitated and quick to anger like a sociopath? The sooner I find out, the sooner I'll have an edge over him."

Jack tapped a finger atop the table. "Hmm …"

"What?" she asked with pinched lips. "Spit it out."

"Just be careful. Psychopaths are morally bankrupt, and sociopaths have their own sense of skewed morals. It's a fuzzy line between the two." Jack knitted his brow. "Both can be extremely charming *and* dangerous."

"The Ted Bundys and Adolf Hitlers of the world." With her hand resting on the base of her glass, she swirled the wine against the table.

"Exactly. Now they were definitely psychopaths, killers without a conscience. People were expendable to them."

Kate unfolded her napkin over her lap as the waiter came by with their food orders.

"You're going to enjoy this trip, aren't you, Kate?" Jack sprinkled malt vinegar on his french fries and picked up his steak sandwich.

"Whatever do you mean?" A sarcastic note lifted her voice.

"Oh … you enjoy a challenge." He offered her a fry, and she shook her head. "You're gearing up for a fight, aren't you?"

"I'm going on vacation," she said in a light and musing tone. "I don't need the drama."

"Who are you trying to fool? You hate when people take advantage of others. But remember, it's not your battle."

"Oh, I know that." She stabbed her chicken Caesar salad with her fork. "But if I can help the Pearsons, I will."

"I'm just saying to keep it in perspective. The owners have to work it out with this guy, not you." Jack leaned forward and gave her his serious face. "You're there to advise them, nothing more."

"Of course." Kate took a final sip of her wine and gave her colleague a wry smile. "Why do you think I got into this profession?"

DAY ONE

ARRIVAL

Along with her husband Ben, Nadine flew in with the Pearsons. She was happy to be in Jamaica again, especially since five more inches of snow hit Toronto just after they left Canada.

Several male staffers greeted them as the van pulled into Sunset Villa's circular driveway. A slight man of about sixty-five flashed a grin as he opened the front passenger door. "Welcome back, Mr. Pearson."

"Hello, Harrison, nice to be back. Everything good?"

"Yes, sir, quiet but we are getting work done."

Ben, a big man with a heavy beard and a bandana around his forehead, slid out of the back seat and shook Harrison's hand. A few more male workers bounded out of the property to exchange greetings. Nadine stepped out of the vehicle with Anna, aided by one of the villa's attendants.

An attractive black woman strolled out wearing an apron around her pear-shaped torso. A sense of ease and self-assuredness accompanied her. At almost six feet tall, her full figure dwarfed the skinny men who busied themselves unloading the car. Kind eyes set deep in her smooth face provided few clues to her age. Only her forceful presence and gray wisps around her hairline revealed a mature woman.

"Hello, Mr. and Mrs. Pearson." Her ringing voice accompanied a gap-toothed smile.

"Violet, so nice to see you," Anna said, embracing the large woman. "I hope you are well?"

"Things are good, Mrs. Pearson. Nice to have you back."

Nadine reached her arms around Violet for a hug too.

"Good to see you, Violet," said Nolan.

"You too, Mr. Pearson." She adjusted the bun atop her head and smoothed down her apron. "I best get back to the kitchen and make sure nothing is boiled over."

Nolan chuckled, gave the inside of the van a once-over before closing the passenger door. "We're looking forward to your home cooking."

"I've been starving myself for the past week dreaming of your food, Violet." Sweat clung to Ben's shirt, revealing his generous belly.

The large woman shook her head in amusement. "You boys." She waved a playful, dismissive hand and shuffled back inside the villa.

With the luggage unloaded on the stone driveway, the service staff brought the bags to the rooms as instructed by Anna. Along with Harrison, Nolan and Ben carried several bags filled with wine and other spirits. They headed toward the bar.

"I'll meet you in the room shortly," Ben said. "Nolan wants to show me a few things around the property."

Nadine nodded and proceeded to the main floor suite. Having been guests numerous times before, she chose a room on the ground level due to her husband's arthritis, which made it difficult for Ben to climb stairs. Equipped with a king sized bed and flat screen TV, the room's airy interior looked out to the pool. Plantation louvered doors provided privacy.

"Mind if I talk to you for a moment?" Anna tapped on the door of Nadine's suite, which she had left open while unpacking her suitcase.

"Yes, of course, dear, come in."

Anna entered the room and closed the door, handed Nadine an ice-cold Red Stripe. They sat on the love seat across the bed.

"I never drink beer except when I come down here. I think the heat puts me in the mood for it." Anna tipped the stubby bottle to her lips.

Nadine did the same, observed the delicate features of Anna's face. "It was certainly a hot drive from the airport." They took another swallow before setting the bottles down on the glass tabletop in front of them.

"Nolan's showing Ben the areas damaged by Hurricane Sandy."

"I'll have to take a walk later and survey the place."

"Please do," Anna said, nodding several times, "and tell

me if you see any problem areas. I was here two weeks ago, and the staff has done an amazing job cleaning up all the debris."

"Did I overhear Nolan say he bought a new generator?"

"Oh yes, he had to. The storm damaged the old one. You should see this monster!" Anna laughed. "It's big, gray, and ugly. Nolan has it hidden away and protected, but he's itching to show it to the guys."

"Men and their toys, right?" Nadine chuckled.

"You know him. He doesn't want to be caught in another situation where he has to depend on the neighboring resort for help."

"I agree, better if you don't need to rely on someone else for your business."

Anna hesitated and took a breath, her dark, brown eyes glassy. "That's if … we still have a business."

"Of course you will, dear. Don't think like that." Nadine spoke in a soothing voice.

"I'm trying not to, and I'm so thankful you and Ben were able to come down for the week. Was it a lot of trouble for Ben to get the time off?"

Nadine shook her head. "Sweetheart, Ben loves Nolan like a brother. He'd do anything for him. We wouldn't dream of not coming to support you." It wasn't easy to arrange, but Anna didn't need to know that. Ben had to pull strings to find another professor to take his classes for the week. Seniority in the faculty helped.

"Thanks Nadine, we're both grateful …" Anna shifted her stare to the floor.

"What is it? Tell me what's wrong." Nadine covered Anna's hand with hers.

The dark-haired beauty hesitated, drooped her shoulders. "I'm worried … finances are a mess … no bookings. We need to pay the staff …"

"Oh dear."

"I'm trying to stay strong, but …" Anna's voice broke.

"It's going to take all my strength not to punch out this Matthew Kane when I meet him."

"No, Nadine …"

"I'm sorry." Nadine shook her head. "I'll be civil, but it infuriates me that an asshole like him can damage a business with his callous words. Why do people believe such crap?"

"It's not a bad magazine, really, just this guy's writing … I'm trying to stay positive." Anna picked up her bottle absent-mindedly, set it down again without drinking. "He's scheduled to arrive by eleven tomorrow morning. It'll give me time to talk to the staff. Violet and I will go shopping in the morning after breakfast."

"Is there anything you need from me?"

"No. I'm happy to have some of our closest friends here …" Anna peeked at her watch, "which reminds me, the rest of them should be arriving soon."

"Don't worry." Nadine patted Anna's arm. "If we can't get this guy to write a retraction, we'll get the boys to beat the shit out of him," she said, smirking.

Anna's eyes welled up, and she buried her face in her hands. "Nadine …"

"Bad joke, I'm sorry." She stroked Anna's hair. "Look at me."

Anna raised her head.

Nadine snatched a tissue out of a nearby box and dabbed the young woman's tear-stained, rosy cheeks, removing smudged mascara. "Everything will be fine. You've taken the right step by inviting this jackass—sorry … this *man* back to the villa. It can only improve matters."

Anna blinked away more tears and nodded.

Nadine gently brushed a long, wavy hank of Anna's hair from her eyes. "Everything will work out, my dear. Once this guy meets you and Nolan, he will change his mind about the place."

"I hope you're right. I've only communicated with him via e-mail, and he's not the most reasonable man." Anna rose from her seat and took another tissue to blow her nose. "Maybe he'll be better in person." She stared at herself in the mirror. "Oh god, I look a mess."

Nadine pushed herself off the chair and stood next to Anna. "Let me tell you something, young lady. I am so amazed by how much you've done to this place, and I don't mean what you and Nolan have done. I mean what *you've* done." With a firm hand, she touched Anna's forearm. "It's a huge jump from modeling to the hospitality industry. I'm sure it wasn't easy for you."

Anna blotted her eyes and giggled. "No, it wasn't. I racked up so many air miles flying back and forth that first year I should have bought my own plane."

Nadine let out a belly laugh to lighten the mood, then

said in a calm voice, "You'll get through this."

"It's horrible timing. Nolan scaled back his hours at the University to spend more time here. We had plans to renovate … I'm stressed, that's all."

"Well, don't be. You have a great staff. Things will be fine. Nothing changes the fact you have an amazing resort. People will start coming again, I promise."

When Anna left, Nadine finished unpacking, set aside a few special items she brought for Violet and sat down to calm her nerves. Along with the remainder of her lukewarm beer, she swallowed the anger rising in her throat.

Friends from childhood, her husband and Nolan were extremely close. By the time Nolan turned thirty-five and was still single, he appeared the perpetual bachelor until he met Anna. Within six months, he married her while on vacation in Budapest. Nadine knew they were suited for each other the first time she saw them together, on their wedding day at Sunset Villa more than a decade ago.

An incoming e-mail alert buzzed on her cell phone, startling her. She reached for the device vibrating in circles on the tabletop.

The message from her daughter read:

Hi Mom,

Tyler misses you and Dad already.
Please let us know how things go.
Give our love to Anna and Nolan too.

Have a great time in Jamaica!
I've included new pix of Tyler.
Love you lots,

—Tyler, Chloe, and Steve

Chloe and Steve also married at Sunset Villa. Like her, they were anxious to know how the week would unfold with the reviewer at the resort.
So many wonderful memories here …
Nadine scrolled through the attached pictures and her heart filled with pride. The images showed her three-month old grandson Tyler sleeping in his crib, carried by her daughter, and curled atop a mountain of towels.

Anna's tears had tugged hard at Nadine. In many ways, she was like a second daughter to her, being only a few years older than Chloe. It triggered an urge in her to protect Anna, an instinct already heightened since the birth of her grandson.

Nadine wrote a brief note to Chloe and sent it off as Ben entered the room.

"Hi hon, something wrong?" he asked.

She glanced up at her husband. "What do you mean?"

"I caught Anna going upstairs, hiding her face."

Nadine sighed. "She's pretty upset. The reviewer who panned this place …"

"Yes?"

"Do we have any information on him aside from what Nolan and Anna have told us?"

Ben wrapped his arms around himself and wrenched his T-shirt over his head. He scrunched up the garment like a wet towel and threw it in the laundry basket. "You mean aside from his being a bastard?"

"Yes, aside from that."

"Nolan thinks he has a hidden motive, but he's not sure what it is. Even if he and Anna had been here, they wouldn't have accommodated all his crazy requests." Ben opened his suitcase and removed his swim trunks. "I need to go for a swim."

Nadine heaved out a breath and tossed around evil thoughts. "You brought the drugs, right?"

Ben looked at his wife. "You think I'll need them?"

Nadine shrugged and said in a flat one, "It depends. Let's see how big a bastard this Matthew Kane really is."

THE OWNERS

Following her meltdown with Nadine, Anna ascended the winding staircase to the largest of three oceanfront rooms on the second floor. Decorated in her favorite colors of vibrant blues and greens, an immediate calm washed over her as she entered the room. She loved it here, had spent countless hours choosing the fabric to re-upholster the chairs and cushions. A Jacuzzi whirlpool bath and private entrance to a sundeck adorned the master suite, where she and Nolan honeymooned eleven years ago.

Overcome with bittersweet emotion, Anna teared up when she noticed a vase of red and yellow hibiscus on the corner table. *Darling Nolan.* Even though flowers graced the property everywhere, he knew that she still loved having fresh-cut blooms in their room.

Footsteps by the door alerted her to her husband's presence.

"Sweetheart, you all right?" he asked.

As he drifted toward her, she took a deep breath. "I'm okay, just needed to unload to Nadine."

Nolan pulled Anna toward him and wrapped his arms around her. "Everything will be fine. We need to stay positive and be ourselves. That's all we can do."

She sighed and stroked his cheek. "I love you, and I love this place. Nothing is going to take this away from us. We survived the hurricane and no two-bit reviewer is going to ruin us."

Nolan smiled at his wife. "Not if he knows what's good for him." He kissed her on the nose.

"A part of me wishes this guy wasn't coming now," she said.

"Annushka, … we agreed to accommodate him, remember? We need to make good on our word."

Nolan only called her by her given name when he wanted to appease her. "You're right, darling. I'm meeting with the staff in an hour to go over everything."

Nolan raised his eyebrows. "Are you sure you're up to it? I planned to head into town, but I can wait if you want me at this meeting."

"Go. I'll be fine." Anna met with the staff alone for most of the household matters. Nolan accompanied her if she expected resistance. In this case, she didn't anticipate any problems.

"I'm glad Kate will be here. Have you told her anything?"

"Not much." Anna lied.

"I'm sure you can fill her in if you need to. We don't want to make her work, right? I mean, she is here for a holiday." Nolan kissed her before leaving the room.

Anna hated deceiving her husband, but she didn't find it necessary to worry him. After chatting with Kate before Christmas, she found herself unable to sleep for nights.

Kate's cursory evaluation of Matthew Kane disturbed her.

"Meet his needs as requested, but do not go above and beyond," she cautioned. "If he senses weakness, he will expect more."

"Are we supposed to ignore him?" Anna asked.

"No, don't ignore him, but diffuse his power. Treat him as you would any other guest. He doesn't have to know friends are surrounding you that week."

A few days after the phone call with Kate, Matthew Kane accepted the offer to return to Sunset Villa. By separate e-mail, he sent a document listing his "special requirements." Anna read the list aloud to Nolan. They both shook their heads in disbelief.

What he sent read like the demands of a diva-esque celebrity.

Page one listed his dietary concerns, right down to the temperature of the water he could drink. Page two itemized his sensitivity to products used in cleaning his room. And page three ranted on about his environmental issues: smoke; perfumes; paints; and more.

When Matthew Kane booked in the summer, he had indicated a few dietary needs. Only later did Anna discover he had run the workers ragged, though they never once complained to her.

The staff of twelve already knew bookings had slowed down, actually halting in the last two months. Hurricane Sandy explained much of it but could not continue as the excuse any longer. Sunset Villa was back to normal, looking better than ever, in fact.

Nolan had broached the subject of laying off the house cleaning staff until things improved, but neither of them had the heart to follow through with it.

Anna sighed. The tightness of current finances felt like a noose around her neck. They'd already postponed renovations they had planned for the coming year. Even though they hadn't missed any payments to the bank or the employees, she knew the moment of truth was approaching.

What happened by the end of the week could decide the fate of Sunset Villa.

FRIENDS

Anna surveyed the table, arranged with translucent porcelain plates, crystal glasses, and gleaming silver utensils. A dainty glass vase of pink bougainvillea sat in the center. Set back from the Caribbean Sea, the indoor dining area was the perfect place for dinner on a warm night. A gentle breeze skimmed the back of her neck as she crossed into the adjoining living room. After choosing one of the many set lists Nolan compiled for dinner parties, she turned on the music player. The upbeat sound of Jimmy Cliff singing "I Can See Clearly Now" flooded the room. It lifted Anna's spirit. A good omen, she thought. The song played the day she and Nolan signed the contract to buy Sunset Villa five years ago.

The meeting with the staff had gone well. With the goal to erase any confusion the workers might have, she addressed each of Matthew Kane's restrictions, both dietary and otherwise. A photocopy of his requirements now hung in the housekeeping quarters and in the kitchen.

Her last words to them were, "Mr. Kane is a guest like every other guest. We need to treat him with respect and courtesy, but I don't expect nor want you to go above what you would do for anyone else. If you have any concerns with his requests, please come see me or Mr. Pearson. We will deal with it."

Though uncertainty still pervaded her mind, Anna felt lighter after talking to the staff.

The melody of "The Tide is High" sung by the Paragons pulled her back to the present. She opened a drawer on a nearby lamp stand and retrieved a rectangular, luxury matchbox. Anna re-entered the dining room, pleased to see Harrison had set out the candles she requested. On occasions with more guests, she preferred the multi-wick pillars. They sat sturdy on the table and did not obstruct anyone's view of the person across from them. Tonight, however, she opted for the elegance of tapered, silver candles. She found two boxes purchased for the Christmas holidays. In previous years, she could not stock enough of them.

"Let me do that for you."

The deep voice interrupted her pensive mood.

Greg.

She swung around and faced her best friend.

"Hello gorgeous," he said.

Anna skipped in to his open arms and nestled against his wide chest. "Hmm ... I'm so happy to see you," she said, snuggling a bit longer before handing him the matchbox.

He removed a long, aspen wood splint and lit the two candles in the middle of the table.

"How was your flight?" she said as Greg blew out the match.

"Uneventful, just the way I like it. We were able to upgrade to business class, and my back thanks me a million times over."

Anna knew Greg hated flying. At six feet three, she guessed that even the more expensive charter seats offered little comfort on a four-hour trip.

Greg twirled a strand of Anna's raven hair. "Are you okay?"

"I'll be fine." It was hard to fool Greg. He always knew when she was feeling down. She shifted her thoughts away from business. "Where's Tom?"

"He's probably with the rest of them at the bar. I took a nap." Greg held her cheeks and said, "I know you're worried, but whatever you and Nolan need … anything."

"I know." She covered his hands with hers and stared into his eyes. "I know—"

"If you weren't a married man, I'd say you were trying to make a move on my wife."

Anna swung around to see Nolan and Tom stride into the room. She giggled, reached out to her husband. "Hi darling. Greg was just cheering me up. How are you, Tom?"

"Hi Anna, you're lovely as always." Tom leaned in to give her a hug.

"So glad you made it." Anna had stood up as Greg's "best man" at his and Tom's wedding, a momentous occasion weeks after New York State legalized same sex marriage.

"Did Greg give you our gift yet?"

"Shush, you weren't supposed to say anything." Greg scolded his husband, who stood a foot shorter than him.

"Oh come on now." Tom pleaded with his eyes. "I can't keep a secret."

Anna lifted her shoulders and clapped like an excited girl. "Oooh … Please tell me it's one of your designs!"

Greg shot Tom an exasperated look. "Yes, we have a new line of fabrics we want to show you."

"I can't wait to see it. I need a new OMG dress." She looked up at Nolan. "Don't I, darling?"

"You can always use a new dress," he said, hugging her closer to him. "Has it already been ten years since you started your label?"

"Yes, can you believe it?" Tom said. "I still remember trying to figure out a name for the company, seems so insignificant now."

OMG, a fusion of the last two letters of Tom's name and the first letter of Greg's specialized in new fabrics and innovative styles.

Greg said, "We're going to do one more season before taking a break. We need to devote more attention to our charity for the LGBTQ youth in our community."

"You and Tom will make great mentors for those kids," Anna said. "Who better to teach them fashion?"

Before Greg could respond, Ben and Nadine strolled in from the bar area. "Guess who we found?" Ben said. A short man peeked his head in between the couple, "Howdy folks. Mind if I join you for dinner?"

"Jerry!" Nolan took quick strides to meet his friend. The

two men shook hands before giving each other a manly hug. "You made it. Why didn't you call? We would've had the car service pick you up."

"I've been here enough times to know the drill." A gleeful beam lit up his small face. "I pre-booked a car before boarding at Logan, didn't want to put you out in case things changed at the last minute."

Anna instructed Harrison to bring another place setting and chair, thrilled one of her husband's oldest friends made it in for the week.

As the guests took their seats, Harrison appeared carrying two bottles, one in each hand. After making the round of filling everyone's glass with their choice of red or white wine, he disappeared into the kitchen.

"A toast," Nolan said. "To our closest friends. Thank you for coming to support us. It means the world."

The clink of glasses reverberated around the table.

Anna took a sip, allowed the crispness of the white wine to cool her throat. Surrounded by people who loved her and Nolan, she couldn't fathom not sharing times like this at Sunset for the rest of her life. Their support offered hope that everything would work out. It had to.

She reached for the sterling silver dinner bell in front of her. "Shall I?"

Six smiles gave her the answer. With a dainty swing of her wrist, she rang the bell to let Harrison know they were ready for the first course.

DAY TWO
AT THE AIRPORT

The air conditioning on the plane cooled Kate's skin, but upon landing, she peeled off her sweater and swapped her runners for sandals. A loose-fitting cotton dress outlined her slender figure. Shouldering a laptop bag and dragging a medium-sized suitcase behind her, she weaved her way with ease toward the exit. Customs proved quick and efficient due to her early morning arrival.

When the doors separating the airport to the outside world slid open, she strutted into a blistering wall of heat. The thick, stagnant air choked the oxygen out of her, forced her to slow down her pace.

Welcome to Jamaica.

Kate shielded her eyes with sunglasses and turned toward the area for airport transfers. Perspiration beaded her skin, the heat a welcome break after a cold start to winter. From around her wrist, she removed an elastic band and pulled up her hair in a cheerleader's high ponytail. A couple of porters approached her; she dismissed them with a shake of her head. Chin held high, she peered across makeshift barriers at the rumple-shirted men holding signs scrawled with strangers' names. Some of them appeared hopeful; others looked bored and weary. In the middle of the throng, she caught sight of a familiar face—a medium-built man in his sixties with graying hair. She waved to him. With a nod of acknowledgement, he threaded his way toward her.

"Good to see you again, Sam." Kate shook his hand. "You picked me up last year at this time."

"Greetings, ma'am, I remember," he said, baring a grin which revealed straight teeth against coffee-colored skin. "Welcome back."

"Thank you."

Sam took her luggage, and she followed him. Together, they moved away from the growing crowd of new arrivals. "I'm parked close by," he said, "and two more people will join us. They should be coming through soon."

"No worries, Sam, I'm in no rush," Kate said, happy for the warmth on her skin.

Sam stopped by a pillar and depressed the handle of her suitcase, pushing it down until it disappeared. While Kate opted to linger in the sun, he stood under a nearby strip of shade.

"Are things better with your mother-in-law?" she asked.

He pulled in his chin, mouth open. "You sure have a good memory, ma'am. She's doing much better, thank you."

"Excellent." She smiled. The sun beating down on her made it feel much later; it was not yet nine o'clock. They stood talking about the heat for a while until Sam sauntered back to the pick-up area to wait for the other party. Not more than fifteen minutes later, he returned with a couple in their twenties, then excused himself to retrieve the car parked across the street.

"I'm Jessica." The attractive, young woman introduced herself to Kate with an extended hand. "And this is my boyfriend Rob."

A man over six feet tall with blond hair plastered to a pointy head shuffled by Jessica's side. "Hello," he said with a flaccid handshake. He immediately moved to a shaded area and lit a cigarette.

"Good to meet you," Kate said to Jessica. "I detect an accent. Tennessee?"

"Yes, Knoxville. Have you been?"

"No, I had a roommate in College from Memphis. Your accent is not as pronounced as hers though."

Jessica's face lifted. "That's really good to know. I wouldn't mind losing my accent altogether."

Rob made a snorting sound and spit.

His girlfriend shot him a look of disgust but said nothing.

"Your first time in Jamaica?" Kate pretended not to notice the hostile interaction between the two.

"Yes, first time anywhere really. First time on a plane." She passed her forearm across her brow. I've never been in such intense heat."

Kate was aware there was no hint of a breeze. She saw Jessica's fair skin glistening with moisture. "We're surrounded by concrete. It'll be better once we're at the resort near the ocean."

Sam drove up in a mid-sized van and exited the vehicle. He opened the trunk and started loading their belongings in the back. Rob watched the older man struggle with their oversized luggage and a guitar case. He made no attempt to help him.

"Can we get in?" he said. His flushed pallor exposed tiny pink veins in his face. "It's hotter than a whore in church out here."

"Rob, mind your manners!" Jessica snapped at him.

Sam appeared unfazed by Rob's comment. "Yes, sir, the doors are unlocked." He shoved the remaining luggage in the van.

Rob slid open the side door and was about to climb in when Jessica motioned him to put out his smoke. With an arched eyebrow, he opened his mouth as if to protest but stopped short. He took a final, lengthy drag before tossing the still-glowing cigarette. Then, as if hit by a distant memory of good manners, he gestured for his girlfriend to get in the vehicle first.

Kate picked her three words for Rob: *Remiss. Obtuse. Blockhead.*

Sam opened the door for Kate on the passenger side in the front seat. After buckling her seatbelt, she prepared to relax for the two-hour ride to Sunset.

"I see folks here drive on the wrong side of the road,"

said Rob.

Kate heard Jessica swat him on the arm. "Not the wrong side, just different than us." She moved forward in her seat. "It's like the British, right Sam?"

"Yes, Miss, that's right."

The outdoor scene moved steadily past Kate's window as Sam cruised on to the main road that led toward the villa. A1 was a well-paved highway with the occasional pothole, but no worse than many of the streets she'd driven in Manhattan. At least here, the hills and mountains behind a ribbon of hanging mist provided a scenic backdrop.

Clay thatch-roofed homes, some grand, others run down nestled deep in lush greenery and coconut groves. Concrete, windowless buildings sat under an expansive, cloudless sky. Many appeared abandoned, though Sam intimated at Kate's last visit, they were in mid-construction. She recognized a lime-green building with only three walls, its front wall and roof yet to be built, construction material strewn in a heap nearby. Little had changed from a year ago.

Except for the random pedestrian or cyclist, most locals were seen riding in mini-busses, traveling at a fair clip despite overflowing with passengers. On occasion, Sam had to slow down for donkeys and goats venturing into traffic. Wild dogs chasing chickens also kicked up dust on side roads.

For the first half hour, Sam mused on the problems with his mother-in-law. As a courtesy, Kate listened to him tell the same story, even though she remembered it from the last time he drove her. Conversations with Kate often happened that way, but there was no point interrupting to say she remembered the details. Dialogue flowed better if she let others recount from their own memories. Sam talked until Peter Tosh's "Johnny Be Good" interrupted their conversation.

"Nice ring tone," Kate said, her eyes dancing with the clipped melody.

"Thank you, ma'am." Sam kept his eye on the road until he maneuvered out of a roundabout and had clear road ahead of him. "Please excuse me," he said before snatching the singing cell phone out of the cup holder.

Kate grabbed the opportunity to take a catnap. She caught several Spanish words as Sam rhymed off in Jamaican Creole, but the squabbling of the duo behind her overpowered his patois.

Rob fawned over Jessica like a teenage boy who had just discovered girls. That, in itself would not bother Kate, but he spoke with little affection toward his girlfriend.

"Stop pawing at me." She heard Jessica say in a loud whisper. "We're not alone here."

The bickering quieted when Jessica tried to discuss sights they might want to see. Rob's interest in Jamaica's attractions, however, did not last long before he started up again.

Kate cleared her throat a bit louder than necessary. The noise behind her stopped.

Sam returned his phone to the cup holder. "Is it cool enough for you back there?"

"Yes, yes … it's perfect," Jessica said, breathless.

"All right, tell me if you need the air conditioning turned up."

"Thank you."

Kate's sunglasses concealed her smile. Sam's interjection bought them peace, but it was short-lived. A few minutes later, muffled conversation escalated in volume, grew argumentative. Whatever Rob did to Jessica must have hurt. She yelped and cursed him. A scuffle, more harsh words from Jessica, and then a slap resounded inside the vehicle. Kate noticed Sam flinch in his seat and amusement wrinkle the corners of his eyes.

"I warned you to stop it!" the Southern girl said.

"Jesus!" Rob stomped his feet like a six-year-old. "That hurt, Jessica!"

"I'm glad!" She no longer tried to muzzle her frustration. "I said I was serious, didn't I? Listen next time!"

"Fine," he said, his voice dripping with defeat.

Jessica leaned in between Kate and Sam and whispered, "I'm sorry we've caused a scene. It won't happen again."

Sam kept his eyes on the road. "No problem, Miss."

If the couple's behavior annoyed Sam, he didn't show it. Kate respected his cool nature even though the tension behind her was palpable.

Up until then, only low-level talking saturated the airwaves. When Sam fiddled with the dial for a different station, Jessica piped up, "Can you change it to music? I'd love to hear reggae if you know a good station."

"Fine, Miss," Sam said.

A few seconds of static and hissing voices later, a familiar song filled the van. Sam turned up the volume to Bob Marley's "No Woman, No Cry."

From her side mirror, Kate noticed the grim, young lady behind her, head rested against the window, as far away from Rob's side of the car as possible.

Jagged, explosive, and *shrewd* were the three words Kate settled on for Jessica. At first, she reasoned that 'juvenile' might represent the 'J', but Jessica's behavior proved otherwise. *Jagged* would remind her the Southern Belle was edgy and able to stand up for herself. It made her unpredictable but not juvenile.

Rob's rude behavior troubled Kate. That he was oblivious to anyone else but himself revealed something more than immaturity. She considered changing her initial evaluation of him from *blockhead* to *bully* but decided against it. Jessica appeared able to hold her own against him, which meant he did not intimidate her—not in mixed company anyway.

AFFINITY FOR WATER

Both Rob's and Jessica's tempers had cooled by the time they arrived at Sunset. Kate assumed the mellow sounds of reggae for the remainder of the trip had helped keep the peace.

When they exited the van, Jessica's ecstatic expression amused the young men who greeted them and introduced themselves.

"I'm Willy, but everyone calls me 'Chilly Willy.'"

Jessica let out a giggle. "And why's that?"

The tall, skinny Jamaican man smiled and exposed blinding, white teeth. "I'm a laid back kind of guy."

Another excited man jumped in front of Jessica and introduced himself. "And I'm 'Ready Freddy', always ready to be of service, ma'am."

Kate saw Jessica squeal with delight. "Oh my goodness," she said. "I'm seeing double!"

From her previous trips, Kate knew the two men had come by their nicknames honestly. Chilly Willy was as relaxed as Ready Freddy was earnest, an odd dichotomy, considering they were identical twins. Both tended the outdoor gardens, responsible for the upkeep of the foliage at Sunset, a huge responsibility given the dense plant life on the six-acre property.

Rob lumbered out of the van and lit a cigarette. Though appearing nonchalant, he gazed around him with a dropped jaw. Both he and his girlfriend stretched their necks to glimpse the interior of the villa. Jessica twirled around like a wind-up doll, doing a little dance when she spied the ocean in front of her.

"This place looks even better than in the pictures!" she said.

Kate stayed behind to chat with Harrison while the Tennessee couple followed the twins and their luggage upstairs.

"How are you, Harrison?"

"I'm well, Miss Kate. It's wonderful to see you again."

"A pleasure to see you too." She gave him a reassuring smile. "It's been a tough few months since the storm, hasn't it?"

The outer corners of his eyes slanted up. "Yes, ma'am, but we manage."

Kate had a soft spot for Harrison, whose heart-shaped face always brightened her stay. On her way to her room, she noticed tasteful changes made to the property, small decorative touches—new artwork, different pillow coverings, fresh flowers. They all added up and gave the resort a bright, modern feel. As Anna had intimated in her e-mail from December, there would be no sign of devastation left over from Hurricane Sandy by the time she arrived.

As she climbed the stairs to her room, she noticed a man getting out of the pool. Was it Matthew Kane? A picture she found of him from the Internet suggested a man in his late forties, early fifties with a gaunt face and receding hairline.

This figure appeared younger, more fit. He stood with his back to her, drying off before flattening the back of his lounge chair. He draped his towel on top of it and lay on his stomach. Something about the confident way he moved indicated he was not the reviewer. She imagined she would meet Matthew Kane soon enough. Jack was right. Part of her was curious to meet the man who penned such a vitriolic review.

When Kate reached the second floor landing, she heard the sounds of a woman's stifled whimpers, weak at first, then more forceful. It jarred her ears. She paused and listened—Jessica's voice—deduced it came from the room beside hers. She recognized the sound right away. Sex had its own unmistakable cadence.

Kate rolled her shoulders as if to loosen a kink in her neck. With her weight shifted to the balls of her feet, she proceeded to her room at the end of the hallway. Several whines of "Oh my god!" sounded too animated to her ears to be authentic. A sensation of crawling flesh hastened her stride.

By the time Kate reached her door, Rob's caveman-like grunt punctuated the sounds leaking from the room and then—silence.

She shook her head, pondering the fickleness of young

love.

Except for a bright yellow throw on the four-poster bed with a mosquito net draped behind the headboard, her suite looked as it did a year ago.

Kicking off her sandals, she ambled across the smooth clay floor, luxuriated in the feel of cold tiles hitting the soles of her feet. She turned off the air conditioning and switched on the giant ceiling fan. A quiet hum filled the room as the blades cut the air, wobbling until they reached a medium speed.

Kate stepped on the balcony, took in the unobstructed view of the Caribbean Sea.

She was no longer in concrete jungle.

Leaning forward, she rested her forearms on the railing, inhaling warm, moist air into her lungs. A faint taste of salt trickled to the back of her throat.

A half mile to the left of her room, several private residences dotted the coastline. The largest building within her view was an office for Goldeneye, a property purchased by author Ian Fleming after WWII. It was where he dreamt up his famous James Bond character and wrote his novels. From there, the resort sprawled more than forty acres and continued to grow. Sunset Villa, by comparison was tiny, but it lured her with its intimacy. Here, she carved a small piece of paradise for herself, something she would never be able to do in a place as large as Goldeneye.

Due to the corner configuration of the room, her balcony jutted out over the ocean's floor. The shoreline stretched out on either side of her as far as she could see.

Water lapped the beach and created a splash that fizzled quietly. Its hypnotic motion repeated itself in an endless pattern.

Kate had always had an affinity for water, ever since she was a little girl. The reason for it, though, remained a mystery to her. On rare occasions, a memory of water seized her mind—short, unpleasant episodes. It forced her to push the tangled images back into her brain as quickly as they surfaced. Whatever it was about water that called to her laid buried deep in her unconscious. And that's where she wanted it to stay.

Regardless of these past painful incidents, Kate intuitively knew she was safe at Sunset Villa.

Water, a source of life, served as her unwavering and constant companion here.

LUNCH

Lunch was served outdoors on one of the elevated terraces only steps from the pool. Croton, a tropical plant the Jamaicans called "match me if you can" because no two leaves were alike, decorated the pathway leading to the dining area. Hedges of red hibiscus, white and pink bougainvillea in pots and hanging baskets added to the colorful array of foliage.

Though shaded under a clay-roof gazebo, the table enjoyed the warmth of the ocean breeze and offered a panoramic view of the sea. It was the ideal setting for an afternoon meal.

All the guests had taken their seats by the time Matthew Kane showed up at the table. Upon arrival at the villa an hour ago, he had just enough time to shower, change, and take a stroll. Harrison, who greeted him was cordial if a bit standoffish. The elderly man informed him the Pearsons would not be around until lunchtime. The other guests were nowhere to be seen.

From what he observed of the property on his short walk, Hurricane Sandy must have spared Sunset Villa. No downed trees or broken branches crossed his path, no destruction of the buildings. The beach was neatly swept. The only sign of debris were a few twigs and vines in the water, which must have snapped off from the cliffs above. Like litter, they floated in the shallow coral reef.

Polite nods and hellos greeted him as he took his seat. The faces of the guests were different than when he was here seven months ago. Back then, it was a reunion of an English family who traveled from England and other parts of Europe. He remembered his correspondence with Anna before that trip. She had said he might feel out of place being the lone guest not part of the larger group, suggested different weeks for his vacation. Considering he was coming to review the property, he didn't expect it would matter who else was here, so he declined her offer. In hindsight, he had felt excluded on that trip. This time at least, he was not the only stranger in the group.

Matthew expected to talk to the owners in private before sharing a meal with all the other guests. The lack of fanfare upon his arrival surprised him, deflated him somewhat.

Did the other guests know who he was? That he was here at the request of the owners?

The attractive woman seated at the end of the table caught his eye, though he wasn't close enough to have a conversation with her. Instead, testosterone surrounded him.

He sipped his glass of water. From the conversation around the table and an assortment of condiments in front of him, he deduced the lunch menu—hamburgers. When

Earl, the young man serving them brought out the drinks, Matthew inquired if the meat contained Worcestershire sauce, sugar, or vinegar. Earl hesitated and turned to Anna.

"I gave your list of restrictions to Violet, our chef. She will ensure your food allergies are taken care of for each meal."

Matthew nodded in her direction. Anna's accent hinted at an Eastern European background. As stunning as she was, her glacial demeanor made him uneasy. "Yes, I wanted to make sure. I know how these things can slip through the cracks."

"Of course. Nolan and I understand," Anna said. "We trust you will find the food prepared to your satisfaction."

"I hope so," he said.

Anna's lips curved up as she looked past him to her husband at the opposite end of the table. Maybe she detected his hint of sarcasm.

"How rude," said a deep voice in his direction.

"Pardon me?" Matthew stiffened as he stared at the man sitting across him. With his swarthy complexion and a stubbly growth darkening his chin, he conjured an image of a Middle Eastern terrorist.

The man repeated himself. "I said your response to the lady is rude. I've never heard of anyone with such peculiar allergies."

Matthew snorted and took another sip of water, which he'd requested at room temperature sans ice. "Sorry, what was your name again?"

"It's Adam."

Matthew turned away from him and looked to the end of the table. "If I was rude, Anna," he said, "please accept my apology. I didn't mean it to come off that way."

Anna lowered her gaze. "No harm done."

Did her bottom lip quiver because he intimidated her? It didn't matter anyway, as now he shot a glance at the woman sitting near Anna. Kate—one of the few names he remembered after the lightning round of introductions. Her long hair cascaded below her shoulders, appeared damp as if she had stepped out of the shower or had a swim. He forced a smile in her direction but failed to draw one back from her. Did she think he was rude too?

Earl finished pouring drinks before disappearing toward the kitchen. The way he deferred to Anna meant she probably managed the staff. He would have preferred to deal with her husband. The e-mails he had exchanged with her revealed an efficient woman, but there was something cold about her. Her words informed, but her tone came off icy, just like she did in person.

"Great place you have here," Adam said, addressing Nolan. "I haven't had time to check out the property yet. Any issues from Hurricane Sandy?"

"Quite a lot of damage," Nolan said." You don't see evidence of it now because we've been cleaning up for the past two months. This roof above us was blown off."

"Really? I thought the storm lost steam by the time it came this far north." Adam leaned back in his chair and lifted his eyes upward. Everyone else did the same except for Matthew, who took the opportunity to check out the terrorist again. He wondered what Adam did for a living.

"Actually, after it made landfall near Kingston, it picked up strength once it hit the Caribbean Sea. Anna and I were at home, glued to the news, on the phone to the staff every half hour. It was tense until we were able to assess the damage for ourselves."

"Gracious me! How terrible," Jessica piped in. "Knoxville was spared for the most part, but the Southern Appalachians had power outages, more snow than seen in years, especially for October."

"Bad in New York State too," Greg said. "The storm flooded streets, tunnels, and subway lines, cutting power around the city. They had to cancel the New York City Marathon, first time that's ever happened."

"And they say Canada has bad weather!" Jerry said.

Laughter spread around the table.

"We were not as badly hit as one of the large resorts in Ocho Rios …" Nolan scrunched his face and looked to his wife. "Which one was that, Anna?"

"Umm … it was Sandals." Anna nodded toward Earl as he approached the table with food. "All their guests moved to Montego Bay or other hotels on the south coast unaffected by the storm."

"Right, it was Sandals. Our damage was not as extensive, but we're remote here." Nolan unfolded his napkin over his lap. "That was our biggest problem."

"I see, getting materials in was the challenge," Adam said.

"Yes, especially since we lost power for a few days.

Our staff did what they could to clean up the grounds and beach area, but we needed to haul away the big stuff. The storm uprooted several large palm trees."

"The place is still awfully nice, plenty of flowers and plants growin' from what I see," Rob said.

Matthew heard a strong Southern accent from the man sitting beside him, who also couldn't stop fidgeting and playing with his utensils.

"True," Ben responded to Rob, "it's still lush, but then everything grows quickly in the tropics."

"It's the fertile soil," Nolan said. "This roof took the most time, but we had November and December to rebuild it."

"But wasn't that your high season?" Jessica said. "Did y'all have to cancel many bookings?"

Earl unloaded his cart of food on the table—platters of hamburger patties, buns, wooden bowls of salad, and baskets of fries.

"Thank you, Earl. Please help yourselves, everyone." Anna started by passing a dish to Kate. Ben took one of the salads and moved it down his side.

"Jesus, I'm starvin'!" Rob shook in his seat like an excited kid.

The aroma of charbroiled beef and the hunger of eager guests could have explained the non-response to Jessica's questions, but Matthew doubted it. Perhaps Nolan and Anna chose to ignore her. When the owners invited him back at no cost to him, he suspected his review had hurt them. Now that he learned Hurricane Sandy had closed them down for two months on the heels of his article, things could only have become worse. When he estimated he may have wiped out close to six months of their business, smugness pasted a smile on his face.

Serves them right.

For the moment though, conversational silence blanketed the table. The sounds of "Please pass the …", "I'll have more of …", and "Thank-yous" accompanied the flurry of activity. Lunch was a casual affair, Matthew remembered, and nothing defined casual eating more than hamburgers. Earl appeared beside him and placed a large plate with two meat patties in front of him. "This is for you, sir. Violet does add a bit of sugar to her hamburger recipe. She has prepared these for you without it."

"I see." Matthew studied the meat on his plate. Rob handed him the basket of buns, which he promptly passed on to Jerry.

"You're allergic to buns too?" Adam asked as he prepared his burger, squeezing ketchup and layering tomato and pickle slices on top of his meat.

"I can't have leavened flour, so I don't eat white bread."

Adam ignored him and asked Jessica to pass the salt. She seemed more than happy to oblige him.

"Do you want the pepper too?" she asked in a sugary tone.

"No, this is perfect. Thank you," Adam said, winking at her.

Nolan accepted a serving dish of burgers from Tom, transferred two patties to his plate and set the platter in front of him. He raised a glass. "I want to propose a toast and thank everyone for coming. Welcome to Sunset Villa and the first of many meals together."

Everyone grabbed their glasses and toasted one other.

Matthew cut into his meat with knife and fork as if he were eating a steak. After chewing a piece, he turned in Jessica's direction. "I'll take the pepper if you don't mind."

Without the flirtatious smile she had given Adam, she grabbed the mill and slid it to him. Her big eyes and sensuous lips attracted him. Nice rounded breasts didn't hurt either. Southerners always came across dim-witted to him, but Jessica appeared knowledgeable and did not speak with a pronounced drawl or lilt. Certain words and phrasing betrayed her though. Saying "y'all" was one of them, the way she dropped the r's in her words another. Southern belles were not his type anyway, but he didn't mind her so much.

Her boyfriend, however, was a pig. Slovenly and probably not well educated, he confirmed every stereotype Matthew had ever learned about Southerners. With Rob's first bite of his hamburger, half the fixings slid on to his plate followed by a generous swirl of relish and mustard. Rob picked up the tomato slices, pickles, and onions with his fingers, shoved them back between his buns, and mopped up the runny mess with his burger.

Matthew turned away from Rob, so he didn't have to see him. If he were not so hungry, he would have lost his appetite. He made a mental note to himself. *Do not sit beside this hick at another meal.*

"What's the name of your disease, Matt?"

The table, which entertained several conversations up to that point hushed. Heads turned toward him. He loathed being called Matt. Adam's presence felt like an invasion to him.

"Adam ... correct?" Matthew pretended he forgot his name.

"That's right."

"There's no name for my illness," he said. "I just know I don't feel well after eating certain foods or when exposed to particular substances." He punctuated his statement with an air of self-awareness.

Adam took a swig of his beer, set down his glass. "Do you break out in a rash or a sweat? What happens to you?"

"I wish it were that easy, I don't have a conventional allergy. Nothing manifests that you can see."

Who was this guy with a hate-on for him?

"Oh ... so what you're saying is, nothing to prove anything," Adam said.

Matthew's pulse sped up. "What are you implying?"

"You have no symptoms."

"Of course I do, but I call them reactions. They can happen right after exposure or minutes later, maybe even hours later."

"I see," Adam's voice flattened into a robotic monotone. "And we can't see these reactions, we only know of them when you say you don't feel well."

Matthew tried to sound superior and professorial. "Yes, because unlike most people, I'm in tune with my body. Who else knows it better than me?"

"Sounds as if you're *too* in tune with your body." Adam shrugged. "Convenient."

Matthew wanted to reach over and smack the dismissive look off Adam's face, but before he could summon up a worthy response, Nadine grabbed Adam's attention.

"Are your burgers all right?" Nolan asked Matthew, snapping him out of his flustered state.

"Yes ... yes, they're fine." Angry with himself for allowing anyone to cast doubts on his illness, he wiped his mouth hard with a napkin. How dare Adam make it seem as if his condition did not exist.

"Violet will be happy to grill more for you if you want," Nolan said, pouring himself a glass of water.

"All right, thanks." At least Nolan accommodated him, probably to compensate for the haughty behavior of his wife.

When Anna had contacted him through the magazine after his review was published, he had not bothered to answer her, had not felt the need to defend himself. She persisted in e-mailing him and surprised him with the offer to return to Sunset Villa at no cost. It wasn't at all what he had expected. Most places that received poor reviews from him tried explaining their behavior and begged for a retraction. Some threatened to sue him and the magazine. A few even offered to secretly pay him for a favorable second review.

This was the first time a resort asked him to return without any attached conditions. Nothing explicit anyway, though he knew the Pearsons wanted something. If it were to make amends, they would need to work at it before he'd consider writing a follow-up review, *if* he wrote a follow-up. Matthew knew his well-informed voice defined the magazine, even if he and the editor-in-chief of *Travel in Style* frequently battled over his caustic articles. His column built up their reputation as the go-to periodical for honest travel reviews. As long as he didn't slam any of the companies that advertised with them, he had free rein to write whatever he wanted.

As the meal continued with conversations that excluded him, he turned to Jerry. "What brings you here?"

Jerry served himself more fries and offered the basket to Matthew.

"No, thanks."

"I'll take those taters." Rob reached across Matthew's plate and grabbed them from Jerry.

"It's a vacation for me." Jerry unscrewed the top of the vinegar and shook the liquid on top of his fries.

Matthew coughed loudly, bent over in his chair.

"Are you all right?" Jerry asked.

Snatching the napkin off his lap, Matthew covered his mouth. "That stuff reeks. It's curling the hair in my nose!"

Jerry frowned, twisted the cap back on the bottle. "It's malt vinegar. Nothing bad about it."

"Maybe not for you …" Matthew coughed again before trying to sit up. Nolan poured water into his glass, which he gulped. The liquid was too cold for him but it would have to do. "I'm allergic to vinegar, even the smell makes me a little ill."

"Sucks to be you," Adam said, as he grabbed the vinegar from the table. "This stuff's fantastic."

Matthew seethed as Adam shook the brown liquid liberally on top of his fries.

Rob picked up the bottle after him, turned to Matthew. "You gonna be all right? I'll try not to add too much."

"Fine, put the cap on when you're done … please."

"Would you like more water, Matthew?" Nolan asked.

"No." He caught his breath, watched Adam eat his fries and talk to Jessica across the table. The asshole was flirting with the girl, and her boyfriend was too busy stuffing his face to care.

Jessica, who appeared oblivious to his near choking incident blathered on. "Mama and I have watched 'The Price is Right' ever since I was a kid. I never imagined I would get on the show, let alone win a trip to Jamaica!"

"I was in the audience screamin', goin' outta my mind!" Rob said.

Matthew had to admit Jessica's bubbly personality grabbed his attention. She recounted how she played one of the more popular contestant games, Plinko.

Kate turned to Jessica. "Plinko?"

Matthew met Kate's eyes for a fleeting moment when she glanced in his direction.

"Yes, you guess the prices of small items to earn Plinko chips, these huge chips the size of …"

"A hamburger!" Rob said, on his third helping.

"No …" Forming a circle with her hands about six inches wide, she said, "They were more the size of a dessert plate. I won four chips, which I released at the top of a big game board. Each chip fell into a slot with different dollar amounts. In total, I won $22,000!"

Rob raised his left arm with an open palm. Jessica hesitated but then slapped him a high-five. "Hell, Jess was amazin'! Twenty-two thousand buys a whole lotta guitars!"

Matthew caught Adam's smirk as he gazed in Jessica's direction.

"Rob's a real guitar fan," she said, dropping her chin.

Ben nodded. "Great, come play with us tonight. Did you bring a guitar?"

"Umm … yes." Rob looked at Jessica. "I reckon I need practicin'."

"Don't worry, we're not professionals, right boys?" Ben yelled to his friends across the table.

"Speak for yourself, Ben." Jerry taunted. "Rob, we need young blood, so join us. We set up over there." He motioned to a covered space with an electric drum set and a couple of miniature speakers underneath it. "That's center stage."

"Sure," Rob said, his gravelly voice hesitant. "Who's the drummer?"

Both Jerry and Ben pointed to Nolan.

"An accomplished drummer *and* a marine biologist rolled into one," said Jerry with an exaggerated grin.

"Oh stop it." Nolan waved off the compliment. "We jam after dinner, Rob, we're the live entertainment. It'll be fun, always nice to have another musician join us."

"Sure … I'll check it out." Rob returned his attention

to his food.

"So, y'all still want to hear how I won the trip here?" Jessica asked.

"Of course," said the fifty-something woman, Nadine, who had given Matthew a curt hello when he arrived at the table. He had a strong feeling she didn't like him.

"Well, since I was one of the day's big winners," Jessica continued, "I wound up on the showcase showdown at the end. I passed on the first one filled with appliances and stuff I didn't want. The second showcase opened with a set of luggage, so I had a pretty good idea it was going to include a trip. The next item was a year's supply of suntan lotion. Can you imagine? A year's supply of lotion!" Jessica's exuberance made everyone laugh. "I knew at that point it had to be a trip to a hot destination. I just prayed it wasn't Florida since I've been there already. When the curtain opened and announced it was a trip to Jamaica, I couldn't stop jumping up and down! I've never been anywhere outside the States. I'm still shocked I won. This place is amazing."

Matthew couldn't believe how the woman could talk without taking a breath.

"Great story," Nadine said. "I used to love watching that show when Bob Barker was the host."

"And the funny thing is," Anna said, "We offered Rob and Jessica the choice to have the villa to themselves, but they preferred to share it." She raised a glass. "In many ways, this is your week and we're your guests, so cheers to you both."

"This is our first trip together," Jessica said. "We wanted

to meet the owners and new people. So far, I love it."

"We're happy to have you here," Anna said, "Rob, did you have enough to eat?"

"Yes, ma'am, fuller than a tick at the moment." He leaned back and rubbed his stomach.

Not long afterward, Earl returned to the table and cleared the dishes. A slight hunger pang jabbed Matthew's side. His burgers were delicious; the best he'd eaten in a long time, though he would never admit it here. Before the vinegar nauseated him, he wanted to ask for one more. Too late now.

"Great lunch, thanks Earl." Adam pushed his chair back and stood up.

"You're welcome, sir."

"Greg, I'd love to learn more about your fashion label. Maybe we can do work together."

"Absolutely, Adam. Tom and I could use a man of your expertise."

The three men left the table, already chatting.

"Enjoy the day, everyone," Nolan said. "It's going to be hot." The guests rose from their seats, strolling off in different directions, some in pairs, others in a group.

Matthew walked off alone wondering what Adam's expertise was.

ZEN GARDEN

Under a never-ending sky, the sun glanced off the water lily pond in the Zen Garden. Two women took a stroll to catch up with each other's news.

"Matthew is a man with limited power who believes he deserves more," Kate said. "Call it arrogance, conceit, or hubris, but he likes the sound of his own voice. That much is obvious."

Anna nodded. "And he doesn't play nice when others disagree with him."

"No, he doesn't." Kate kicked up tiny pebbles on the path. "His review, like the man himself, shows a flair for the dramatic. His ego is easily bruised."

Anna paused her steps. "And what do you make of Adam?"

"Did you know him before he arrived?"

She shook her head. "No, he was a last minute guest. I was worried about how he would fit in with everyone, but we couldn't afford to turn him away."

"No need to explain," Kate said in a soothing tone. "I understand."

"I know, and I hate to admit it, but …" Anna retrieved

a hair band from her pocket. "I found myself tingling with delight when Adam told Matthew off. The man pulls no punches."

"He's every bit as arrogant as Matthew, but in a different way." Kate heard the gentle sound of running water.

Anna tied her hair into a ponytail and pointed to what resembled a swarm of bees. "Look," she said.

Squinting to focus, Kate pressed a hand to her chest. "Beautiful," she whispered.

No larger than the size of thumbnails, the black butterflies glowed with bright yellow bands across their hind wings, a stark contrast against giant palm leaves.

As she and Anna stood on the ivy covered bridge, Kate felt as if she had stepped into a Monet painting. At that moment, she could not imagine a more beautiful place on earth.

"Freddy told me butterflies were plentiful when he was a kid. When we bought the place, I didn't see any for the first couple of years."

Kate slowly let out her breath. "Butterflies are never seen in the city anymore, almost as if they've become extinct."

"True. Both Freddy and his brother have been experimenting with different plants to attract butterfly breeding. I was skeptical, but it's worked. We're also not spraying with pesticides anymore."

"Oh?" Kate pursed her lips. "Have you gone completely natural with pest control?"

"Yes, it seems to have helped. I've seen more butterflies

in the last year than ever before." Anna let out a sigh.

"Are you all right?" Kate placed a hand on the other woman's arm.

"I'm fine." Anna stared straight ahead at the fluttering insects. "There's so much we love about this place, we haven't scratched the surface yet … and to think we could lose it."

"You made the right decision by inviting Matthew Kane here."

"Do you think so?" Anna gestured for them to continue along the garden path. "He's such a mean-spirited bastard. I think he's paranoid I'm going to poison him."

Kate chuckled. "Yes, he is a strange man. I've not come across such peculiar allergies, if that's what they are."

"Yes, I just learned recently of his preposterous demands from his trip last summer."

"Like what?" Kate slanted her head.

"He'd requested Harrison ask the family not to wear perfume and use only unscented soap and shampoo. The nerve!"

It astounded Kate too that anyone could be so self-centered. "What did Harrison say?"

"Exactly what I would have said, which was *no*. The villa is open and airy, he justified to me, with multiple spots for Mr. Kane to get away from smells and people he didn't like."

"Smart man, that Harrison." Kate halted her steps. "These so-called allergies are not the crux of Matthew's problem anyway."

"Oh? What do you think it is?" Anna stopped and turned to face her.

"In simplest terms, Matthew Kane is a bully, and it's not a stretch to say he's a narcissist. He has no empathy for others and little regard for the consequence of his actions." Kate lifted her hair and twisted it into a bun to cool the back of her neck. "For him to feel good about himself, he needs to put others down."

"Hmm …" Anna frowned as if weighing Kate's words. "That makes sense considering more than eighty percent of his reviews are bad, though ours had to be the worst."

Kate nodded. "Not surprising. From what I've seen, he lashes out to hide a shortcoming, be it low self-esteem or lack of control. Maybe it stems from a childhood trauma or another pivotal event in his life." She rocked on her heels. "Unconsciously, he may have even harbored resentment or envy toward you and Nolan when he wrote the review." She gave a *who knows?* shrug.

"We weren't even here at the time. In fact, we were with Ben and Nadine. Nolan was helping Ben with his university's Environmental Studies program."

"Right, you were the absent owners unavailable to satisfy him."

Anna rolled her eyes. "We never even knew the issues."

Kate touched Anna with a reassuring hand. "I'm not saying any of this is logical because it's not. Someone who is a narcissist projects his own feelings of inadequacy onto others. In Matthew's case, he blamed you and your staff. To let you know, he hit you where it would hurt most. It's probably the only area of his life where he has any power."

Anna scrunched her face with a look of bewilderment. "What I don't understand is *Travel in Style* is a respectable magazine. He's not even a good writer."

"I don't disagree with you there." Kate swatted a mosquito buzzing near her and they continued walking. "He's a horrible writer, but you only need to see the type of media that attracts the widest audience. Newspaper tabloids, gossip rags, reality television, they all purport to have journalistic appeal. Why should the travel industry be immune to this nasty media?" She saw a pained expression contort Anna's face.

"Nasty media is the new leisure activity."

Kate sighed. "I'm afraid so."

"Oh Kate, I feel horrible I've involved you. You're supposed to be here on holiday."

"And I want to continue coming here." Kate surveyed the beautiful surroundings. "I spoke to a colleague before Christmas, and he said I hate when people get taken advantage of. He was right." She looked Anna in the eyes. "I want to support your business in any way I can."

Anna stopped and gripped her arms. "Thank you. Both Nolan and I have the greatest respect for your insight. We so appreciate your being here."

After exiting the garden, they made their way toward the main house behind the swimming pool. Adam, Jerry, and the OMG boys were in the pool tossing a volleyball back and forth across a net. Ben lounged on a chair nearby, Nadine beside him with her e-reader. It was the perfect day to be outdoors. No sign of Matthew.

"Any final words on this guy?" Anna asked.

Kate shook her head and took a breath. "You and Nolan don't need to do anything that goes against who you are. Meet his needs, but don't allow him to commandeer or dictate any conversations with you. You'll be fine."

Anna nodded. "Let's hope he writes a retraction. Many of the bookings made in the summer canceled as a direct result of his review, that much I know."

"Don't worry." Kate bit down on her lower lip and released. "I'm sure he can be persuaded."

FOR MEN ONLY

Alone with his laptop in the living room, Matthew navigated through multiple searches before he found Adam's profile on the Internet. He overheard key words such as: capitalist; male power; and Chicago from Adam's conversation with Greg. It wasn't easy to eavesdrop and not show interest, especially when the Neanderthal, Rob, sat next to him flapping his jaw like an ape.

A few more taps of the keyboard and Adam's picture popped up on screen. He appeared younger, an old photograph, but it was him—Adam Naderi.

Adam's skills, whatever they were, impressed Greg and Tom so much they left lunch excited to work together. Now Matthew was about to find out what Adam did. Several articles all said the same thing. *"Adam Naderi's influence affords him more clout than the mayor of the city."* He referred to himself as part anarchist, part capitalist, believed in free enterprise, loathed government interference, and loved to travel. Indeed, pictures of him from all over the world were posted on several sites. Many had him posed with different women—young, attractive women.

Big name advertisers took up prominent real estate on his website. A string of testimonials from large energy companies, telecommunications firms, and numerous airlines accredited Adam with improving their business and increasing profits.

But how? What the hell did he do?

What his business services were remained a mystery even after Matthew tabbed through all the site's pages. On Adam's active blog, to which he only had limited access, articles ranged from poor airline service to unusual diets to exercise regimes. Matthew hated admitting to himself that the writing impressed him, what little he was able to read. To access full articles or to engage with Adam, a questionnaire had to be completed and membership granted after an interview with Adam or one of his representatives. Rates ranged from one hundred dollars a month to a thousand dollars for the year. Five thousand dollars bought a lifetime membership.

Matthew widened his eyes and reread the line. *Really?*

Even if he had not met Adam in person, he would've assumed the same thing—scam artist. Meeting him only reinforced his suspicion. Sure, Adam had some business savvy. Recognizable companies slapped their logos on his flashy website. In the age of online businesses, anyone could write anything on a website, including glowing testimonials.

It didn't mean it was true.

Unlike the average person who believed everything they read on the Internet, Matthew knew better. With palms pressed to his cheeks, he shook his head in disbelief, thankful he was a journalist who questioned everything. Positive reviews could not convince him Adam was anything other than a crook.

He toggled back to the Bio page to check out pictures of the women—all beautiful, young, model types. In scrolling through the photo gallery, a tinge of jealousy rippled through his stomach. Perhaps it was a hunger pang, but Matthew could not believe all the gorgeous women draped over a weasel like Adam. Just thinking of the man made him want to spit.

As he was about to sign off the computer, he noticed a small, animated button on the right sidebar. It pulsed from a deep cherry red to pink and back to red again. No label accompanied the button, so there was no way of knowing its purpose.

Was it an error in the site's design? Was it even functional?

Matthew hovered it with his mouse; the color changed to electric blue—an active link. He stared at the throbbing button, which for some strange reason, reminded him of a woman's clitoris. Was it a trap? If he hit it, was there a way his information could be captured on the backend? He moved his mouse away from it, rubbed his chin, sat back.

After staring at the pulsating button for a few more seconds, curiosity got the better of him, and he clicked it.

A warning screen popped up that read:

For Men Only.

Do you want to proceed?
Yes or No.

He clicked the *Yes* button.
The next screen read:

> You are about to learn the secrets of being a man,
> to get what you want in life on your own terms.
> Women, money, power.
> Are you ready?

Matthew snorted at the ridiculous scam. Now he had to go through with it. He hit the *Yes* button again.

The next screen requested an e-mail address before he could proceed.

Shit.

Lucky for him, he had multiple e-mail addresses. He input a generic one that would have no connection back to him or his work: *Anthem (dot) Tweak (at) mail (dot) com*. After confirming it, he re-entered the website and started reading.

Three sections divided the page:

> How to be successful with women.
> How to gain unlimited power.
> How to earn what you're worth.

Matthew scrolled to *How to be successful with women,* and

pored through the words, mouth hanging open. Certain passages resonated truth, but they were so outrageous no one would dare speak them, let alone write them down. Yet, here they were: *Adam's Commandments*.

After reading it twice, he flung his head back, slapped his thigh so hard, he flinched from the sting. Laughter arose from some uncontrollable place in his stomach up his chest.

What an egomaniac!

Adams's writing read like the rants of a mad man disguised as words of wisdom. Matthew was able to unscramble the fancy wordplay, but he still could not believe Adam's nerve.

"What is so funny?" The woman's voice startled him.

He slammed his laptop shut. "Oh … hi," he said. "I didn't think anyone was around."

"Sorry, I didn't mean to sneak up on you. Care to share?" Anna swept by and took a seat across from him.

"Crazy things they post on the Internet these days."

"Oh, one of those jokes," Anna said. "You don't have to worry. The guys can get pretty raunchy here at times. I've heard it all."

Peeking out from her wrap-around skirt, he observed the smooth lines of her perfect thighs. "Nothing I can repeat to a lady, I'm afraid."

"No worries." She chuckled to herself. "I was hoping to catch you before you disappeared for the day. Sorry Nolan and I were not around to greet you when you arrived. Is your room okay?"

"It's fine. I wish I had Wi-Fi access though."

Anna smiled. "It's on the list to upgrade. All the rooms will eventually have it." She crossed her legs in the opposite direction.

Matthew followed her thighs up as far as he could see. "It's large and airy, that's more important."

"Yes, that's why I reserved it for you. It's a bit removed from the main villa here, but the advantage is you have your own pool. I know certain smells bother you, and I didn't want you to feel ill again while here."

Matthew narrowed his eyes. Was she trying to be nice to him, finally? "I prefer it a bit more remote. I don't enjoy swimming in a pool, so that's not important for me."

Just then, fast-walking footsteps came up behind him. Anna lifted her chin past his shoulders and acknowledged whoever it was. Nolan breezed by Matthew and joined his wife on the couch.

"What are you up to today, Matthew?" he asked.

Only then did Matthew notice the age difference between them. Nolan was probably a few years younger than him—late forties. Anna did not even look thirty. His jealousy meter rose as Nolan placed a hand on his wife's knee, and she leaned into him.

"I don't know yet," he managed to say without sounding too distracted by their affection for one another. "I was going to meditate and take a walk later, not much of a swimmer."

"Understandable. I don't meditate. The drums are my way of relaxing."

Nolan's charm eclipsed his wife's and made Matthew

feel at ease. "That's a form of meditation, I suppose, a loud one." He let out a stilted laugh.

A flash of humor crossed the couple's faces. "Well, you just arrived, so settle in," Nolan said. "Tomorrow, I'm taking the young couple from Tennessee on an excursion to Dunn's River Falls if you care to join us."

"Oh? How far is that?"

"Not far, less than twenty minutes. You passed it on the way in."

"Right …" Matthew sat erect, trying not to break eye contact with Nolan but noticed how he flexed his fingers atop Anna's knee.

"It's a spectacular sight," he continued. "You can climb as high as six-hundred feet to see the river empty into the sea. The Dunn's River beach was featured in the James Bond movie, *Dr. No*, if you're a James Bond fan."

Matthew wasn't, and he couldn't imagine sitting in a car with Rob. With his fear of heights, climbing a slippery wet surface did not appeal to him either. "I'll think about it. Thanks."

"Sure. We'll leave after breakfast to avoid the tour busses if we can, pack a lunch and spend the day." He turned to his wife, as if to signal they had somewhere to go, but then stopped. "Oh, by the way, Matthew …"

"Yes?"

"If there's anything you need while here, just ask. We're pretty casual, and we want you to feel at home."

"Uh … okay." Not what he expected. "I gave Anna the list of my restrictions. If I think of anything else, I'll let you know."

Nolan gathered Anna's hand in his and entwined their fingers. They traversed the dining room and headed toward the beach, chatting quietly to one another.

What did Nolan have over him?

Matthew pressed his palm against his chest to assuage a slight burning sensation. He expected much more of a pitch, something that involved retracting his review or writing another one. When he considered their finances were probably hurting because of him, both maintained a composed exterior, especially Anna. Nolan caught a cool one with her, with legs that seemed to extend forever. How did that iciness translate to the bedroom, he wondered.

Matthew opened his laptop and Adam's website reappeared. He shook his head again at the absurdity of what he read. The man had balls, he had to give him that.

ALPHA BETA

"I'm not sure what your problem is, but I've been doing a bit of checking on you," Matthew said.

Adam floated in the pool on a rubber mat. "Don't you have anything better to do?" With a pinch of his thumb and index finger, he pulled down his sunglasses from atop his forehead.

Matthew's ire increased as Adam appeared unaffected by his request for a confrontation. "I was surfing my social networks and you happened to come across it." He slanted his baseball cap lower.

"Happened to come across it?" Adam flipped up his glasses and sat up on the raft. "You don't fool me. I've been on social media long before the term was coined, when bulletin boards were the only form of online interaction." He jumped off the mat and splashed Matthew when he descended into the water.

"What is your problem with me?" Matthew did not intend to let the matter go. Somehow being in the pool cooled his temper and made him feel brave.

"I don't have a problem with you, so don't flatter yourself. I haven't given you a moment's thought."

"You dislike me." Matthew's bitterness grew louder. Visions of punching the smug from Adam's face crossed his mind. "Why?"

Adam moved into the deep end and treaded water while facing Matthew. "I dislike your rudeness if you must know, and your writing is dreadful."

Matthew grabbed two Styrofoam noodles and propped himself up on them. He didn't want to dip his head into the chlorine. "Oh, so you know who I am."

"Yes, I do."

"I guess you're a friend of the Pearsons, and you don't like me because of my review of this place."

"Wrong on both counts. I chose to come here *after* reading your review. I had no idea you'd be here and would've preferred you not be."

"Why's that?"

"You're a shitty writer."

"What do you mean?"

"How many ways do you want to hear it? You're a shitty writer. Period."

"You can't say that and not offer reasons!" Fury bubbled inside Matthew, catching in his throat.

Adam moved to the side of the pool and leaned his back to the wall. "Reasons?"

The man's calm only infuriated Matthew more. "Yes, you can't call me a shitty writer and then not back it up. It's slanderous!"

"You want reasons?" Adam stuck out his thumb, then his fingers, counting them off one at a time. "Here are three for you. One: Your review had little to do with the resort. Two: You came across as a whiny, loathsome man. Three: Your writing style bores me. Shall I fire off more?"

Blood rushed to Matthew's head. "And I suppose your blog is a showcase for your stellar writing?"

Adam floated on his back and shielded his eyes with his sunglasses again. "It is. I get more than five thousand unique visitors daily. People with strong intellect who are not easily offended appreciate it. You're not of that camp." He extended his arms out and glided atop the water. "Why are you here anyway if you hated it so much the first time?"

"None of your damn business." Matthew slumped over the noodles and pushed up to keep the water below his armpits. His gut churned from the overwhelming smell of chlorine.

"You initiated this conversation, not me. I was happy to have the pool to myself."

"Well, I'll leave you alone, but tell me one thing." Matthew moved to the side of the pool and held on to the edge. "How does an asshole like you get all the young ladies? And I mean really young." He wanted to punch himself in the head to unfog his mind caused by the toxins in the pool.

Asshole was the best epithet he could come up with?

"That sort of thing is not challenging for someone with money and resources," Adam said.

Matthew hated how Adam had an answer for everything. "I think you're incapable of dealing with women your own age." A hollow laugh tinged with triumph escaped him, and he liked how the insult rolled off his tongue.

Adam swept water underneath him and righted himself in the pool. He created a big splash, which Matthew was certain he did on purpose. "You know how pathological you sound, Matt? You're not even close to being my equal, which makes you an unworthy opponent. It would be unfair of me to crush you."

"You're the biggest … the most … arrogant bastard I've ever met!" Matthew sputtered.

"I believe it, but I'm not always arrogant. You, on the other hand, are a beta, and you will always be a beta. If you don't know what it means, look it up, because for some reason, I fascinate you." Adam dipped under and propelled himself in the opposite direction.

Matthew swatted at the water, which splashed him in the face. He swore under his breath, threw the floatation device at Adam who was already at the other end of the pool. Anxious to shower the chorine off his body, he waded along the edge and stepped out. When he grabbed his towel to dry off, he viewed Kate headed his way, her long swathe of sun-kissed skin flawless in a black and white bikini.

DAY THREE
MEDITATION

Matthew Kane sat in a half-lotus position in the Zen Garden. A palm tree shaded him, but he also wore a straw hat. He didn't need any more sun on his already tomato-red face. With eyes closed and hands folded in his lap, he concentrated on his inner calm. The sound of water from a nearby fountain helped him focus.

Peace. Calm. Tranquility.

The run-in with Adam had rattled him. The man was an obnoxious megalomaniac. Matthew guessed him to be ten years younger than him, slightly more handsome, though that was subjective. He reasoned he'd aged well since he rarely ate junk and didn't drink much. At forty-nine, he'd never had to exercise, while Adam probably did so every day. Earlier this morning, he saw him in the gym running on the treadmill like a lab rat on a wheel.

The nerve of the idiot to call him a beta.

Matthew had heard the word before, but not in the way Adam used it. After researching several Internet sites, he figured out how Adam meant it to describe him. A dishonest, manipulative, and sexually repressed beta male was the opposite of the alpha male. He complained incessantly and was unsuccessful with women. It shocked Matthew to see pages and pages of sites devoted to the differences between alphas and betas, and how betas could learn to become alphas by transforming their mindset.

When he read that, he twigged to the connection of Adam's Commandments, his rules for success with women. Adam taught courses in it. How any of that connected him to the companies who endorsed him escaped Matthew.

The meditation usually relaxed him, calmed violent thoughts in his head. All he had to do was concentrate on breathing, directing his energy toward this instinctual life force. By doing so, he lived in the moment. Today, staying in the moment proved impossible. His mind wandered like an unleashed, wild animal.

All he could think of were Adam's Commandments.

They had invaded his brain since reading them, beginning with the bold statements about the nature of alpha and beta males.

> Alphas are assertive.
> Alphas never take things personally.
> Alphas remain calm under pressure.
> Alphas have mastery over themselves and their women.
>
> Betas are passive.

Betas make excuses.
Betas are insecure.
Betas do not have mastery over themselves
and cannot master their women.

Part of him refused to believe he could improve his chances with women by becoming more like Adam Naderi. He loathed the man, but there was no denying women were attracted to him. The Southern girl certainly was. Probably Kate was too. It was a shame, because Kate really interested him.
As much as he hated to admit it, Adam's Commandments held a glimmer of truth to them and tugged at his thoughts.

He cracked one eye open just enough to glimpse his watch.

What the fuck? He'd only been sitting for ten minutes, with fifty more minutes to go. It felt as if his body had been contorted in this position for hours already.

The commandments filled his mind again, repeating themselves in his brain.

1. Be unreasonably self-confident.
2. Touch a woman boldly on the first date.
3. Connect with her emotions.
4. Always maintain control.
5. Make her your sexual slave.

The last one made him laugh aloud when he read it. Yeah, right, as if any man can make a woman his sexual slave, unless he paid for it. He would never be able to pull it off, especially not with Kate, who both intimidated and aroused him in equal measure. To think he could force her into submission gave him a rampant erection. In reality, he knew nothing about her, but his mind filled in the gaps, transforming her into the sexiest woman alive.

To stop from fantasizing about Kate, Matthew squeezed his eyes tighter, but it only made the images more vivid. Meditation was supposed to calm him, but he could neither pacify his mind, nor the uncomfortable swell in his groin.

Just breathe.

His mind skipped to the Pearsons.

The owners were trying to endear themselves to him finally, though their casualness irritated him. They didn't appear all that concerned to make amends for the hardship he experienced here the first time. Maybe he did require more attention, but he expected to be with people who were open-minded and considerate.

Breathe for God's sake.

Canadians owners.

He wasn't fond of Canadians, not after staying in Vancouver during the 2010 Winter Olympics, the one and only time he was in Eskimo country. Claude, the concierge could not accommodate his request to change rooms. Of all the people to help him, he had to get a bloody French Canadian.

Concentrate ... breathe...

Faint voices in the background grew louder, drew him

back to the present. Footsteps moved closer to where he sat, which was invisible from the main path. He discovered the serene nook the first time he was here, enjoyed the shade combined with the sound of running water. Hidden in the brush behind a ceramic statue of a meditating Buddha, he claimed the spot as his sanctuary.

Whoever wandered by stopped not far from him. The conversation continued, low male voices. He strained to listen. There were at least three of them.

"Nolan is stressed, but he's staying strong for Anna's sake. That asshole's review has put the business in jeopardy. Their reservations are non-existent."

"Seriously?"

"Yeah, they planned renovations for this year, but they had to cancel. Nolan said they're in maintenance mode right now, and of course they have to pay the staff."

"Do you think we should offer financial help?"

"No, he would never accept that. He's too proud."

The flicking of a lighter sounded.

"I have half a mind to beat the crap out of that pompous bastard."

Cigarette smoke wafted toward Matthew. He scrunched his eyebrows. His nose twitched.

"Come on now. Don't let Anna hear you saying that."

"I know. She's upset enough already, I would never say it in front of her."

"Have they talked to this guy? I mean, is he reasonable?"

Matthew perked up his ears while prickly sensations moved up and down his stiff back. As he got caught up in the conversation, the top of his head started itching. He wanted to rip his hat off and scratch his scalp raw. It sounded like the gay couple and one other man, a voice he had not heard before.

More cigarette smoke blew in his direction. It smelled like … *Shit!* Now they were smoking a joint. His mind fogged up as he tried to concentrate on what they were saying about him. He didn't dare open his eyes even though his insides shook and smoke gripped his throat.

"Nolan said he might try to talk to him, but frankly, I don't know if that's going to help."

"Why do you say that?"

"The guy's an old woman! I've never met anyone who has so many imaginary fucking problems."

"Hey, you're insulting old women! My mom's eighty, and she's lower maintenance."

Belly laughter and someone coughed.

"He's that bad?" said the unfamiliar voice.

Matthew detected an accent. French? German?

"Yeah, no perfumes, no scented cleaning products for his room. I saw a laundry list as long as my arm for all the things he can't eat."

"Poor Violet, she needs to alter every meal just for him. He's a goddamn hypochondriac if you ask me."

Definitely Greg speaking.

"Sounds to me like he's allergic to life, maybe he needs to live in a bubble."

More spirited laughter. More smoke in his direction.

"And when not talking about his allergies, he shoehorns

the name of his magazine into every conversation."

"You caught that too?"

Someone snorted.

"How could I not? Fucking *Travel in Style* this and *Travel in Style* that. He has a nerve thinking anyone would buy his magazine."

"The man is delusional."

Silence.

"Hey, want to light up another jay?"

Oh, Christ!

Matthew pleaded and whimpered in his head, prayed the answer would be *no*. He blew out an inaudible breath as a stitch crept up his right leg. As quietly as possible, he alleviated some of the pain by making a minute adjustment to his position. He struggled to breathe normally, swallowing the acrid taste of fear in his mouth. Only with monumental effort did he not have to clear his throat.

"Save it. Come by my place after dinner and we can smoke it then."

Holding on to his discomfort and fear of discovery a little longer, he bit down on his lower lip.

His place? So this stranger must be staying at another villa because he didn't sound like a local.

Matthew heard them finally meander down the path. When he was certain they were far enough so they would not hear him, he unraveled his legs and kicked them in front of him. A wave of relief washed over him as the cramp subsided. Leaning back on the heels of his hands, he continued shaking his legs to stretch them out of their twisted memory. To make matters worse, his other leg had fallen asleep.

When he opened his eyes, he almost feared a cloud of toxic gas surrounded him, but he didn't see that. The air was clear and the sky bright. He exhaled a sharp breath and tried to imagine emptying himself of the fumes he had inhaled. Fuzziness pulsated his brain.

Fucking faggots and whoever was with them, the nerve of them to call *him* an old woman. It was obvious the owners didn't intend to curry favor if they were talking about him behind his back to other guests.

He shook out the pins and needles in his foot and winced from the pain.

The Pearsons would regret they ever invited him back here.

BITTEN

A chill crept over Kate's body, manifested as goose bumps dotting her arms.

Had the sun gone down already? It was then she realized the presence of someone nearby.

"I took the liberty of spraying more tanner on your back. I didn't want you to burn."

That voice.

She flipped on her back, shielded her eyes with a forearm. He stood in front of her, blocking the sun.

"What … what time is it?" she asked, pushing herself up.

A dark figure sat at the foot of her lounge chair, his skin touching hers.

She froze.

He stroked her shoulder, trailed his fingers behind her neck, down her back. Her bikini top mysteriously flew off, her breasts colliding with his hairy chest. His firm lips pressed against hers, invading her mouth with his tongue.

With his legs spread on either side of the lounge chair, he grabbed her heels to rest against his shoulders and peeled off her bikini bottom. Pearls of sweat formed in the basins of her collarbones. She clutched the side of the lounger and closed her eyes.

A buzz sounded near her ear. She wanted to scream but only guttural, strangled noises escaped her throat. When the rattling of the chair grew louder, the annoying buzz returned, now drowning out the sound of everything else. She swatted the air and felt herself falling off the chair.

Kate bolted up from her lounger.

A dream. Just a dream.

A stinging sensation immediately moved down the back of her head. "No, no … not here …" With nails digging into her scalp, she rocked back and forth in the chair. "Please … not here."

In front of her, old tree branches twisted like giant, distorted limbs, casting generous shadows in the shape of monsters. Ivy climbed the walls of the embankment. It took her a moment to remember where she was—on the small terrace carved out of the cliff's edge, just beneath the pool area.

She wrapped her arms around herself and clawed her sides. "Shhh," she said to herself. "Relax." A warm breeze caressed her back.

The prickling on her skin stopped, but a headache formed quickly, causing her right eye to throb with each beat of her heart. She reasoned she had been out in the sun too long, was dehydrated.

Exhaling a jagged breath, Kate pressed a hand to her stomach, unnerved and shaken. Though a mild episode, nothing like this had ever happened to her here. Sunset

Villa was her sanctuary, where bad memories had never intruded on her thoughts.

She tried to conjure up the fading image of the man from her dream. An object had obscured his face. Was it the sun or a hat? Who was he? Try as she might to hold on to the memory, the silhouette disappeared into her subconscious.

The buzzing returned.

Her eyelashes shot up. Unblinking, she followed the sound, rage building inside her. With flattened palms hovered on either side of the pest, she held her breath. Her eyes ping-ponged to capture the insect in an imaginary spot, awaiting the perfect moment.

Waiting. Waiting.

She readied herself and then hard and fast—*Smack!* Upon spreading open her palms, the twisted remains of a mosquito lay squashed in the middle of her left hand. Kate heaved out a self-congratulatory breath. Relief. That was, until she glanced at her other hand. Smeared across the heart line was a splotch of red.

Too late, she had already been bitten.

DINNER GUESTS

Kate approached the dining room, and both men stood up. Seated at opposite corners with no one else at the table, she sensed the tension between them. Matthew pulled the chair out for her when she took a seat next to him. It would have been awkward for her to proceed past him and sit elsewhere.

"How was your day, Kate?" Adam asked from across the table.

"Good, thank you. I swam and read for most of it. The library here has more than a thousand books left behind by people who've stayed here. I picked up Ian Fleming's *Live and Let Die*."

"Ahh … James Bond. Are you a fan of thrillers?"

"Yes, Fleming wrote it next door more than sixty years ago." Kate took a deep, satisfied breath. "I like the mystery of his connection to this place. I've read he wrote in a monastic room with the shutters closed, didn't even have a chance to appreciate his ocean view." When Harrison poured ice water in her glass, she mouthed a *"thank you"* to him and adjusted herself in her seat.

"I've read that too about Fleming, and I know what you

mean about the mystery here." Adam nodded. "I started *The End of the Affair* this afternoon."

"Graham Greene?"

"Have you read it?"

"No, but I read *The Quiet American* years back."

"Me too. I would read that again, such a—"

"I'm not much for fiction," Matthew interrupted Adam. "I prefer non-fiction and journalistic criticism."

Kate turned to the man beside her, his thinning pate of salt and pepper hair on the cusp of a bad comb-over. "Even while on vacation?"

"Especially while on vacation." Matthew projected his adenoidal voice for a much larger audience. "The mind needs to be at work so it doesn't stagnate." With both hands in the air, he gestured as if he were giving a lecture. "Fiction for me is mindless entertainment."

Kate cocked an eyebrow. "I see, and you don't think there's any value to fiction, not even as a respite from … journalistic criticism?"

"Well … I suppose I relax in other ways. Meditation is how I feed my mind."

"At least you're not allergic to *that*," Adam said, leaning back in his chair with exaggerated apathy.

"I … What are you saying? Why don't you … what gives you the right to—" Matthew's words came out as a stammering mix of offense and indignation.

"I heard you played tennis with the guys today," Kate said to Adam, seeking to diffuse Matthew's outrage.

Adam carved his fingers across his thick head of hair.

"Right, Nolan and I against Greg and Tom. Jerry took Tom's place for a set."

"And?" Kate knew Nolan was a good player because he and Anna took lessons from the local tennis instructor. She had no idea about the others.

"It was a close game, but we won, even though Greg plays damn well in flip-flops."

Kate laughed. "Yes, he was mumbling about not having proper shoes. He would've beat you otherwise, he said."

"Yes, that's our story and we're sticking to it!" Jerry entered with Greg and Tom behind him.

Chatter escalated as the others wandered into the room. Kate noticed Matthew wringing his hands in his lap.

"Hello Adam, Matthew, Kate," Anna said, taking her place at the head of the table. Nolan pulled out her chair for her. "You're early."

Kate flashed a smile. "I'm hungry. All day, I've been dreaming of Violet's famous jerk chicken."

Nolan threw his head back in laughter. "She makes it like no one else. We're lucky to have her. Nadine is helping her put together a cookbook of her recipes."

"It's a labor of love." Nadine sat down across from Kate. "I even brought a few ingredients for her that are hard to find here like cream cheese and candied cherries. She's using them in a dessert this week."

"I can't wait," Kate said.

"Me neither, and the best part of doing the book is I'll be tasting every dish."

Kate moved in closer to the table. "Lucky you. If you need an additional taster … I'll be happy to help."

Nadine chuckled, draped her napkin across her lap. "Violet is so excited about it."

"When will we be able to buy a copy?"

"It should be available by the end of the year."

The guests played musical chairs. It reminded Kate of attending wedding receptions on her own. Accustomed to sitting with strangers, she considered social functions like therapy, a lot of talking and listening with little attachment. At Sunset, sharing food was a good way to meet and talk to guests without feeling any obligation to spend time with them otherwise.

When everyone was seated, Nolan rang the bell. Harrison appeared in a white, short-sleeved shirt, a pressed pair of black pants, and wearing smart white gloves. He circled the table pouring wine into each guest's glass. Kate noticed Matthew accepted only half a glass of red.

"I'd like to propose a toast," said Ben, clad in a loose fitting floral green and orange shirt. The big man reminded Kate of Francis Ford Coppola with his larger than life presence and warm smile. He raised his glass and everyone did the same. "To Nolan and Anna, for being such gracious hosts."

"Hear, hear," was the overriding response.

When the first course of soup came out, the aroma of sweet tomatoes filled the dining room. The wine flowed, counterpointed smoothly by Miles Davis and dinner conversation. Matthew leaned to say a few words to Anna, but other than that, he remained quiet and did not partake in the table chatter.

Kate noticed Ben and Nadine avoided eye contact with Matthew. Except for a few words when Anna mentioned to Matthew that Nadine was a gourmet cook with several books out, no conversation flowed between them.

It intrigued Kate to narrow down the many traits of Matthew that rubbed people the wrong way. She weighed her own assessment. Maladjusted and awkward described him in group settings. Unless holding court, he did not get along with others. As for being a tantrum-thrower, she had already witnessed his sulky attitude on more than one occasion. To convince him to rewrite his review for Sunset, she had to spend time with him alone. At the very least, get him away from Adam.

Aggressive, dominant, achievement-motivated were the words Kate settled on for Adam earlier in the day. From his brief exchange tonight with Matthew, he did not disappoint.

Harrison returned to clear the soup bowls. Kate wiped her lips with her linen napkin and turned to Anna. "Great soup, just the right amount of tartness."

"I love a good tomato soup as well," she said. "I hope you enjoyed it, Matthew?"

He turned to Anna and appeared surprised she spoke to him. "Yes, I'm great with fresh vegetables and fruits. I don't do well with certain foods, like anything processed. I prefer only organic if I can get it …"

Nadine tapped Anna's arm and murmured a question.

Anna politely excused herself from Matthew.

He appeared unfazed as Anna turned her back to him. Instead, he swung his chair around to face Kate. "Is this your first time here?" he asked.

Kate moved her head in his direction. "No. I've been here several times."

"Oh?" He leaned away from her as Harrison approached to take away his soup bowl. "You must like it here."

Kate wondered if he was fishing for information. "I do." She smiled at him and brought her wine glass to her lips.

Harrison wheeled out the main dish on a trolley and the tang of jerk chicken drifted by Kate's nose. A piquant fragrance filled the air. "That smells so good," she said to no one in particular. Several people chimed in and agreed.

"I've never had jerk chicken. Is it spicy?" Rob chugged his white wine like beer.

Kate caught Jessica's eye-roll, but Rob did not appear to take notice of her. When Harrison set down his plate in front of him, he sat up straight over his platter of chicken "Wow, that looks fantastic."

"Wait until you taste it," Nolan said, who passed along a basket filled with oblong dinner rolls. "Here's something to go with the chicken if you find it too hot. They're called festivals."

It amused Kate that Rob rattled his chair with excitement. Given the shape of his belly, she had already suspected food as one of his vices.

He grabbed two festivals, eager to take another when Jessica shot him a stern look. Rob glimpsed her expression.

"What?" A grimace spread across his face.

In a voice that could melt frozen butter, she said, "Sweetheart, why don't you pass along the buns until everyone has taken one?"

"Oh yes … sorry." Rob reluctantly handed the basket to Jerry. "These remind me of hush puppies from home." Like a curious child with a new toy, he held one up and scrutinized it.

"Good call, Rob," Nolan said. "They're similar since they both use cornmeal, though festivals are sweeter."

"Oh lordy, these are much better than hush puppies!" he said after taking a bite.

The table burst into laughter, except for Jessica who looked mortified.

"Take as many as you like. I'm sure Violet has made plenty," Anna said.

As everyone helped themselves to platters of chicken, salad, and festivals, Harrison placed a plate in front of Matthew. A drumstick, a thigh, and a medium-sized breast seared to perfection sat on it, decorated with several sprigs of thyme and roasted slices of garlic. It did not have the dark brown color or the smoky scent of the jerk chicken.

"This is for me?" Matthew asked Harrison.

"Yes, sir."

"You get the special treatment, don't you?" Kate said to Matthew.

With his fork, he jabbed at his meat. "Interesting," he said. "I wonder how the cook spiced it."

"There's only one way to find out," Kate said as Nadine

shot her a mischievous smile.

Jerry held a large serving bowl of rice and peas for her. "Kate, would you like some?"

"Love rice and peas." She heaped two spoonfuls on her plate before he returned the bowl to the table.

"The rice doesn't contain anything you can't eat, Matthew," Anna said, "Violet uses real chicken stock."

"Are you sure it's not a bouillon cube or that artificial MSG?"

Kate bristled, not so much from his question but his brusque delivery of it. Anna appeared unruffled. Only a tiny furrow between her brow betrayed her otherwise hospitable demeanor.

"I'm positive," she said in a measured voice.

"Oh, okay." He reached forward and took a small helping for his plate. "Thanks."

Anna's face lightened. "My pleasure."

"Why is this called jerk chicken?" Rob asked, looking to Nolan.

"That's a good question." He gazed down the table at his wife. "There are two theories, one is it originated from the Spanish to describe the process of drying meat."

"As in jerky," Adam said.

"Right." Nolan nodded in Adam's direction. "The second is it comes from the practice of jerking, where holes are poked in the meat to spice it prior to cooking."

"I like that," Rob said with enthusiasm. He winked at Jessica who appeared to ignore him.

"Nowadays," Nolan continued, "jerk describes the

marinade and spices applied to the meat."

"See Jess, jerk is not just a name you call me." Rob's playful stab at his girlfriend brought uncomfortable laughter from the table. Jessica's cheeks turned a deep shade of pink. She unfolded a napkin on top of her lap.

"Rob, please." She tutted him as if humoring a naughty child. "I'm sure no one wants to hear your jokes."

"Oh, but I do," Matthew piped up.

Kate turned in his direction and met a grin on his face. How telling it was that he should jump in the conversation to encourage a subject that embarrassed Jessica.

"Have some salad," Tom said, handing a wooden bowl to Rob.

Rob didn't take any and passed the greens down the table. He pointed a finger at Matthew. "Buddy, you and I should talk. I don't dare say anything with the ladies at this table. I'd hate to be labeled a sexist, or what's that other word ... a massagist."

"A what?" Jessica said in a biting tone.

"You know, that word you always call me, someone who doesn't like women."

Jessica clicked her tongue and huffed.

Kate noticed Jessica either on the verge of tears or hysterical laughter before she interjected, "Rob, I think you mean a misogynist."

"Of course, a misogynist. I knew it began with an *em*." Rob grabbed another festival from the center of the table.

"The world is filled with all sorts of people, Rob. It keeps life interesting, doesn't it?" Kate said.

"It sure does, ma'am, makes the world go 'round."

Everyone quieted while eating dominated the table's activity. Much like the music, the chatter faded to the background. The conversation shifted to less combative topics. The mood calmed. Matthew did not engage with anyone and appeared to enjoy his food.

From her brief interaction with him, Kate gleaned a better understanding of Matthew's behavior. By burdening himself with a health issue no one could confirm, he made himself unique. His vague description of his condition did not fit any of the factitious disorders she knew. Did he believe he had an illness, or did he fabricate one to prey on people's sympathy? His social awkwardness with a vindictive streak bordered on sociopathy.

Kate turned to him and watched as he cut into his chicken breast. "Is it to your liking?"

Matthew finished chewing. "Not bad. It's not jerk chicken, but it's tasty."

"Good to hear."

"I must say the food's much better than when I came here last year."

This time, Kate decided to bite. "You've been here before?"

Matthew shifted his eyes sideways as if he were afraid Anna might hear him. "Yes, one other time. It wasn't the best experience."

"That's too bad." Kate cut up a mouthful of salad. "And yet, you're back."

"Yes, I review hotels and vacation spots for the most

influential travel and leisure magazine there is."

Self-importance with a need to impress suggested a form of borderline psychosis. She added it to the list of his possible disorders. "Are you here to review Sunset Villa?"

"Umm ..." Matthew spoke in an undertone. "I already did after my first trip. Have you heard of *Travel in Style?*"

"Yes, though I've never read it."

"It's a great magazine, and I'm branded highly by the company. I would love to discuss it with you if you have the time."

"So you provide your readers with an honest, objective evaluation."

"Yes."

"I'd like to read it then."

He knit his eyebrows. "Umm ... are you really interested?"

"Yes."

"I have a copy here if you want to see it." Dabbing a napkin to his mouth, he fidgeted with it, then left it crumpled on his lap.

His actions did not match his self-assuredness. Odd, Kate mused. "Of course. I would love to read it. Can you bring it to me tomorrow at breakfast?"

"Yes, yes, I'll do that," he said, smiling.

Matthew appeared cocksure and self-absorbed, but timid when she agreed to read his work.

What was he trying to hide?

NIGHTCAP

Mr. Pearson and his friends worked hard, drank hard, and smoked hard. They also played hard, jamming for more than two hours before they ended at half past eleven.

Harrison welcomed the Bob Marley tunes, even knew a few of the Eagles and Neil Young songs. Of all the songs the band hammered out tonight, the British melodies resonated most with him, especially the Rolling Stones and the Beatles. For the better part of his adult life, he had worked at Sunset for the Woodfords from Birmingham, the owners before the Pearsons. Mrs. Woodford had introduced him to the music of her country.

Lights dimmed near the pool and Harrison detected footsteps coming his way.

"How did we sound?" Ben said, waddling up to the bar with Nadine by his side.

"Very good, sir, getting better every night."

Ben played a fast low-end riff on his harmonica. "I'm winded, need to stop smoking."

Harrison grinned. "Yes, sir."

"That'll be the day," Nadine rolled her eyes and requested water from Harrison.

He pulled open the door of the retro Smeg bar fridge and took out a bottle. "Would you like a glass, ma'am?"

Nadine shook her head. Harrison twisted the cap loose before handing her the water.

Nolan came up to the bar carrying drumsticks. "Did you hear the Donovan song, Harrison?"

"'Mellow Yellow', well done, sir."

Nolan smiled. "A bit rusty. We should improve by the end of the week."

"I think so." Harrison pressed the heels of his hands on the wooden bar. "Care for a drink, sir?"

"Not for me, thanks, it's been a long day. I'm off to bed."

"We're off too." Ben and Nadine said their good-nights and headed inside.

Harrison surveyed the area where the band had played. He saw shadows. With hopes that someone might come in for a nightcap, he rinsed glasses and placed them on the counter. One by one, he polished them dry with a white, cotton dishtowel. If there was one thing Mrs. Woodford had taught him, it was never to serve alcohol in a dirty glass.

The last time he played bartender was for a French family in August, the final booking before Hurricane Sandy hit. He missed having guests at the villa. There was only so much to keep him busy without them. He also missed the Woodfords. Soon after they bought the estate forty years ago, he procured a part-time job with them and had worked here ever since.

The pitter-patter of footsteps and muted voices pulled

Harrison out of the past.

Kate emerged up the steps from the darkness of the pool area.

"Miss Kate," Harrison beamed.

"Hello Harrison," she said, taking a seat at the bar. "I was hoping to see you here. Too late for a drink?"

"Never too late, ma'am. Will someone be joining you?"

"No, I think everyone else has called it a night."

"Fine, Miss Kate. Still drinking scotch, neat?"

"Great memory, Harrison." She set her room key atop the counter. "You've had a few quiet months since the hurricane, haven't you?"

"Yes, ma'am. It's given us lots of time clean up and make the resort beautiful again." He slid a fifteen-year old bottle of Glenfiddich off the shelf.

"I can see that. The place looks wonderful, no one would ever know it was hit."

"Thank you." Twisting the cap, he broke the seal of the new bottle. "How do you drink this with no ice, Miss Kate?"

"It's the only way to drink scotch, at least for me. Ice changes the taste."

"Yes, ma'am." To ensure cleanliness of the glass, he held up a tumbler to the light before pouring two ounces of the golden liquid into it.

"Will you join me, Harrison? Just the two of us tonight."

"Oh no, ma'am, I don't touch the drink anymore."

Kate tilted her head. "No alcohol at all?"

"That's right, not a drop in almost forty years." He slid

the scotch back on the shelf, turned and saw Miss Kate raise her eyebrows.

"May I ask why?" she said.

It always surprised him when guests wanted to learn more about him, that they would even consider his life interesting. "I don't want to bore you, ma'am."

"Harrison, you can never do that."

"Miss Kate, you are my favorite guest."

"And you're my favorite bartender." She took a swallow and set down her drink, swirled the tumbler clockwise atop the uneven wood surface.

"I was thinking while listening to the music I am a very lucky man."

"Oh?" Kate stopped moving her glass. "Do tell."

"Well, ma'am, Sunset Villa has always taken care of me from when I was a young man, ever since the previous owners hired me back in '67."

"The Woodfords."

"Yes, they taught me so much, especially Mrs. Woodford. And Mr. Woodford, he was always generous with me."

The thick base of Kate's glass rumbled as she resumed gliding it in a circular motion. "And now the Pearsons are taking care of you, I hope."

"Yes, they are." A smile lifted his lips. "You asked me why I don't drink anymore."

"That's right."

Harrison observed her dark eyes, which shone like stars cut out of the night sky. "Many years ago, I had gout in my left foot. I did not tell the Woodfords about it. When they discovered my problem, I thought for certain they would fire me."

"But?"

"They hired a doctor to examine me. My condition was not chronic, but rare for my age, I was in my early twenties."

"And alcohol aggravates gout."

"Yes. The doctor treated me with steroids and my symptoms disappeared, but he recommended a change in diet. I don't drink or eat shellfish anymore."

"And everything has been okay?"

"Yes, fine ever since."

"Well, I will drink to that." Kate raised her glass toward him and took a swallow. "You must feel a great debt to the Woodfords. Is it very different working for the Pearsons?"

He peered over his shoulder into the darkness, then returned his gaze to Kate. "It's a strange thing, you see. I loved the Woodfords, never expected to feel loyalty for anyone but them. The Pearsons surprised me."

Kate pushed her drink aside and leaned on the bar. "How so?"

"They looked just like the Woodfords back when I applied for my job with them. Violet and I were the only ones around then. We were both shocked by the similarity. Mrs. Woodford was also much younger than her husband, very smart. Mr. Woodford left her in charge while he took care of his property business in England."

"Like the Pearsons."

"Yes, very much. Mrs. Woodford restored the villa for her and her husband and their friends, but after a couple of years, she decided to expand and rent out rooms."

Kate brought the whisky to her lips. "Were you always the butler, Harrison?"

He noticed the flourish of color brightening Miss Kate's cheeks. "No, I did many odd jobs, landscaping and repairs in the beginning, then Mrs. Woodford hired Violet and me full-time when Sunset opened to the public. Shortly after, she offered me the position of butler."

"Very English, isn't it?"

"Yes, I became the chief steward in charge of all the other male staffers. That's when Mrs. Woodford gave me the sterling silver bell monogrammed with my initials as a gift. It was her idea that I use it to summon guests for the meals, while guests used it to call on me between courses." A lump formed in his throat as memories of his humble beginnings came to mind.

"You and Mrs. Woodford were close, weren't you?"

"Yes, ma'am, extremely close. Through all the important times in my life, she took care of me. It was most hard after my wife died, and I had to care for my son."

"I recall your telling me, your son was young, wasn't he?"

"Not even three years old, I was lucky to have my mother. She moved in and helped raise Lucas while I worked."

Kate extended a hand and touched his arm. "How is your son, Lucas? He has three girls, right?"

"You have a great memory Miss Kate." From his pants pocket, he pulled out a tattered, leather billfold. "He and his family are doing very well. My grand-daughters are growing up fast." Harrison opened the wallet and gave it to Kate.

She flipped through the pictures. "What a gorgeous family." The first photo was with Lucas, his wife and the kids, and the others were of the girls individually in their school uniforms. Harrison pointed at the photos and told Kate each of their names. "They are stunning," she said. The last picture was a faded black and white of a young couple, standing like stiff boards for the camera. He wore a proud face with his arm wrapped around her shoulder. She cast a shy, angelic smile.

"That was me and Sharmaine taken after we learned she was pregnant with Lucas." He caressed the picture with a gnarled finger. "It's my favorite one of us."

"Your wife was beautiful, Harrison, so elegant and poised." Kate closed the wallet and returned it to him. "I'm sure she would have been so proud of how Lucas turned out."

With a bowed head, he said, "Yes, he's head of pediatrics now and teaching too."

"Very impressive."

"My family owes so much to the Woodfords. They and their friends were always good to me. Now Mr. and Mrs. Pearson are taking care of us."

Kate tossed back the remainder of her drink. "You love this place, don't you Harrison?"

"I do. I just hope …"

"What is it?"

"I hope business picks up again soon. I know the Pearsons are worried, even if they don't show it."

Kate pushed herself back from the bar and stepped off the stool. "You'd do anything to help them, wouldn't you, Harrison?"

An understanding hung between them like dense smoke.

"Yes, ma'am, I would." He gave a quick nod. "I most certainly would."

DAY FOUR
INCOMPATIBLE

Dressed in a light cotton robe, Jessica stepped out of the bathroom after her shower to ready herself for breakfast. Anticipating the sound of Harrison's bell any second, she could not wait to get out of the room. Rob sat on the couch with his guitar.

"What's wrong Jess? You seem in a hurry."

"Nothing." It surprised her he even noticed enough to ask.

Sex with him continued to be a disappointment. Rob knew nothing about how to please her. He ignored her mild coaxing and subtle hints, so while he had his way with her, she closed her eyes and pictured her fantasy man of the moment—Adam.

Rob banged out chords interspersed with clumsy finger picking. "Recognize this song?"

Jessica loved the instrument, but not the way Rob played it. "Give me a hint."

"Your musical sense is really poor."

She swallowed her pride but resented his comment. "You know I'm not a fan of country music."

Rob repeated the same awkward pattern and tried humming along. He couldn't carry a tune in a bucket, and his attempt at singing only made it worse for her.

"I give up," she said, slipping off her robe and putting on undergarments.

"It's 'Papa Loved Mama.' Garth Brooks."

"Oh …" Jessica feigned recognition. "Great guitar, isn't it?"

"Sure is." After packing it back in the case, he walked toward the dresser. "I'm not sure about jammin' with the guys though. I listened to them last night, and they're amazing. Jerry smokes that guitar, but he's a lot older than me, had more practice."

Jessica bit her lip. "Whatever you say, Rob." She walked to the closet to pick out a dress. His response brought to mind an expression her step daddy used to say: "Excuses are like backsides. Everybody's got one and they all stink."

Rob was full of excuses.

She didn't want to rub it in that Nolan was older than him too, but he had had no trouble making it up Dunn's River Falls with her and Anna yesterday. Rob had dropped off at one of the lagoons along the way.

The guitar was an early birthday gift for Rob out of her winnings. He chose the Gibson Vintage Sunburst. Even with his employee discount, it cost her nearly four thousand dollars. Jessica encouraged him to take lessons, but he wasn't interested.

"I can learn from watching YouTube videos," he had

said, "plus the sales guys at the shop help me out."

It irritated her that he was so unmotivated to learn, especially after how much she spent on him.

Served her right.

By the time she won the trip and money, she had tired of him and was trying to end their relationship. She bought him the present out of guilt to soften the blow, but she didn't want to come to Jamaica with him alone. This was her opportunity to meet new and interesting people. Rob would have ruined her vacation if it were just the two of them here.

"By the way, Rob," she said, pulling up the side zipper of her dress, "please don't take a huge helping of bacon until everyone else has had their share."

"What?" Rob's eyebrows squished together. "Why are we talkin' 'bout bacon?"

She turned to the mirror, hastily brushing her hair. "I'm asking you to be considerate, that's all. There's no excuse for rude behavior."

"You are somethin' Jess. I don't understand you at times."

Long strands darkened the bristles of her brush. Jessica's natural hair was fine yellow silk. She needed to be gentler on herself or she'd be bald by thirty. "You're not the only one who likes bacon."

Rob opened his mouth, snapped it shut without a word, then shook his head. He rummaged in the dresser drawer randomly pulling out items. "Where are my green swim trunks?"

Jessica turned to him, tried to summon a conciliatory tone. "Rob, is it too much to ask that you not think of yourself all the time? Wait your turn if you want seconds at breakfast, all right?"

Rob's clothes piled high on the floor.

"What's the point?" Jessica threw down her brush. "You're not even listening to me!"

After emptying most of the drawer, Rob snatched the item he wanted. "What's going on, Jess? Are you embarrassed by me?"

"Rob …"

He stepped into the swim trunks, stamping hard on the floor as he yanked them up. "You think these uppity folk are so special, don't you? I've seen you judgin' me since the minute we landed." From the pile, he fished out a T-shirt. "I'm telling you they're no better than we are."

A vein throbbed by her temple when Rob pulled the tattered Kenny Chesney T-shirt over his head. "Would it kill you to wear something more appropriate?"

"I ain't gettin' gussied up for breakfast!" He threw the heap of clothes back in the dresser and slammed the drawer shut.

"Fine." The back of her neck flushed with heat. "Do whatever you want, I'm tired of this."

"I'm not that asshole Adam who has to look like a male model at every meal."

Her ears perked up. "Stop your cussing. What do you have against him?"

"Nothing, except he's got the hots for you."

She scoffed, too quickly. "No, he doesn't. You're jealous of any man who talks to me." Rob's insecurities grated on her nerves. She was tired of defending herself.

"Say what you want, Jess, but I know when another man is makin' the moves on my woman."

His woman? Jessica almost burst out laughing. "You're being paranoid." Adam paid no attention to her except when she initiated the conversations.

"I see the way he looks at you during meals."

"Get a grip, Rob, meal times are for socializing. You might try it if you weren't so busy stuffing your face." Her words spilled out in one long disgusted breath.

Rob took a step toward her.

Jessica balled her hands by her side. "What are you going to do?" she said, flaring her nostrils.

He jerked to a halt. "I ain't gonna tan your hide. I know what happens to men in your family who hit their women … just ask your mama."

A bitter taste rose in her throat. "Don't you dare say another word about Mama … Don't you dare…"

The corners of his mouth turned downward. "I reckon I best keep quiet, then."

She met his eyes with blades behind hers. "I reckon you do."

The breakfast bell sounded as they continued their staring contest, thickening the air between them.

Rob broke the gaze first, stomped to the bathroom, swearing under his breath.

Jessica never swore. Innocent of the arsenal of

profanities until she met Rob, she didn't even like hearing others swear.

They were so incompatible.

She white knuckled the edge of the dresser, staring at her reflection. In just two days in Jamaica, the sun had transformed her appearance. Dark green eyes sparkled like emeralds against golden skin. Her long, usually fine hair fell thick and wavy past her shoulders. Even with fury reddening her cheeks, she looked stunning.

When Rob thundered by her and slammed the door on his way out, every ounce of her filled with murderous rage. She hated him, hated his smoke-filled voice, hated the way he walked, hated his redneck mentality. Her ears burned at the thought of how much he disgusted her.

In an attempt to calm down, she rummaged inside her make-up bag. With a shaking hand, she held a shiny tube of Chanel lipstick, the one expensive item she bought for herself with her winnings. Upon removing the cover, she smelled the pink stick—bubblegum. Jessica applied the color and admired the shimmer. With a gentle twist, she retracted the stick in its gold, metal casing. She grabbed a tissue and blotted her lips; not a trace of it smeared. The lady at the Chanel counter said *Mystique Orchid* was their bestseller. At the time, Jessica mulled over paying fifty dollars for lipstick. Now she understood why. Unlike the waxy, cheap brands from drugstores, this enhanced her natural curves without a hint of heaviness. Expensive lipstick, however, did not cool her rage.

Rob had a nerve bringing up Alana May.

Jessica recognized and feared certain traits of Alana May in herself, but she'd be damned if she was going to let Rob mouth off about her mama.

Alana May never thought twice of spending money on herself. Weeks before her trip, she had a long talk with Mama at her waterfront estate, the Knoxville property she bought following her second divorce. They drank Bourbon and peach punch inside the screened-in porch off the kitchen.

"Jessie darlin', you must treat yourself, money is for spendin.'"

"I will, Mama, but I haven't thought of anything I need." Jessica had deposited her winnings in the bank until she figured out how to best invest it.

"Need? Girl, who's talkin' 'bout what you need? I'm talkin' 'bout splurgin'. There must be somethin' you want."

"Mama, I'm taking a trip outside America for the first time. I'm nervous about flying. Shopping is the last thing on my mind."

"You bought the guitar for Rob."

"Yes, but …"

"He doesn't deserve you. You were goin' to break it off, weren't you?"

"It'd be too mean to do it now … when we get back. He's so excited to go on the trip."

"You're too considerate." She tipped the pitcher and refilled her glass. "It don't matter when you end it, it's goin' to hurt, the sooner the better."

As Jessica stared at her tanned complexion and Chanel lips, she realized Mama was right. Mama was always right

THE REVIEW

"No Warm Glow for Sunset Villa"
Rating: 1 star out of 5
Matthew Kane
Senior Travel Correspondent
June 2012

Sunset Villa, a vacation spot in Jamaica wants to be your destination of choice, it says. It states this on its website as its mission statement. The problem is, it wants to do this on its own terms, without any regard for your needs.

Given the multitude of five-star reviews on various sites, my review is going to sound harsh. It sounded harsh even to me after I wrote it. I thought of changing a few words to soften the blow, but my mandate for this column is not to make it easy for the resorts. It's to make travel better for vacationers, so they don't get duped when they spend their hard-earned money. I changed nothing of my review because it's an honest account of my week at Sunset Villa.

The hotel provided the car service to the resort from Montego Bay's Sangster airport. Here was the first problem. The car appeared nice and clean until I opened the door. A smelly deodorizer hanging from the rear-view mirror made me sick the minute I tried getting in. I asked the driver to please remove it from his car. I told him I was allergic to artificial perfumes. He seemed a bit offended by my request but did remove it. I offered him a plastic bag to seal it in, but he just threw it in the glove compartment. The strange scent could only be compared to rotting strawberries, and its odor leaked into the car for the two-hour ride to the resort. I had my window open the entire time. This seemed to suit the driver, probably because he didn't have to turn on his air conditioning.

I slept most of the way, though was jostled awake several times. Large potholes line the main road, so make sure you've got a strong bladder. The car looked new but had no shocks to speak of.

Upon arrival at Sunset Villa, about fifteen minutes from Ocho Rios, I was prepared to fully relax, especially after a long ride in the car.

I was greeted by several of the staff who seemed friendly enough upon meeting them. The concierge/butler advised I would be staying in a room on the main level overlooking the gardens. It would be quiet and removed from the only other party booked at the villa —a family of eighteen who hailed from England and other parts of Europe. They were at Sunset Villa for a reunion. I was the outsider as I usually am when I go on assignment for the magazine. I never advertise where I'll be as my anonymity ensures the business will not treat me in a special way to incur a favorable review. I go about my business and mingle with the guests and staff as if I was on vacation. I am usually a chameleon, great at mingling with crowds, but not here.

For example, three meals were served daily, and I was expected to eat with the family. I didn't mind eating with them even though I felt a bit ostracized. I found their humor quite unsavory, so I didn't participate much in their conversations. When I inquired if I could take all my meals an hour earlier, the butler said it would make it very difficult for the chef to accommodate me, given she was cooking for so many people. Her reasoning was she made all the food fresh and wanted it hot and ready just before serving. He suggested instead that I take my meal in a separate dining area if I didn't want to eat with the family. In the end, I decided this was not a huge issue. So long as I did not linger after the meal was over, I did not have to listen to the boorish discussions afterward. Dinner was a problem when the family took a long time in between courses because they wanted to stretch out the meal. I was there to eat.

Another example where I received no consideration caused me severe discomfort. I have specific allergies to foods, smells and chemicals, so my requests were not meant to be troublesome but health-related. I asked housekeeping not to use any harsh cleaners in my room and to separate the washing of my linens from those of the other guests. I have an acute sense of smell, and several of the women from the other party doused themselves with fragrance, which would undoubtedly mix in with the linens. I requested the staff use non-fragrant detergent to wash all the laundry, especially mine. I know they had some of it because I made the butler buy a box for me. Unfortunately, there were still several days I didn't feel quite right, and I suspect it was because my laundry got mixed in with the others.

One day while taking a walk around the property, a strange odor filled the air. It came from the privately-owned adjacent property. I was unable to see inside the compound, which was fenced in. It smelled like noxious fumes. The butler said Americans owned the place, but they were not there. Work was being done to the place, mainly painting. I asked him to request they immediately stop as I was allergic to oil-based paint. I remember he seemed a little stunned, said he would try, but that he had no control over what the property did next door. He even suggested I not walk by that area, which only irritated me more. Thankfully, I was not able to smell it from my room or while inside the villa, otherwise I would have insisted I speak to the workers myself.

From what I gather, the owners of Sunset Villa are new and bought the place five years ago. I doubt they came from a business background, nor do they understand the meaning of customer service. They were not present when I was at the villa. The behavior of the staff shows they only want to take your money. If you want to be catered to in the least obtrusive way, don't expect any special treatment here, even if your health may depend on it.

After perusing all the five-star reviews on the various

travel sites for Sunset Villa, I had to give it a try, but what a disappointment it was! My experience was the polar opposite of everyone else's. I realize opinions are subjective, but given my credentials and having traveled to countless hotels and resorts, I consider my opinion more credible than the average tourist.

The criteria by which I measure success covers the five Cs of the hospitality industry: character, charm, calm, courtesy, and cuisine. And although Sunset Villa passes on each one except for courtesy, I cannot in good conscience recommend it.

Do yourself a favor and don't let the small and intimate setting fool you into thinking you will be pampered. It's quite the opposite. Save your money and go to a big resort with experienced owners and staff who will indulge your needs, not ignore them.

The above are merely several reasons why I would not recommend Sunset Villa as your destination of choice. If I were to list every one of the problems I had with the resort, I'm afraid this review would fill up the entire issue. You wouldn't want that!

Flip through the pages to see some of the places where you should go, and until next time, happy travels!

AT THE BEACH

From where Matthew sat, he watched her take confident long strides toward the ocean. Her lean body in a pink two-piece swimsuit was sexier than any naked model he'd seen in a magazine. There was something about what he couldn't see that excited him. Muscular limbs moved with elegance, her arms by her side. Each time the foamy white caps rushed in to push her back to shore, she rebalanced herself and moved forward. Kate called out his name, her eyes begged him to join her. When he held up a bottle of sun tan lotion he wanted to apply, she nodded and turned back to the sea.

With the grace of a dolphin, she dove in. He squinted toward a random point beyond where she disappeared, waited to see a sign. After what seemed like a long time, her head bobbed out of the water about two hundred feet out.

Impressive.

While the sun played hide and seek behind cloud formations, he slathered himself in lotion. As an added precaution, he applied zinc oxide on his nose. They had spotted only one other couple as they made their way here. Afraid the beach might have been crowded at first, it pleased him that it was almost secluded. What surprised him more was that he was here with Kate at her invitation. It delighted the hell out of him.

To block out the sun's rays, he tugged on the bill of his baseball cap and scrutinized his hairy legs. During peak sun hours, he had avoided being outside while at the villa. Nonetheless, he perceived a slight difference in skin tone where the band of his swim trunks met his stomach and the area below it.

Though he'd never read any of Ian Fleming's books, he'd watched the James Bond films as a kid. *Dr. No* was one he remembered for its pivotal scene filmed here at James Bond Beach. As he sat watching Kate swim farther out, he smiled at his change in luck.

This morning, he had intended to leave the magazine with Kate for her to read on her own time. Instead, she read it immediately after breakfast with him beside her. On the edge of his seat the entire time, Matthew waited for her to oppose a line or passage. He had prepared to justify his views with a cascade of reasons after Adam berated his writing.

When she glanced at him after leafing through the magazine, he felt his defenses crumbling.

"You're not afraid to be a contrarian." With wide eyes, she had looked at him. "What I love is simple honesty. Love a place or hate it, but be truthful about it. It's always important to be truthful," she had said.

He remembered grinning ear to ear, and then she invited him to spend the afternoon with her if he had no plans.

Win! Kate preferred him to Adam!

Yesterday, he was ready to fire off another scorching review of the place, but he reined himself in. He needed to be smart, not act on his impulses. Not yet. After speaking with Kate at dinner, he reconsidered his words and outlined a second review that wasn't as harsh. With a few more days here, it could go either way. As long as every experience satisfied his needs, he would consider giving Sunset Villa a better review. That is, a better review according to him, not anyone else.

In the distance, he saw Kate riding wave after wave carrying her back to shore. Grabbing her towel, he stood up and made his way toward the water. She dropped from sight for a moment, only to reappear closer to him. For the remainder of the way in, she swam with a steady and even pace. Just as Ursula Andress did in her famous "coming out of the ocean scene" in *Dr. No*, Kate rose out of the water like a phoenix. She lifted matted strands of hair off her neck and flicked her mane back. Matthew quickened his steps toward the ocean, erasing the distance between them. Kate's hips swayed side to side as she approached him. He offered her the towel.

"How was it?" he asked.

"Beautiful, so warm and refreshing." Kate buried her face in the towel, tilted her head to one side, then the other, shaking water from her ears.

They walked back to their spot on the beach where she dabbed her body dry and rummaged inside her bag.

Matthew helped her spread her towel next to his.

"You're a terrific swimmer," he said, sitting down.

"Thanks." Kate kneeled beside him with a bottle of water. An odd smile crossed her face.

"Is something wrong?" he asked.

"You look funny, that's all."

Before he had a chance to figure out what she was referring to, Kate tapped his nose and showed him the chalky white on her fingertip.

"Oh yeah … the zinc oxide …" With the back of his hand, he smudged the cream off his nose. "I guess I do look ridiculous, but I'd look worse with a burnt nose, so I—"

"No need to explain, Matthew, I'm just playing with you." She broke the seal of the bottle.

"Did you take swimming lessons as a kid?"

Kate unscrewed the cap off the water. "No … my father taught me."

"Oh, how old were you?"

His question must have caught her by surprise. She did not answer right away, but took her time gulping down half the bottle of water. "I was five." For a finger snap second, she acknowledged him with her eyes, but her flat tone hinted she might not wish to pursue the topic.

He decided to push anyway. "Your father must have been a great teacher."

Drinking the rest of her water, Kate stared at the ocean and did not answer him.

Uncomfortable with the silence, he said, "It's just me

and my dad left."

"Oh?" Kate turned to him, her expression softened. "Are you an only child?"

"Yes, didn't have time for sports as a kid. Parents were pretty strict about academics."

Kate nodded and wrung more water from her hair. "I'm an only child too." She handed him the sunscreen. "Would you mind putting lotion on my back?"

"Not at all." Matthew read the bottle's label while Kate lay down on her towel. "This is an SPF four. I have a sixty I can use on you."

"No, that's okay, I prefer mine."

Matthew flipped up the cap. He squeezed beige cream on his palms and rubbed it into Kate's back. "You don't burn?"

"No, I don't, but I started with a fifteen earlier in the week, so I'm good."

"I see." Her beautiful dark skin felt like silk against his hands. While moving the lotion across her back, he massaged along her spine from her lower back up to her shoulders. "How's that?"

"Feels good."

"Would you like me to do the backs of your legs?"

Did he really say that?

"No, I'm good there, but can you do my neck and shoulders?" Kate lifted up her hair and moved it to the side.

That's when Matthew noticed the ink on her body.

Squeezing more lotion from the bottle, he gently

spread it across Kate's slender neck. With her eyes closed, she appeared to be smiling, as if reveling in the sensation of his hands on her.

Adam's second commandment suddenly popped into his head.

Touch a woman boldly on the first date.

And the reason was to make a man's sexual intentions known right away, but was this even a date considering she initiated it? He really liked Kate and didn't want to blow it with her.

"I think that should do it," he said, after he rubbed down her arms until the lotion disappeared.

Kate took a deep breath. "Thank you. That was good."

"You're welcome," he said, hesitating a second while ogling her long golden body. "You have a tattoo."

With her head propped on an elbow facing him, Kate readjusted her position. "You mean the one at the base of my skull."

"You have more?"

"Yes, but you can't see it … not here anyway."

His heart froze a moment before it pounded hard in his chest. He slid down his blanket, stretching out beside her. "I don't know how to interpret that."

Her chin lifted and her eyes met his with a mischievous twinkle. "I think you do."

The flecks of green against dark brown pupils hypnotized him, beckoned him closer. With her face so close to his, he could almost taste the sweetness of her lips. Even her coconut suntan lotion, which would normally make him nauseous, merely tickled his nostrils. Kate smelled sweet and delicate. Natural.

"Kate, I …" Footsteps shuffled sand behind him just as he leaned forward to kiss her. He broke their gaze and spotted a couple strolling beside them holding hands. The man carried an old-fashioned wicker picnic basket, while the woman clutched a couple of beach blankets under her arm. They said "hello" as they walked by.

When Matthew returned his attention to Kate, she was sitting up. Stretching her back, she gathered her hair and clipped it in place atop her head.

"Uh … sorry, Kate …" Even as he said the words, he wasn't sure why he was apologizing. Damn that couple for making an appearance at the most inopportune time.

"There's no rush," she said. Her smile warmed him. When she hugged her knees to her chest and looked at him with her doe-like eyes, he had an overwhelming urge to kiss her anyway, but he didn't. The opportunity had passed. A wave of anger and regret rolled through him as he sat up. "I thought we were the only ones here."

"Not anymore, the lunch crowd is coming in." She tossed the lotion and empty water bottle in her bag. "We should be getting back soon anyway. I have a badminton game with the girls later this afternoon."

More people filled the beach, but he didn't want her to leave yet. "Your tattoo, what is it?"

Kate stood up with her towel. "The Wheel of Dhamma," she said, wiping sand residue from her legs and shaking it from her towel.

Matthew rose as well, familiar with the symbol of the small wheel containing eight spokes. "Are you a Buddhist?"

"No, I'm an atheist. I had it done in Asia years ago."

Matthew had no affinity for tattoos on women. The trend toward getting full sleeves of them down a limb did not appeal to him in the least. On Kate, it was different. Hers, no bigger than a nickel, added another layer of mystery to her.

"So, what does the tattoo symbolize?"

Kate folded her towel then removed a stick of lip balm from her bag. "Simply that life is a spinning wheel. We can live miserably for many lives, or …" She pursed her lips and applied the balm across them, "we can stop the cycle of misery in this life."

Matthew's eyelids drooped. Her luscious lips grabbed his attention like a Venus flytrap.

"Are you all right?" she asked.

"Fine," he said, "must be the sun." He considered himself agnostic, believing there had to be a god, but could not commit to one religion. "Don't you believe in a higher being?"

"No."

"Aren't you afraid of what will happen after you die?"

Kate chuckled as they strolled on the beach. "There's enough to think of in this life. I don't worry about what will happen next."

"I see." He scratched his head. "And you're fine knowing there might be nothing else after this?"

"I'm betting my life on it," she said in a resolute manner.

"Until someone can prove to me otherwise, why should I sacrifice my happiness now?"

"I suppose I choose to believe in the absence of proof."

"Blind faith."

"I prefer to call it optimism."

"Is that what you call it?" She raised her eyebrows at him.

"Yes, so I guess that makes you a pessimist." Matthew took pleasure in their playful banter.

Kate threw her head back and laughed, narrowed her eyes as if assessing him. "Hardly. I'm a pragmatist."

Matthew stared at her a moment, warmed by how he was able to make her laugh. He wanted to grab her and kiss her. It made him desperate to see her again. "Isn't it funny we've been talking all this time, and I don't know what you do for a living?"

"Is it important?"

"No, but …" His words hitched in his throat. "Your mind works in mysterious ways."

Kate smiled. "Then it shouldn't surprise you I know a lot about it."

LINKED DESTINIES

The villa came up for sale as another deal Anna and Nolan brokered in Negril ended suddenly. In their favor, they already had finances approved from their bankers in Canada, a check in hand for a down payment, and a history with their honeymoon resort. Not in their favor was Sunset's price tag—a cool two million dollars over what the property in Negril cost.

With less than a sliver of a chance to get the place, they ventured to meet the owners of Sunset Villa since they were already in Jamaica. What did they have to lose? In less than forty-eight hours, Anna and Nolan negotiated the successful purchase of the resort.

"Tell me the whole story," Jessica said. "Hard to believe you wanted to buy this place for so long."

"Yes, ever since we married here, we wanted to own a place in Jamaica. Nolan and I never dreamed Sunset would come up for sale."

"And you only discovered it after your plans for the other place went south," Nadine said.

"That's right, the timing couldn't have been stranger." Anna fidgeted with a birdie as the women sat on the lawn by the badminton net, their rackets piled beside a small cooler. The sun sat high in the sky, the day not even close to reaching its maximum temperature, forecasted at 100 degrees Fahrenheit. Anna shouldered the heat, felt at peace sharing with the women here. They waited for Kate to show up for their doubles game.

"What happened with the property in Negril?" Jessica asked.

"The craziest thing. A Brit and a Jamaican co-owned the small hotel. Nolan and I met with the Jamaican man in person at his home. Along with our lawyer, we flew in ready to sign papers. Their lawyer was present as well. As we were about to connect to the Brit on video Skype, the phone rang. That's when the deal fell through."

Jessica pulled up her knees and clutched them to her chest, eyes wide as if she were in a story circle at the climax of the book. "Goodness gracious, what the heck happened?"

Nadine giggled.

"The Brit changed his mind."

"At that moment when you were supposed to sign?"

"Yes, damn Englishman, he couldn't part with the property. It shocked everyone, especially his Jamaican associate who swore he had no clue of his partner's change of heart. Nolan was so upset. I'd never seen him that angry before."

Nadine nodded. "Nolan rarely gets angry, but you'll know it when he is. He doesn't even have to say a word. He just has to look at you," she said, hugging herself in a mock shiver.

"I'm glad you told me." Jessica appeared mesmerized by Anna's story. "But then you found this place, so it worked out."

Nadine and Jessica said hi to Kate as she approached and sat down next to them, forming a wider circle.

"Sorry I'm late," Kate said.

"No problem. I'm telling Jessica the story of how we acquired Sunset." Anna crossed her legs in a lotus position.

"Oh yes." With elbows propped on her knees, Kate rested her chin in her palms. "It's one of my favorite stories of this place."

"So when did you stumble upon this place for sale?" Jessica asked.

"Nolan did, the same night after our deal fell through. When I returned to the room from a power walk, I thought he was surfing the net, but he had been checking a Jamaican real estate site. A new listing had just popped up."

"Oooh … let me guess … Sunset Villa?"

Jessica's giddiness made Anna laugh. "Yes," she said, "but it was way over our budget.

"But …" Jessica started a confused shrug, "you bought it, right? Did you borrow more money?"

"No, there was no more money to borrow. We were tapped out at that point, could not afford another red cent."

"I don't understand." Jessica bit her lip, appeared in deep contemplation. Kate and Nadine smiled at her but said nothing. "How were you able to buy this place then?"

Anna remained quiet and didn't offer a hint, knowing Jessica was smart enough to figure it out.

The Southerner scrunched her face for a moment then lifted her brow as if slapped. "Are you saying … the Woodfords sold to you at two million dollars below the asking price?"

"Yes."

"Oh my!" Jessica gave a shake of her head. "You and Nolan must have really impressed them!"

Kate folded her legs in the opposite direction and shifted her position. "I think so."

"You shared a kinship with the Woodfords." Nadine stood up and stretched her legs. "That's my favorite part of the story."

"Kinship?" Jessica appeared puzzled.

"Yes, they said Nolan and I reminded them of themselves. At the time, we were the same ages they were when they bought this place. There were so many odd coincidences." Anna uncrossed her legs and stood up next to Nadine, picked up her badminton racket. "We shared similar traits and temperament, liked the same foods, even enjoyed the same music. They showed us photo albums from when they first bought the place. Nolan and I flipped through the black and white pictures as if we were staring at ourselves, only they were taken forty years ago.

Jessica pressed a hand to her heart. "That is so eerie."

"Very much so, and for the Woodfords too. When we looked at them, we were sneaking a peek at ourselves forty years later. They were staring into their past. Something unexplainable connected us, as if we had traveled through time to find one another."

Kate rose and offered to pull Jessica up. "I'm a scientist, but I believe in karmic forces bringing people together at the right time, linked destinies if you will. You and Nolan losing out on the other property, Nolan seeing the ad as it popped up ... All that had to happen to get you here."

"You're right." Anna bounced on her toes. "We were destined to have this place." She exchanged a knowing look with Kate. "And I'm going to do whatever it takes to make sure we own it for as long as the Woodfords did."

A FRIENDLY GAME

Anna yelled a warning at her partner. Jessica saw it coming at her, spinning in slow motion aimed right between her eyes. A wave of dizziness wobbled her legs, nailed her to the spot. She lacked any strength to shift out of the way or raise her racket to block the shot. The force to her forehead coincided with a pop in her eardrum. Her body seized. The last thing she remembered was Kate clasping a hand to her mouth and Nadine running toward her. Then she was falling backward, stiff like a plank of wood. A heavy thud sounded when her head hit the ground. Her sunglasses flew off. Blood strummed in her ears like waves pounding rocks.

Garbled, hushed voices floated above Jessica as if they belonged to people talking behind closed doors.

"I didn't think I hit it that hard!" she heard Nadine say.

"No, you didn't knock her out. The heat must've got to her."

Jessica recognized Kate's smoky voice, tried opening her eyes but static hit them. She immediately clamped her lids shut.

Someone slipped cold objects into her open palms.

Time ticked by slowly even though muffled conversation swirled around her like a turbine. When she squeezed the items in her hands, she realized they were bottles of water.

Thirsty, she was so thirsty.

"Here, take these and press them against her cheeks. Place a couple on her forehead too," she heard Kate say.

Glug glug glug. Water poured out of a bottle.

Jessica flinched as a cold compress touched her forehead.

The sounds were becoming clearer and louder.

"Nadine, can you remove her shoes and socks?"

"Yup, on it."

"Should we turn her on her side?"

Anna's concerned voice.

"No, she fainted. I saw her eyes roll up even before the birdie hit her. Her breathing isn't labored. Let's just keep her cool."

"I see her eyelids fluttering."

"That's a good sign."

"Jessica … can you hear me?"

Water trickled down the side of her neck.

"I think she's coming to."

"What …?" Jessica swirled the space between her brows.

"Can you open your eyes?"

Kate. That was definitely Kate asking her to open her eyes.

Jessica processed the words, but took several more seconds to understand their meaning, took even longer before she could crack open her lids. When she did, three faces stared down at her with only a snippet of blue sky behind them.

"I'll help her up. Let's try to get some water in her." She felt Kate encircle her neck and lift her head.

From above her, she saw Nadine pass Anna an open water bottle. "Drink this," Anna said, tilting the bottle to her lips.

The cool liquid coated her mouth and soothed her parched throat. Jessica drank as if she had not swallowed a drop of water in days. The fog began to lift.

"Can you sit up, Jessica?" Kate asked.

She croaked out an *I think so*. Anna supported her as she rolled onto her side and pushed herself into a sitting position.

"You okay, hon?" Nadine asked.

"Yes …" She took a moment to catch her breath.

Kate examined the back of Jessica's head. "Hmm … you might have a goose egg from the fall. You landed pretty hard, thankfully the ground is soft." Kate rubbed her back. "Lean your head forward."

Jessica dropped her head toward her legs, folded in a semi-lotus position. Silence and stillness were a welcome relief. "Wow … I don't know what happened," she said.

"Are you in any pain?" Anna asked.

"No …" She lifted her head. The spinning stopped. "The last thing I remembered was you telling me to watch out for Nadine's serve … then I must have blacked out." Jessica finished the water. "Nadine, you have a killer swing!"

Nadine examined Jessica's forehead where the birdie struck her. "I'm so sorry. Must be the competitive streak in me."

"Next time, I should wear my glasses instead of propping them on my head. Who knew badminton was such a dangerous sport?" Jessica giggled nervously.

"There's a tiny pink mark above your brow line," Anna said, "nothing a bit of concealer won't hide."

"Let's get you out of the sun," Kate said. "Do you have a history of fainting?"

"No … the only other time was when …" An involuntary contraction caused Jessica to grab under her ribs. "Oh darn it."

"What is it?" Nadine asked.

"I'm afraid it's getting close to that time of the month, wasn't expecting it until next week."

"Aunt Flow?"

"Yes, I was hoping not to have it while on vacation."

Kate sighed. "That could explain the fainting. How's your head?"

Jessica patted the back of her skull. "It's a bit tender."

"I'll come by later to check on you," Kate said, "just want to make sure it doesn't lead to a concussion."

Jessica stood to her feet with the help of Nadine. She leaned against the sturdy woman for support. "I'm sure I'm fine."

"I'm sure you're fine too, but I'd like to be on the safe side. Someone should check on you for the next twenty-four hours. Can you have Rob wake you periodically tonight to make sure you're able to regain consciousness?"

"How embarrassing to faint during a badminton game. Rob will never let me live this down."

"Don't worry, honey," Nadine said, hugging Jessica close to her. "Everything's going to be okay. Does she really need to tell Rob?"

Jessica looped her arm around Nadine's, experienced a real kinship with her. The two of them turned to Kate.

"It's precautionary." Kate offered a warm smile, her pitch mellifluous as she spoke slowly. "I'll give you a definitive answer after I check you, okay?"

"Thanks," Jessica said. To push the heavy feeling from her chest, she exhaled hard. "I'd really prefer not to say anything to Rob."

ALL WORK AND NO PLAY

Matthew sat by himself in the living room, head down, pecking away with two fingers on his laptop. It was late afternoon, and he was overdue on an article to *Travel in Style* he promised for yesterday. In addition to writing vacation reviews, for which he was compensated, the magazine required he blog twice a month and receive no monetary payment. He hated blogging. It was beneath him, but all the writers were expected to contribute.

The blog originated with the online version of the magazine a year ago. The owner handpicked its editor, Carlton Moss, due to her success in launching two other online magazines.

A woman named Carlton. They hated each other from the start and clashed at every turn. Her parents must have wanted a boy so much they gave her a masculine name. She had probably spent her entire life trying to live up to it.

Part of her goal was to amass buyers for the travel apps of the magazine, which served as the main source of revenue for the online division. The blog was her way of attracting more readers and advertisers. This month, he had to write on the topic of Food and Drink.

"I know food's not your thing," Carlton said, antagonizing him before he left on his trip to Jamaica. "I want stylish, bold, and delicious. Give us something colorful and I don't want recipes. All the other mags have recipes. And for god's sake, I'd better not get any of your Birkenstock granola crap."

He procrastinated, assumed incorrectly she might cut him a break since he was out of the country. *Bitch.* A flurry of hateful messages back and forth started yesterday evening after he missed his deadline. He banged out a fourth note in response to her last e-mail.

So engrossed was he in his venomous wrangle, he failed to hear the slapping of sandals coming up behind him.

"Howdy, pardner! Whatcha up to?" Rob said in a booming voice.

Matthew's hand flew to cover his heart. "Shit! Don't sneak up on me like that."

Rob walked by and sat across from him. "Sorry, you tryin' to write somethin'?"

Matthew took a few seconds to regain normal breath. "Yeah…" What the hell did this country bumpkin want with him?

"Nice day, ain't it?" Rob took a swig from his beer.

"I'm working." Matthew returned his attention to his laptop.

"Anythin' I can help with?"

Christ! This man could not take a hint. As if Rob could help him with anything, let alone writing. "Uh … no, I doubt it." He raised his head. "And isn't it a bit early for that?"

Rob held up the bottle of Red Stripe as if he were posing for an ad with it. "What, this?" He snorted a look of disbelief. "Never too early for beer."

"I guess not … not for some people anyway." Matthew pressed several times on his space bar, pretending to type. "I have an article to submit by tonight, and I wanted to do it now while it was quiet, no Internet in my room." Rob did not budge but continued to look at him. The man was definitely thick.

"You a writer?"

Matthew took in a deep breath and held it, then released a loud exhale. It was something he did when stressed. "I'm a journalist. I write for *Travel in Style,* the number one travel magazine in the country."

"Impressive."

He raked his fingers across his scalp. Droplets of perspiration dotted his palm. "I'm sweating. Does it feel like the air conditioner is on?"

"I think so," Rob said after a swallow of beer. "I feel a breeze comin' from the ocean, this open concept's great."

Matthew grabbed a brochure from a nearby stand and fanned himself. "Even with open spaces, you can't stop the humidity. I really feel it today. Someone needs to turn up the air conditioning."

"I ain't hot," Rob said.

"You *are* not hot."

"What?"

"*Ain't* is not proper English."

"Says who?"

"Says … oh never mind." Matthew shook his head and blew out an exasperated breath.

"Listen, I stopped by to be friendly and all, but if you don't wanna talk …" Rob rose to his feet and picked up his beer.

"Rob… sorry… sit down. I'm in a foul mood, need to get this article off and I haven't a clue where to begin." Matthew shocked himself with his sudden change of heart toward the man. Perhaps he felt sorry for him and his simplemindedness. After all, he couldn't help being born in the South. At least they were both American, not like those horrible Brits he had to contend with his last time here.

The large man sat down again, rested his forearms on his thighs and leaned forward. "What's the topic? I used to do writin' in school, maybe I can suggest somethin'."

"Uh …" Matthew surveyed the poor slob. Rob probably felt as much of an outcast as he did amongst the men here. What did he have to lose? He explained what the editor wanted for the article, trying hard not to let disdain for Carlton Moss curdle his tone. After he finished his story, Rob pounded his chest with his fist.

"Are you kiddin' me?" Rob said, taking a gulp of beer. "You wanna talk food and drink, I'm your man!"

"Yeah, I can see you love food."

"I live to eat!" Rob bounced in his seat. "This body didn't get this way from dietin', I can tell you that."

Matthew tried to keep calm, wondered why he was even making the effort with Rob. "I don't eat like normal people and I'm not much of a drinker, so you can imagine it's not a subject I particularly want to write about."

"Yup, you sure do have a lot of strange food issues." Rob reached behind his shorts and pulled out a pack of cigarettes. "Mind if I smoke? You're not allergic to these, are ya?"

Matthew sighed. "I am. Smoke makes me sick. Do you mind not smoking?"

"All right, just cuz you're having a hard day," he smiled through yellow-stained teeth, "but just this once."

"Thanks," Matthew replied in a sullen manner. "Yeah, the editor hates me. She wants me to fail, so she can hire someone else. I'm sure of it."

Rob threw the pack of cigarettes on the table. "Well, we're gonna put her in her right place, show her what yer made of."

Matthew could not believe his sudden alliance with Rob. He had to be desperate, but the more he spoke with him, the more he realized the man was not so stupid after all. If there was one subject he knew well, it was eating and drinking. As he talked it over with the Southerner, he came to understand his reluctance for blogging. Any writing devoid of his opinion seemed pointless to him.

"Just the facts," Carlton reminded him the four times he had submitted a blog post. "I don't need your commentary. You're not writing one of your fucking reviews."

She didn't conceal her dislike for him, or what she thought of his writing. On more than one occasion, she had threatened to bring in another travel writer to take his place. It was all talk. Carlton didn't oversee his reviews, which he knew sold the magazine.

Rob gave him the perfect idea for the blog post, and he could stick it to Carlton too. After their brainstorming session, Rob left him alone to write the article. Matthew guessed he needed a smoke and another beer.

He penned a thousand words about a detoxifying juice he discovered in Jamaica made with tropical fruit, leafy greens, and scotch bonnet peppers. To embellish further, he added how it cleansed the colon and increased energy too. Though plausible, the drink was a figment of his imagination. She'd have to prove he made it up.

After he finished typing, he reread his essay entitled "Jamaica's Secret Jungle Juice." He shut down his computer after sending off the article.

Just the facts, right Carlton? Choke on it.

TEMPERATURE CHECK

Jessica took up residence at one of the smaller inner terraces. Bright and airy, it provided a tranquil place to read and offered protection from the sun's unrelenting blaze. She rested on one of four cushioned loungers and placed a glass of lemonade on the table beside her. From where she sat, a clear view of the ocean welcomed her. With a book propped on her chest, she stared out to sea.

The gentle waves provided a soothing backdrop. The hush of the water reminded her of early afternoons on Mama's property when the lake was calm. Many times, she had sat on the veranda daydreaming of faraway places and interesting people, just like what she experienced here. She inhaled the warm ocean air and blew out a mix of satisfaction and regret. Except for the fact that she was here with Rob, she was living the dream life.

"Jessica, Jessica …"

A gentle nudge woke her. "Huh … what …?"

"I wanted to make sure you're all right."

She pushed herself up and rubbed her eyes. On the chair beside her, Kate sat with a glass in hand. A set jaw outlined her face. The sun hovered lower on the horizon than she last remembered. "Did I fall asleep?"

"You must have."

"Wow, I don't remember …" The sound of a motor revving drew her attention away for a moment. She stood up in time to see a couple of workers speed off in a four-person motorized dinghy. Nolan and Ben stared after them from the beach. "What's happening down there?" Jessica lowered herself to her seat and smoothed down her flyaway hair.

Kate blew out a breath. "You missed the excitement. Nadine went snorkeling after our game and a stingray confronted her. It kept circling her and wouldn't let her get back into shore."

"Oh my god, is she hurt?" Jessica touched her fingers to parted lips.

Kate shook her head. "No, she's exhausted because she was out there for a while, but she'll be fine. No one has ever seen a stingray here before."

"That's what killed the Crocodile Hunter." Jessica felt the blood drain from her face.

"Right, Steve Irwin." Kate nodded.

"I must speak to her." She wrapped her arms around herself. "See if she's all right."

"I'm sure we'll hear all about it at dinner. She's resting now." Kate looked down on the floor and picked up something. "Yours?" She handed Jessica the book.

"Oh … yes." Jessica took the paperback and tossed it in her bag. *How Not to Speak Southern* was a bad title for a good book. Written by a businesswoman from Alabama now living in Chicago, it told the story of her hardships based on how she spoke. "I'm trying to lose my Southern accent, or at least speak with a less pronounced one. It's a bit embarrassing for you to discover me with the book."

Kate tucked in her chin. "Why?"

"You're a New Yorker, sophisticated and polished. If I'm to succeed in the corporate world, I'll need to improve on my speech."

"I think you speak very well."

She blushed. "Thanks, but I have a long way to go. It's not easy growing up in the south. People have a certain perception of us based on how we look or talk. It can be difficult for someone like me."

"How do you mean?"

"Big boobs, squeaky voice, blond." She tugged her hair and watched the realization spread across Kate's face. "Yeah, this chestnut-brown comes out of a bottle."

Kate nodded. "Nothing wrong with that. It suits you."

"Thanks." Melancholy bubbled up her throat. "I started coloring it after Mama suggested I try out for the Miss Tennessee pageant. Her intentions were good, but she made me realize no one wanted to see me for more than a dumb blond. I decided I had to make changes to my life if I wanted to get anywhere." She felt on the verge of tears.

"You're hard on yourself, Jessica." Kate's fireside voice exuded calm. "I don't know the reality of living in the south, but I do know this. You're a bright woman no matter what color your hair is. If dark hair helps you stand out in a sea of blonds, then why not? Everyone can use an advantage."

"That's how I see it. One day I'll show my blond roots again, but not until I've made it." Her stomach somersaulted. Jessica flinched from the spasm.

"Are you all right?" Kate furrowed her eyebrows.

"I'm fine, just feeling bloated. I still don't have my period yet."

"Take it easy tonight. Dinner's not for …" Kate glanced at her watch, "… at least another two hours. I think you can sleep without any worries."

"It's kind of you to check on me." Jessica picked up her lemonade with condensation dripping down the glass. "So I don't need Rob to wake me during the night?" Her gaze dropped to the floor. "He and I are not getting along at the moment."

"I think you'll be fine."

"Good." She took a sip of her juice, grimaced from the warm, acidic taste. "Kate, may I ask you a personal question? You've been so kind, I don't want to take up more of your time, but …" Jessica saw Kate's eyebrows knit in curiosity.

"What is it?" the doctor asked.

"I've been meaning to seek counseling, and since you're a psychiatrist, I thought …" To make sure no one was nearby, she sat up and looked around. "It's … it's about Rob."

"Jessica, whatever you tell me stays between us, don't worry."

"I envy you, you're so well put together. I feel lost." Words dried up in her throat. As much as she admired Kate, something about the doctor intimidated her. She always seemed so poised and calm.

"It'll be easier once you start talking," Kate said, as if she read her mind. "Starting is the hardest part."

Jessica lowered her eyes. "Okay, here goes nothing." She took a deep breath. "Rob … he's my first real boyfriend. We've been together eight months now, but I intend to break it off when we get home. If I had my druthers, I would have preferred he not be here … I'm sure you've noticed we're not exactly compatible."

Kate tilted her head, responded in a soft tone. "It's not for anyone to judge your compatibility. Does Rob know you intend to end it?"

"No."

"You're an ambitious woman with a brain. It's important …" Kate locked eyes with her. "No, it's *imperative* that you not allow anyone or anything to stand in the way of what you want in life. That would be such a waste."

Kate's words hit Jessica like a slap she couldn't duck. Up until that moment, Kate's intelligence had a detached, analytical quality to it. Jessica did not expect such a definitive response. "I suppose … I'm not sure how to end it with Rob. He's not a bad guy. There's no abuse or anything, but we're just not right for one another."

"You don't have to wait until he abuses you to know you're not meant for each other. Too many women stay until it gets really bad."

"Yeah … I suppose that's why I've delayed it, almost as if I'm waiting for him to do something horrible, so I'll feel less guilty about ending it."

Kate spoke firmly. "Don't wait for something horrible to happen to you. Leave because you want to, not because you have no other choice. Staying in a bad relationship is also a choice."

Jessica placed her glass back on the table, wondered if Kate was talking from personal experience. "Mama has encouraged me to leave him too."

"You respect her opinion?"

"I … yes, but …" Jessica stared off in the distance.

"But …?"

"Mama is a wonderful woman, but she's never had to work in the outside world. She's where she is because of the men in her life. Three marriages, two divorces, and well, the last one ended in …"

"In …?"

"Mama killed him … in self-defense of course."

Kate raised a brow and leaned in closer to Jessica. "What happened?"

"He beat her. Mama took it for a while until he …" The space behind her eyelids throbbed, "… until he came on to me." Her belly sank like a bag of rocks.

Kate placed a hand on Jessica's arm. "Are you all right?"

"Yes. You must be good therapist, I've never talked about this to anyone except Mama."

"When did this happen?"

"I was fifteen at the time."

"Did you ever receive counseling for it?"

"No, I wanted to be with Mama, she took care of me."

"Your mother sounds like a strong woman."

"She is, but she's resolved never to marry again. I can't blame her." A pain rippled through her mid-section, caused her to wince and take an extra breath. "It scares me. There are days I fear my temper may push me over the edge too."

"Killing is not something you inherit like eye color. Of course, everyone has a tipping point."

"I fear I do have it in me to kill. I get so angry at Rob sometimes."

"It's not easy to change ourselves, even more difficult to change others. Think about it if you intend to stay with Rob." Kate lowered her chin to meet Jessica's eyes. "Okay?"

Jessica hung her head in reflection.

DAY FIVE
MORNING SWIM

Kate dove into the pool with a quiet splash. She loved swimming this time of day with no one else around. Only the ocean waves lapping the shore and the hushed wake-up call of birds accompanied her. With a steely determination, she focused on slicing and kicking to propel herself forward.

As she stared at the sky in backstroke, her attention crept to yesterday's conversation with Jessica. The young woman was a bit confused but mentally strong. Despite an ordeal at such a young age, she had acquired strength through trauma and appeared well adjusted

Kate understood childhood trauma, how it affected people. The lucky ones, or those with strong psyches and support, used it as a springboard to move forward. Others never moved beyond the pain. Self-harm, substance abuse, and withdrawal were some of the consequences. Over time, these destructive behaviors depleted them of their desire to live, to love, and to want.

She had witnessed it as a pattern in many of her patients, but had never wallowed in her own misfortune.

"You either sink or swim," her father had said to her.

Sink or swim.

At the age of five, she learned the phrase from her father. He was a man who saw the world in black and white, compromised on nothing, and considered grieving an activity for the weak. He had little time for self-pity and even less for sentimentality. Despite being absent for most of her childhood, he taught Kate to be tough.

Damn it. How did her father creep into her thoughts? She pushed off the pool's wall and proceeded at a feverish pace in freestyle.

After one lap, carbon dioxide built up in her lungs. She wasn't gliding between strokes. She was over-rotating, moving too frantically.

Exhale. Don't hold your breath. Glide, exhale, glide, breathe.

Don't fight the water. It will always win.

Why was she thinking of her father anyway? Fuck her father. *Fuck him!* In the water, he could never reach her. He had tried, but he never could. His words of wisdom rang in her ears, but she didn't need or want them. Not anymore.

Kate continued at a merciless speed. Kicking from her hips, she flared out her arms and swept back harder with each stroke. Water was her haven. Despite her heart pounding out of her chest, she knew she was safe here.

EARLY WAKE-UP CALL

Jessica's eyes flipped open, not a gentle fluttering of eyelashes toward consciousness, but a scary clown's click of the eyelids. At the far edge of the mattress, she rolled on her back. From across the bed, Rob's snoring penetrated her earplugs, forced her to fold the pillow over her ears. A sliver of moonlight slanted through the windows enough for her to make out shadows. With hopes of falling back to sleep, she stared at the ceiling fan, tried counting the rotation of the blades like counting sheep. Round and round it went. Perhaps it would make her dizzy.

Jessica glanced to where Rob lay diagonally beside her, his frame hogging up most of the king-sized bed. Seconds later, the snoring grew louder. Under her breath she grumbled, and a bitter tang coated her mouth. Naked and lying on his back, Rob's chest rose and fell with each grunt.

She grabbed a fistful of her hair. He couldn't even snore properly!

It wasn't a low rumble or rippling sound. His was a high-pitched noise that came in fits and starts. Using her feet, she tried pushing him on his side but could not budge him. Visions of pinching his nose, sticking a fist down his throat, or suffocating him with a pillow erupted in her brain.

Where did these violent and desperate thoughts come from?

Rob's arm suddenly lurched in her direction and she recoiled. The smell of alcohol and cigarettes flowed out of his mouth and his pores, creating a stench cloud that hung over the room. They had avoided each other yesterday, though she saw him hanging out with Matthew, of all people. When she came to bed, the two were still sitting with the band. Matthew had on a surgical mask because he said the smoke bothered him.

Freak!

Jessica sat up and squinted at the bedside clock next to her. It was not yet half past five. In about an hour, sunrise would flood the room, but for now, she cherished the quiet shadows. She got out of bed and tiptoed to the couch, opened her laptop. The snoring continued.

Jessica started a blog after countless people asked her what it was like to win big on a popular game show. *Jessica's Journey* chronicled her experience on *The Price is Right*. One blog post each week grew to two, and soon she was posting every other day. Her writing evolved. People gravitated to her—a girl from Tennessee who didn't even own a passport before this trip.

Imagine that.

Though she didn't need the passport for entry to Jamaica, she decided to get one anyway. Soon, she found out her naiveté charmed her readers. Her blog connected her to young, ambitious people around the world and only confirmed her wanderlust. Hundreds of daily hits and comments on her posts proved people enjoyed her writing. She even surprised herself with her ability to market her blog.

Her ultimate dream was to travel and open her own business one day. Whatever she did would involve entrepreneurship, that much she knew. Unlike Mama, she never wanted to depend on a man. Through her writing, she reached people, and it gave her confidence like she never had before.

"Jess, where are you?" Rob shouted from the bed.

She snapped her head up from the computer screen. "You startled me!"

Rob grunted, pushed himself into a sitting position. "Shit, it's still dark. What are you doing?"

"I'm checking my blog."

Rob propped several pillows against the headboard, stared at her for a few seconds. "Let's not fight anymore, all right, Jess? I'm tryin' to be more polite to all the folks here, even helped Matthew write somethin' yesterday for his magazine." He scratched himself. "You know he's a journalist?"

A laugh escaped her, sounded almost like a cough. "Umm … yeah."

"Why do you say it that way?" He let out a lengthy, forceful yawn. "Maybe he can teach you somethin' for your blog. He's teachin' me to speak better English and less like a Southern boy. Isn't that what you want?"

She wasn't sure if he was serious or not but detected no sarcasm in his tone. A small part of her felt sorry for him, but only for a moment. "Rob, for the record, I don't want you to stop speaking like a Southerner."

"Well, Goddamnit Jess, what is it you want from me?"

Nothing.

That was the problem. She wanted nothing from him, only she couldn't say it right now. "Let's just try to make the best of it while we're here, Rob."

"All right, I promise to be more considerate."

Rob sounded less than contrite, but she didn't want to fight anymore. In less than a week, she would end their relationship. After her talk with Kate, she was confident she could do it.

Led by a semi-hard erection, Rob got out of bed. "Gimme me some sugar when I come out, all right? You know they say make-up sex is the best."

Jessica watched him swagger toward the bathroom and cringed. After he closed the door, she turned off the laptop.

Nausea rolled through her like seasickness as she pictured Rob's hands on her. She would need to steel herself for another emotionless, mediocre romp. If there had been one positive thing about fighting with Rob, it was that she didn't have to have sex with him. Now, she would have to make nice for the remainder of the trip, unless … She stood up and slid her fingers down the front of her panties.

Jessica held her breath, silently praying Mother Nature had intervened.

SCENTED RESENTMENT

After dinner and before the band took to center stage, Anna excused herself and called it an evening. Before heading upstairs, citing fatigue, she kissed Nolan and said her good-nights to everyone.

Anna lied. She was tired, but she was more angry than anything.

Up in her room, she stood in the shower stall and allowed the hot water to beat down on her.

Symbolic, as she did feel beaten down.

It was the only place where she had privacy. The sound of the shower muffled her crying, and the water camouflaged her tears.

She squeezed a dollop of scentless shower gel onto a sponge and scrubbed herself.

Scentless soap. Like a mentally unstable person without a care in the world, she let out a thunderous, unladylike laugh.

Before Matthew alerted her to his issues with perfumes, she had never bought such a thing. Even though outwardly, she showed him no special treatment, she wanted him to enjoy his time here, with the hope he would write a better review. It seemed ridiculous now. She had failed—miserably—despite going out of her way to accommodate him.

Her mind shuttled back to earlier in the day when she booked a yoga class with a local instructor. Anna provided the yoga mats and towels, just enough for the girls and Tom. To her surprise, Matthew showed up and asked to join the class.

She was pleased to see him, gave him her mat and towel to use and sat out the class herself.

The hour-long session was held on one of the open terraces with a breeze coming off the ocean, neither too hot nor too cool, perfect temperature in fact. Everyone seemed to enjoy themselves.

Shortly before dinner, Matthew approached her in her office. "I feel horrible after that yoga class," he said, leaning his body against the door frame.

"Oh?" Concerned he had pulled a muscle or sprained a joint, she ushered him into the room, even saw an opportunity to finally bond with him.

Matthew stepped in the office, his hands tucked in the pockets of his shorts. He chose not to take a seat but remained standing by the door. His face appeared flushed and sweaty. His jaw clamped tightly as he spoke.

"Your towel. It was your towel."

"What?" Her head snapped back. "What are you talking about?"

"Your staff washed your towel in a detergent I'm allergic to, or maybe they used a horrible fabric softener sheet." He rocked back and forth, heel to toe, toe to heel. "Either way, I don't feel well."

She stood up from her desk but did not move toward him. Something in his manner reminded her of a small dog, the type that barked at larger dogs and hid behind their owners when confronted. "Matthew, I—"

"Anna, I didn't think it was too much to ask that my needs be met for the week. Obviously it is." He stared at her blankly, as if she were someone who couldn't possibly understand him and was unworthy of further explanation.

"I'm sorry you feel that way," she said, trying to keep her voice unemotional even as her anger mounted. "That was my own personal towel from home, not washed by the staff here."

Matthew heaved out a loud breath. "Well … that doesn't help me, does it?" Venom loaded his tone. "I'm not joining you for dinner. I need to lie down for a while." He pulled his hands out of his pockets and crossed his arms in front of his chest.

The look on his face told her nothing was going to appease him. It took all her strength to remain civil toward him. "Why don't you call us when you wake up? I'll have Harrison bring dinner to your room."

"Fine." Turning to leave, he hesitated and looked back at her with a robotic smile. "And I was just beginning to like it here too."

* * *

Anna exited the shower, wrapped her hair in a fluffy white towel, and slipped into a bathrobe. When she looked in the mirror, it reflected swollen, tired eyes. Her throat clenched. To prevent more tears from flowing, she tilted her head back.

She could not let Nolan know how upset she was.

She had instructed her staff to treat Matthew Kane a certain way, and yet, she had gone against her own advice. Why? Because she had rationalized she needed to try harder than anyone else to protect Sunset Villa. It was her baby.

In addition to buying scentless cleaners and hygiene products for Matthew's room, she went so far as to replace his linens with brand new ones. Anna even purchased hypoallergenic pillows and blankets, having become paranoid that it was not good enough to just clean the old ones. She did all of this because she felt she had to.

And I was just beginning to enjoy it here too, he had said.

Asshole.

The thought of him made her stomach lurch.

Anna entered her bedroom and removed her robe, draping it at the foot of the bed. Outside her suite, the sound of crickets chirped their nightly tune to the rustling of a gentle breeze. The ocean roared intermittently.

She'd had more than enough of Matthew Kane. No one even missed him at dinner. In fact, his absence made the evening more relaxed. She now regretted inviting him, resented even having him here for the remaining days.

His needs. His wants. That was all Matthew ever

thought of. She had pandered to them, thinking it would help Sunset. How foolish of her.

The only thing that would satisfy her now was to remove him from the property. Anna took a heavy breath and allowed her tears to spill out. In front of her on her dresser, she spied creams in a colorful array of bottles in different shapes and sizes. She had avoided using them on this trip because the scent might bother Matthew.

No more.

She removed the lid off her favorite jar by Christian Dior and scooped out a generous amount. With manic energy, Anna rubbed the moisturizer into her legs, then she spread it over her arms and stomach. When she finished, she shimmered and reflected light like white pearls.

To hell with Matthew Kane and his problems. It was time she looked after her own needs.

CONSEQUENCES

Adam accompanied her past the bar through the villa. They stood at the base of the steps leading upstairs. It was close to midnight. The music had stopped a half hour ago according to Harrison, who was still tending bar with Kate as his sole customer.

Jessica had intended to return in time to listen to Rob play, but then she received a much better offer. Adam invited her for a walk …

"Sweet dreams, Jessica," Adam said. "I'm glad we were able to spend time together."

Her heart jumped, and heat rushed to her face. "Me too," she said. The power he had over her was like nothing she had ever experienced.

As she climbed the stairs, Adam walked toward the bar. A pang of jealousy hit her. It was ridiculous given the incredible time she just had with the man. She shook off the bitter emotion and psyched herself up for a possible confrontation with Rob.

Upon arriving at the top of the steps, she removed her sandals and crooked her index finger through the straps. An empty hallway greeted her when she peeked around the corner. Up on her toes, Jessica advanced toward her room, comforted by the familiar sounds of the ocean and night critters. Everything seemed normal. Once in front of her door, she curled up her shoulders and pressed her ear to the surface. For once, she was hoping to hear snoring.

Silence.

Rocking slightly on her feet, she looked around, assessing. No light escaped from under the door—a good sign. Harrison said everyone went to bed a half hour ago. That was time enough for Rob to fall asleep. She listened for noise from the room again. Nothing.

Should she wait?

In her mind, she bargained and pleaded with some imaginary power. She laid out the entire path of walking in the dark toward the bathroom, cleaning up, slipping into bed. She'd be more than happy if Rob kept her up all night with his snoring. It would give her time to think of what to say to him in the morning. With that conversation rattling in her head, she inserted the key into the doorknob and turned.

Please let Rob be asleep.

The door cracked open, but only as much as she needed to slink into the dark room. Once inside, she exhaled a breath that hit her in the face like a blast of hot air. A menacing waft of cigarettes wrinkled her nose.

Click.

On went the lamp next to Rob's side of the bed, flooding the room with light.

Jessica jumped back with her hand to her throat. A

thwack reverberated as her sandals hit the floor. Squinting against the glare, Rob's appearance twisted her insides into a knot. Sitting in bed naked amidst a cloud of smoke and a half empty liquor bottle, he glowered at her through heavy-lidded eyes.

"Sneaking in, Jess?"

"Jesus, you frightened me!" She stared at Rob, unblinking.

"Where you been?"

Jessica propped herself against the door and steadied her legs by grabbing the doorknob behind her. "I went for a walk … lost track of time."

"You went for a walk …" His head drooped. A trickle of drool hung from his bottom lip and pooled on his stomach. "And who the hell did you go with?"

"What?"

Rob snapped his head up and faced her. "Who … the … fuck … did you go fer a walk with at this hour?"

"I …" She took a breath and stood up straight, almost considered lying. "Adam … but I guess you knew that already."

"That Yankee asshole!"

The quickness of his remark made Jessica think he had already formed the thought, had been waiting to use it. "Rob …" His pitiful state tugged at her, but she had to remain strong and alert. When he picked up the bottle and took a deep pull, some of its contents spilled on his flabby chest.

"I can't believe you did this to me, Jess. You fucked

him, didn't you?" His scowl made her feel dirty and cheap.

"Rob ... no, of course not." She forced a kittenish smile, the one that usually appeased him. "You've had too much to drink."

He swung his legs over the side of the bed, grabbed the bottle and sucked down the remainder. It sent him into a coughing fit.

"I'm getting you a glass of water." Against her better judgment, she took several steps toward the bathroom.

"No!" Spitting out a sticky glob in his palm, he wiped it on the sheets before tossing the empty bottle on the bed. "Yer not goin' nowhere."

"Rob, it's late. I'm sorry I didn't make it back to hear you play, okay?" She had never seen him so inebriated, so volatile.

From a dish on the night table, he picked up a cigarette and curled his lips around it. Jessica recognized the soap dish from their bathroom. After a long drag, he blew the smoke toward her. Crimson splotches covered his cheeks as if someone had punched him. She didn't dare remind him he wasn't supposed to smoke in the room.

"I waited for you," he said, swaying on the edge of the bed, gazing at her with watery bloodshot eyes. "I played well tonight. All the guys said so."

Jessica transferred the weight from one leg to the other, no longer within reach of the door. "I'm glad you played well, and you're right, I should have come back ... Can we please call it a night and talk about this in the morning?"

"You'd like that, wouldn't ya?" Fury darkened his

expression, his chest heaving as if he were about to be sick.

Jessica's heart thundered in her ears. The heavy scent of sweat and alcohol assaulted her nostrils with each breath Rob took. She observed his mood becoming gloomier by the second. Her eyes darted to the bathroom around the opposite side of the bed, back to Rob who looked daggers at her. She prayed his alcohol-induced haze would slow his reflexes. The metal taste of fear coated her mouth.

A moment of silence connected them until she bolted for the door. Rob lunged at her and yanked her by the hair. She instinctively grabbed his wrist to prevent him from ripping into her scalp. Buckled against him, she lost her balance and stumbled. Her nails sliced into his chest. He dragged her to the bed and threw her on it face down. Her arms shot out as she crumpled in a heap, immediately scrambling on all fours. Rob collapsed on her with the impact of a wrestler's splash.

Her head snapped back and struck something hard behind her. A blinding pain ripped across her skull.

Heavy hands shoved her face deep into the mattress. Darkness. She couldn't breathe, strained to turn her head to the side. Pain and panic constricted her throat. Fingers compressed the sides of her neck. Her left arm flailed behind her. Her fist made contact, probably with Rob's shoulder. She continued punching, but each blow became feebler, had no impact of toppling him. Her right arm was useless wedged beneath her torso. She thrashed about to rock Rob off her, needed to dislodge her right hand. If only she could grab the bottle …

Hair stuck to streaks of tears against her cheeks. Strands caught in her mouth. She tried spitting them out, gasped for any amount of trapped air. Along with the horror of what was happening, she gurgled more tears, which threatened to choke off all her oxygen. Her legs were numb, pinned under Rob's two hundred pound frame. She couldn't breathe. Just as she felt herself passing out, Rob released the chokehold around her neck.

Immediately, she lifted her chin and whipped her head to the side, almost hyperventilated as she gulped air into her lungs. The bottle lay within her reach, but her arm was still trapped.

Rob forced his hand underneath her and groped a breast, pinched her nipple. "I'm gonna take back what's mine," he whispered, his rancid breath near her ear.

She scrunched her face as if he were spewing acid at her. The new horror coiled her intestines tighter than the bedsprings beneath her.

Blood rushed up her throbbing neck. "I'll kill you … I'll kill you." The threat sounded weak, even to her.

Rob fumbled under her skirt. Jessica bucked against him as hard she could. She felt his fingers hook the elastic waistband of her panties. "Fuck!" she said. The word sounded foreign to her, as if it were coming from another person.

Rob grunted. "Yer feistier than you been with me in a long time, Jess." He wrenched the underwear off her buttocks. "I'm gonna enjoy this." Pawing between her legs, he inserted one, then two, then three fingers inside her.

"Stop! Rob … please stop!" She thrashed like a wildcat to escape his painful jabs. "Stop … you're hurting me!" A tremulous cry wheezed past her ears in a voice she didn't even recognize.

"So wet, Jess, so wet …" A muffled groan, a snicker, "you must really be turned on, I know I am," he taunted.

A rush of sour bile crept up her throat, along with a hatred she never imagined possible for another human being. Her ribs felt crushed, her insides wounded. Even as exhaustion eroded the last of her reserves, she knew she could kill him. She understood this with crystal clarity.

When he withdrew his fingers from inside her and fumbled to replace them with something else, fury erupted like a volcano in her head. Consumed by a seismic rage, she jerked out her contorted hand. The pain ripped a high-pitched scream from her. She continued screeching as she grabbed the neck of the bottle and smashed it against the wrought iron bed frame. A wide swing behind her connected to what she hoped was Rob's head. She kept on slashing but only cut air. He was still on top of her. Her struggling and wrath had been for naught.

As tears and hair blinded her, her surge of strength dissipated. She croaked out a sob and braced herself for the inevitable.

BAR BANTER

Kate smiled as Adam took a seat next to her at the bar. He requested his usual from Harrison.

"How did it go?" she asked.

"You were right. Jessica's a smart girl."

Kate shifted on her stool and rested her forearm on the bar, facing Adam. "Where did you end up going?"

"We took the road around the perimeter of the property. It's a nice walk."

"You had a good talk then?"

"We did. She impressed me with her ideas, has a true entrepreneurial spirit." Adam gave Harrison a *thumbs up* when he returned with his drink in a flared cocktail glass.

"Shaken not stirred, sir."

Adam clinked his glass against Kate's and took a sip. "You make a mean Martini, Harrison."

"Thank you, sir." Harrison excused himself.

Adam set down his glass. "Jessica's blog has huge potential for monetization."

Kate nodded. "I concluded the same when I read her work."

"Thanks for the referral. I think we'll be able to do

business together." Adam bit off one of three green olives skewered on a black plastic toothpick.

After her conversation with Jessica yesterday, Kate figured out a way to help the ambitious woman. Greg alerted her to Adam's talent for using social media to build his businesses. He and Tom would be hiring Adam's company to help with their fashion and fundraising projects. Matthew confided he had stumbled across Adam's website as well, but he had only unflattering remarks for the man. Contrary to Matthew's thoughts, she knew Adam's professional platform would be a good fit for Jessica.

"I think Jessica has a good head on her shoulders. She could use a man of your influence."

Adam stared straight ahead for a second then turned back to her. "May I ask you a question, Kate?"

"Sure."

"As a woman, you're not offended by some of the things I've written?"

Kate swirled her empty glass on top of the bar, dipped her head when Harrison gestured a refill. "Just a splash," she said to him before turning her attention back to Adam. "You're referring to your views on women and relationships."

"Yes."

She felt Adam fix his gaze to hers like a hunter to its prey. For several beats, she didn't say a word. "You push the boundaries, and your views may be outrageous, but ..." Kate took a sip of her drink. "I don't think you're wrong.

There are many men like you in successful relationships, even multiple successful relationships, however …"

"Yes?"

"I also know men like you who are psychopaths."

Her blunt response must have caught him off guard. He paused a moment before throwing his head back in hearty laughter. "That doesn't surprise me, I've been called a psycho on occasion."

Kate smiled. "Don't worry, I don't subscribe to the notion that all powerful, intelligent, ambitious men are psychopaths, even though they may show symptoms for it. It's too simplistic a view."

Adam turned his body leisurely toward her. "Agree, and besides, you can't blame men if women are attracted to these types, right?"

"Touché." Kate found Adam to be a worthy adversary, as she expected he would be. She was correct in her original assessment of him as *aggressive, dominant*, and *achievement-motivated*. Add to that a charismatic, powerful presence, and she imagined few women would be able to resist him.

"I like that you don't jump to conclusions, Kate."

"Oh I do, sometimes … but the heart wants what it wants. Attraction isn't led by logic." She stretched her back and took a deep breath. "There's a gulf of misunderstanding between men and women as it is. I never judge what consenting adults do."

"Neither do I. I'm needs-oriented. If my needs aren't met, I lose interest. It sounds crass, but there's no point carrying on with a woman unless we are both disgustingly happy. Don't you agree?" Adam roamed her face, down to her neck just above her cleavage, and slowly back up.

"I do indeed," she said, taking note of his deliberate mannerisms. The way he devoured her with his eyes was reminiscent of a bygone era—a time when a woman would have slapped a man for looking at her in such a lascivious way. Like the men of those times, Adam was impossible to ignore.

"And you, no man in your life?" Adam's voice pulled her out of the past.

"That's forward of you to ask." Kate rubbed her jaw.

"You know psychopaths aren't shy." He returned a playful gleam in his eyes. "I've freed myself from the social norms of politeness."

"Have you now?" She blinked at him with curiosity, shifting in her seat.

He touched her bare arm. "Yes."

Kate ignored the fingers stroking her skin. "I had guessed Jessica to be more your type."

"I never go after another man's woman."

Kate wet her lips with her tongue. "Ahh, so you do have morals after all."

"One of my commandments. Some things I just don't do." He withdrew his hand from her arm and grabbed his drink, polishing it off.

"Admirable."

He shrugged. "Jessica is a sweet girl but not a challenge. I can already tell she wants to get in my pants."

Kate lifted an eyebrow. "Really?"

"Yes." He gave a stiff nod. "I know these things."

"If you say so." Kate stifled a chuckle.

"You haven't answered my question."

"Ah yes, your question." Her voice grew deeper with the alcohol. "The answer is there's no one in my life at the moment. It's a fool's game to fill empty spaces with people."

"Sounds lonely."

"At times …" Her chin lowered, "but people fail one another even with the best of intentions. It's a good thing I enjoy my own company."

Adam appeared amused. "My commandments weed out people I don't want in my life, but let in those I do. You should try it."

"Thanks, but I'm guided by my own code of conduct."

Adam leaned in. "It's important to have a moral compass."

Kate drained her scotch and savored the pleasurable burn down her throat. "Who said anything about *moral*?"

Adam squinted at her with vaguely predatory eyes, his mouth slack. He paused as if to digest what she said before turning to Harrison. "I think we're going to need another round," he said.

Kate followed Adam's hand as he caressed up and down her calf, his fingers resting in the nook behind her knee, drawing small lazy circles. "No more for me. Two is my limit tonight," she said to Harrison when she saw him reaching for the scotch.

"Yes, Miss Kate." A sympathetic flicker crossed his face.

He looked to Adam. "Sir, would you like another Martini?"

"Please," he said. Adam gave her knee a light squeeze. "I like you Kate. You're a beautiful, sensual woman."

She extended him the tiniest of smiles. It would have been so much easier to experience that swelling of ego, followed predictably in many women by a need for humility. But she didn't feel it, not for Adam. She gave him a slight nod, but he wasted his compliment on her.

At that moment, the sound of footsteps and voices cut the silence between them. The OMG boys, Jerry, and a man she had never met approached the bar as she stepped off her stool. It was the perfect time for her to call it an evening. Jerry introduced the stranger as Daniel, a British ex-pat who lived nearby.

The silver curls grazing his temples hinted at a man in his mid to late-forties. Light-brown hair framed a cleft chin and chiseled features, but they were hard lines. The furrows between his brow hinted at an intense thinker. Despite that, a lightness appeared when the corners of his mouth lifted in an easy smile. He was not handsome in the classical sense, but he possessed something much more important for Kate—that indefinable quality that attracted her to a man. Had he not shaved for lack of time, or was it just his rugged look? Her superfluous observation was merely to avoid one thing—the lure of his hypnotic eyes.

He bowed toward her hand, which she offered in greeting, grazed it above the knuckles with his lips. The stubble across his chin brushed her skin as he lifted his face. His indigo eyes never left hers.

"Oh …" she said, as a rush of heat swept up between her breasts to rest on her cheeks, "an English gentleman." The contact was delicate, yet so pleasurable, with an intensity that shocked her as if no one had ever touched her before.

"You, Kate, are seduction personified." He held her fingers a moment longer before letting go.

Daniel's charm sneaked up on her like sarin, stunning her into immobility.

"How I regret not coming sooner," he said.

Her skin tingled where he had kissed her. "That's kind of you to say."

"Perhaps another evening, Kate."

She turned to him with a sideways glimpse. "I would like that," she said.

Daniel's presence silenced the other men. It was as if time had trapped them in a vacuum, while she and the Englishman danced around each other with words.

After she bid the men good-night and headed toward her room, she felt eyes at her back. The men would probably stay up until dawn passing liquor and stories back and forth. She was happy to leave them as an uneasy feeling swelled inside her.

Caressing her hand where the stranger's lips had skimmed it, she ascended the stairs to her room. When she stood outside her door and fumbled for the key in her purse, Kate reflected on the royal blue of Daniel's eyes. It unnerved her at how easily he was able to trap her in his vertigo. It flooded her with thoughts of a man from her past, someone who …

The scrape of a door opening made her turn around. Kate saw the disheveled, young woman step out of the room beside hers. Jessica moved backward in a tentative manner, as if she were sneaking out after a night's illicit affair. Her head and shoulders hunched forward. She gingerly pulled the door until it clicked into a locked position. When she raised her head of tousled hair and caught sight of Kate, she blinked back tears through a mess of smeared mascara. Her bottom lip trembled as if she wanted to say something, but no words came out. She started to shake.

Kate ran to Jessica and grabbed her.

CLEANUP

Jessica leaned her palms on the sink. To mask the sob bubbling in her chest, she turned on the tap to full capacity. In an attempt to clean the tangled mess on her head, she scooped handfuls of water and scraped the caked blood off unruly strands. Her hair, which had appeared full and shiny only a couple of days ago, now fell limp like wet straw.

A deep line etched the left side of her jaw where it had ground into the firm mattress. Streaks of make-up ran across her face. She tasted blood in her mouth and spit in the sink, watched the red mucous blend with the water and fade to pink before it swirled down the drain. Opening her mouth wide in front of the mirror, a large blister revealed itself on one side of her tongue. She sucked the blood pooled around it, spit again, and rinsed her mouth. The cold water relieved the sting. She remembered the exact moment she bit her tongue—when her chin hit the mattress after Rob threw her on the bed, right before he started choking her. While swallowing more water to soothe the rawness inside, she gingerly stroked her throat. Discoloration around her neck was evident, particularly in two spots where dark pressure marks had left indents in her skin.

Jessica turned to the full-length mirror behind the door. God, she scared herself.

One side of her sleeveless yellow blouse hung off a shoulder, torn where the soft pleating had met the neckline. Reaching a hand behind her, she discovered the button missing from the keyhole opening. Jessica grabbed the hem of her blouse, winced from the pain below her ribs when she pulled the top over her head. She undid the clasp of her bra and slid off the garment.

Bruises, the size of strawberries, appeared where Rob's fingers had dug into her flesh. The red marks and darkened nipple contrasted with the milky white of her other breast. She bit down on her lower lip to stifle a whimper. Now was not the time to cry.

She removed the belt around her waist and wiggled the skirt down to her ankles. It was only then that the smell of blood hit her nostrils. The sight of red streaks on her skin wobbled her legs. Just before her knees buckled, she turned to clutch the counter. With her head bowed, she shut out the light and watched the room spin behind her eyelids. It seemed like minutes before the dizziness subsided, and she was able to open her eyes.

Moving slowly, she threaded her panties down her thighs and stepped out of them. After wrapping the undergarment in tissue, she placed it in the plastic-lined compartment of her beach bag beside her suntan lotion.

Jessica pulled out a face cloth and held it under the water, wrung it until it stopped dripping. She wiped her genitals and the insides of her thighs, bracing herself to feel a sting from an open wound. None surfaced. How she managed not to cut herself was a miracle, considering she found pieces of glass lodged in her hair. Several rinses later, she wiped the blood clean and revealed her smooth, tanned skin.

Even though she conducted her clean up on autopilot, her mind swirled in madness. No matter what, she had to keep moving. If she stopped for a second, a hurricane of emotions would overcome her. Of this, she was certain. *Keep moving.*

Just as she began to feel confident she was holding it together, several drops of blood hit the floor, barely missing her feet. A cry percolated inside her chest, threatened to overwhelm her. She clutched her stomach and clamped a hand over her mouth.

Tears streamed down her cheeks. She could not allow herself to come undone. Not now.

A knock on the bathroom door made her jump. With her heart in her throat, she pressed against her chest to calm her frayed nerves. Fear had followed her here.

"Jessica?"

"Yes … yes, I'll be right out."

In the hopes of reducing the redness, she pressed ice-cold water into her eyes. With several squares of toilet paper, she dabbed her cheeks dry. After she finished dressing, she gathered her things and threw them in her bag. A survey of the room showed nothing out of place, but she used several more tissues to wipe down the counters and clean the floor again.

Never had she felt so dirty and humiliated. The last thing she wanted was to leave evidence of her shame in this room. Jessica took a deep breath to compose herself before opening the bathroom door.

Upon seeing Kate, she teared up again. The doctor rose to her feet and escorted her to a chair. "Sit down."

"I'm sorry Kate. I didn't mean for this … here with you. I …" Jessica collapsed her face in her hands.

"Look at me." Kate grasped her shoulders. "Just tell me what happened."

"Rob … he was so drunk … He attacked me …" Her raspy words spilled out in gasps.

In a soothing voice, Kate asked, "Where is he now?"

"In the room on the bed … I had to get out … too scared to even use my own bathroom …" She erupted into sobs, inserting bits of babble alongside bursts of crying. Kate poured a glass of water for her.

"Here," she said, handing her the glass. "Drink this. Now tell me what happened."

Jessica's words cascaded from her like a waterfall as she recounted Rob's jealous rage and how he had tried to rape her. "He was crushing me. I hit him with a broken bottle as he was about to … you know …" She sniffled. "That's when his body went limp." She gulped more water, coughed from swallowing too quickly, then took deep breaths to calm down. "His full weight dropped on me and then nothing." She pressed on her mouth with a fist. "I killed him. Oh my god, Kate … I killed him."

"Calm down." Kate patted her arm and handed her a

box of tissues. "Tell me what you did next."

The doctor's touch stopped her from shaking. "I don't remember. It took all my strength to claw my way out from underneath Rob." She dabbed tears away from the inside corners of her eyes. "I had an overwhelming urge to get out of there otherwise I was going to be sick. I quickly grabbed a few things for my bag … and left."

"You did the right thing, and I'm glad I came along when I did." Kate opened up her medical bag.

"I was going to sneak downstairs to the washroom by poolside. After that, I'm not sure …"

"It's okay, you're safe now. Let me take a look at those bruises."

Jessica took a breath and allowed Kate to touch her neck.

"Does that hurt?"

"It's tender," she said, forcing a smile, even though she felt as if her face might crack from the tightness.

"I'm going to get you a bucket of ice. You're staying here with me tonight."

"Kate … I can't impose, I—"

"Jessica, it's late, and you need to rest. You'll be safe here." Kate pulled on a pair of gloves, closed up her medical bag. "I'm going in your room to check on Rob."

"No, Kate … no …" she bleated pathetically. "What have I done?" Jessica hugged her arms around herself. "Oh my god, what have I done?"

"You're going to be fine. Don't worry." Kate rested a reassuring hand on her arm. "Don't open the door for anyone."

PLAYING DOCTOR

Kate scrutinized the man lying on his stomach, his head twisted at a peculiar angle, his body not fully visible from where she stood by the door. His flabby body spilled across the bed perpendicular to how one would sleep, his calves overhanging the side. At first glance, nothing appeared out of the ordinary except for a broken liquor bottle with slivers of glass on the bed. A few fragments had scattered on the floor, but then … she saw the blood.

She and Jessica were almost the same size, could share a wardrobe if they wanted to. The sight of Rob splayed out like this confirmed how much bigger he was than her. It disgusted Kate to think of him overpowering Jessica as she had described.

The air conditioning kicked in, ruffled the tendrils against her shoulders. The room was an icebox—much too cold for her liking. Still, it could not mask the pungent smell of body odor and blood.

Kate circled the body, careful not to step on broken glass. She stopped when she reached the opposite side of the bed where Rob lay facing the wall. Withdrawing a digital camera from her bag, she took several pictures of the body from different angles.

The last time she saw Rob was at center stage listening to music. By the time the band packed up, Rob retreated upstairs with his guitar case in one hand, rum in the other. The bottle was already half empty at the time. Ben, Jerry, and Nolan had all been drinking from it during the jam session, which meant Rob could not have consumed its entire contents.

Bending forward, she observed his slack-jawed expression, winced from the smell of his breath. With two fingers pressed to Rob's neck, she counted his heartbeat—steady, no sign of respiratory distress. Aside from a low rumble, his breathing was normal, but it would take a lot to wake him now. She estimated he would sleep for at least another eight to ten hours.

Kate picked up the largest piece of glass by Rob's body and placed it on the night table. More sharp fragments littered the bed. With several tissues, she swept the shards into a pile, dropped them in a plastic bag.

"You fat fuck," she said, loud enough for him to hear her if he were conscious, but he wasn't.

Tears moistened her cheeks as she stared at the body. To stop the tingling at the top of her scalp, she took several deep breaths.

"No," she whispered.

A memory threatened to unlock itself from her brain. It tapped at the door of her consciousness, dampening her back in perspiration. Her head felt on the verge of exploding. To prevent the thoughts from surfacing, she squeezed her eyes shut.

"No," she whispered again, louder this time to hear an echo in her ears. The knocking inside her head continued. Heat swept up her neck.

She grabbed the largest pillow at the end of the bed and stood over the body.

"No!" she shouted. Her husky voice bounced off the walls.

The prickling sensation on her scalp abated, relieving her of the burning urge to scratch her head raw. Her breathing returned to normal. The unwanted memory retreated to a dark corner ... for now, as did her physical and emotional discomfort. Kate dabbed her face with a tissue, composed herself to carry out the job she came to do.

Even with a remote chance of alcohol poisoning, she needed to minimize the odds that Rob might choke on his own vomit. Kate took a firm hold of his shoulder and rolled him off his stomach. With one pillow wedged by his chest, she added a second to prop him higher. A supporting wall of cushions at his back anchored him in a semi-fetal position. He grumbled at one point while she adjusted the pillows near his mid-section, but then his snoring took over.

Phew.

A gash on his right forearm confirmed Jessica's story. It was where she caught him with the jagged edge of the bottle. An odd place to cut. It would have made more sense if Jessica slashed his bicep or higher.

Did he raise an arm to defend himself?

She examined Rob's wound. The blood surrounding it had already started clotting, not deep enough to require stitches. For this, Kate was grateful. Rob did not stir, not even when she tore open a sterile alcohol pad and wiped the area clean.

Once she dressed his wound, she inspected his right hand. Dried blood caked his fingers, but the blood did not belong to him. It was Jessica's menstrual blood, which also trailed across the bed. According to Jessica's story, he was about to rape her after she failed to topple him.

So why didn't he?

Kate doubted he had passed out from the alcohol. Even in his terrible physical condition, his heightened libido and increased adrenalin should have pushed him to finish. The blood trail on the sheets happened while Jessica was struggling to get out from under him. But that was after he had already passed out.

All the evidence was in place, but something did not make sense.

Similar to a wildcat circling its injured prey, she moved around the bed, tried to picture the scene unfolding from Rob's perspective. What caused him to stop? The flesh wound Jessica inflicted would have done little to deter him. What happened right before that?

The position of the body. The pattern of the blood. What did Rob see that prevented him from continuing the assault?

Then it hit her.

Like a picture buried within a picture, once the hidden image was seen, it could not be unseen.

A quiet, yet triumphant breath seeped from her lungs.

Kate surveyed the room once more, turned down the air conditioning and increased the fan to a medium speed. When she observed goose bumps on Rob's skin, she draped him in a light blanket.

Out of her bag, she retrieved a pad of paper. Kate penned a note and tore off a sheet. She left it next to the bag of broken glass.

DAY SIX
A BRAND NEW DAY

Immediately after Kate left her, Jessica's sobs exploded with fury and settled in her throat. At one point, she could no longer catch her breath. It prompted her to run into the bathroom as a wave of nausea rolled over her. Her ribs hurt from coughing.

"Everything will be fine. Everything will be fine …" she repeated to herself while staring at her doleful expression in the mirror.

She was losing her grip on reality. One moment, high from her talk with Adam, a man of the world who wanted to discuss business with her—the next, assaulted in her room by her own boyfriend.

It seemed just as the doors were opening for her, she was turning into Mama.

She could already read the scathing headline: "A Mother and Daughter Killing Team."

It wouldn't matter that the court had found Mama not guilty of mariticide. It wouldn't matter that she had killed Rob in self-defense. The press would jump all over the story and spin it for as long as they could sell papers. In the meantime, Mama would be dragged back into the spotlight. Adam would want nothing to do with her. Her blog would be history.

When Jessica exited the bathroom, Kate was sitting on the couch. A stainless steel bowl filled with ice sat on the table.

Jessica poised frozen in place. Adrenaline pumped in her veins. She was unable to speak, as if fear had stunned her into silence. She stared at the other woman for a stuttered moment but found nothing in Kate's expression that eased her dread. An air of anxiety filled the space between them.

Kate stood up and drifted the few steps to where Jessica stood paralyzed. Only her trembling emotions suppressed her gag reflex.

"Everything is going to be fine." Kate held her by the shoulders. "You did not kill Rob."

Her mouth dropped open and she sank to her knees. "Oh god … thank you god … oh …"

Kate knelt close to her. "Listen to me." The doctor clutched her shaking arms.

Jessica blinked rapidly while she whimpered. Her thoughts jumbled in her head.

"Are you listening?" Kate repeated.

She snapped to, steeled herself to focus. "Yes … yes …" She nodded compulsively.

"Here's what we're going to do," Kate said.

* * *

Jessica's upper body ached, but the cramping had stopped. Disoriented and in mild discomfort, she rolled on her side. Her morning breath warmed the pillow. Light slanted through the windows, and she remembered where she was. No sign of Kate.

Balling her hands, she rubbed underneath her eyes. The room was cool, but not freezing from an overactive air conditioner. Despite it, she tugged the sheet toward her and folded it under her chin. When she pressed on her ribs, they no longer hurt. She stretched her neck, reached behind her and squeezed lightly at the base of it. The tenderness had subsided. Compression with the ice had helped.

Jessica grabbed the cell out of her bag and clicked out a text.

> Mama,
> You won't believe all that has happened.
> I have so much to tell you when I come home.
> The big news is it's over between me and Rob.
> He will be taken care of.
> You taught me well, Mama.
> I miss and love you.
> —Jessie

Send.

The clock on her phone read quarter to seven, today's sunrise time.

She rummaged in her bag and pulled out a compact mirror from her make-up case, examined the bruising around her neck. A sense of relief washed over her. The crimson of Rob's fingerprints had faded, now replaced by a blue shade. Though it didn't look much better, she knew she was on the mend.

What upset her more was the reflection of fleshy bags that stared back at her. The image was shocking, made her look older than her age.

Sadness.

Endings.

Several tears dropped on the looking glass, blurred her vision. She placed the mirror beside her and wiped her face.

When she saw clearly again, a swatch of rainbow colors greeted her on the opposite wall. Perplexed, she picked up the mirror and realized her tears on its surface had created a prism. It caught the light shining into the room.

Like a motivated student in science class, she pivoted the mirror playfully against the light to see an arc of dancing shapes. When looking in the mirror again, eyes smiled back at her.

It was a brand new day.

THE VISITOR

Tap, tap, tap on the door, neither too boldly nor too lightly, just loud enough for her to hear. Back straight, chest out, he loosened his arms by his side.

The door opened. "Come in," she said.

He entered, followed her inside, noticed she was barefoot. Her room was spacious, airy, configured differently than his. A quick scan revealed a few things that personalized it. Her shoes lined the door to the balcony, a floral wrap draped the back of a two-seater couch, and a hairbrush on the dresser sat next to a small mound of jewelry.

She appeared angelic in a veil of dark silk that fell down her back. A sheer, pearl pink dress with spaghetti straps and two undergarments separated him from her naked body. While they stood by the foot of the bed, he found himself transfixed by her.

"This is unusual." He felt as if she had invited a wolf into her room.

She nodded, licked her full lips until they glistened. "I know."

He took a step closer to her. With most of the slats

turned down on the windows, only a fraction of the light filtered the room, framing her lithe body. There was at least another hour before sunset; the mood in the room was already dusky and mysterious.

While observing the flutter of her eyelashes, he traced the long sweep of her neck, searched her face for any hint of resistance but saw none. "Yesterday …"

"Shhh …" Her index finger pressed to his mouth. "You don't have to explain."

Was she one of those women who could separate desire from rational thought?

"It's just that—"

"It's not important." She placed a hand against his chest and drew tiny circles near his heart.

His breath caught in his throat from the pleasure of her touch. Her scent, warm and honey-sweet, wafted up to him. Blood pumped into his groin, created a predictable, pleasant swell between his legs.

He slid the right strap of her dress off her shoulder, bent to kiss her neck while sliding off the other strap. Her dress inched down her body, helped along by an impatient tug from him. She held him in a hypnotic stare until the dress formed a puddle at her ankles. She stepped backward out of it, swept the dress aside with her foot. His gaze fell upon her, drifting over her body. Underneath a pale pink bra nestled two perfectly shaped mounds, but even more pleasing were how the nipples tented the thin fabric.

Her buttocks settled firmly into the curves of his palms. When he grabbed her hard, it prompted an indistinct squeak of surprise from her. Lips parted, she swayed against him. His heartbeat raced. Only yesterday, he would have bet his life this would never happen. Now … here he was with her in her room.

Nothing mattered anymore. He didn't care how this happened, only that it did happen.

With blood thrumming in his ears, he covered the bitterness of his guilt with the pleasure of her lips upon his.

* * *

With arms pinned by her side, he nuzzled her neck, licking down to her glorious breasts. She locked her thighs around his waist, applied pressure to his lower back with her heels. The strength of her grip did not surprise him. He had observed her colt-like legs in her swimsuit.

A wave of heat hit him, trickling sweat down his forehead. Was the air conditioner broken? The whirl of the ceiling fan and cold air circulating over his buttocks suggested otherwise. Before he could contemplate it further, the room spun. He found himself flipped on his back. He allowed her to scoop his hands above his head as she bit a trail across his chest from one nipple to the other. A mix of pleasure and pain rushed to his loins. Her nails dug into him, scratching hard enough to leave marks.

"Jesus …" He made a half-hearted attempt to struggle from underneath her.

Her long hair fanned across his stomach as she scraped

her teeth down his navel. His erection bumped her chin. She paused, took a firm hold and stroked him—hard.

"Easy there," he said, "easy." Her boldness scared him but excited him more. She lifted her head, and her eyes appeared wild. With a firm grip, she straddled him. He held her at the waist, tried to slow her down while she continued massaging him with her hand. Just when he pictured himself about to explode, she pulled him inside her like quicksand.

A muffled groan escaped his lips. The spin of the ceiling fan mesmerized him, but the whir of the blades sounded as if cotton plugged his ears. The heat in the room felt like a noose around his neck, but it wasn't that hot, was it?

He slid his hands to her hips and held her while she gyrated small circles atop him. The room continued to spin. With eyes closed, he concentrated on her motion. Up and down, she squeezed him in from root to tip, then released him slowly to do it again. Moisture gathered atop his sternum. He should have been in heaven, but she was siphoning the oxygen from his lungs. He coughed to extricate saliva pooling at the back of his throat.

She was doing all the work, so why was he so dizzy? Sweat glued him to the sheets. When he opened his eyes, his dimmed vision saw only a shadow of her. A stinging sensation traveled across his scalp. He feared his head might split open.

His groin muscles twitched hard against her with a spasm that was neither painful nor painless. Whatever it was, it was not the pleasurable anticipation of release. It was like nothing he had ever felt before.

Her shadow came into focus. He concentrated on her face. She looked at him with an odd expression, then leaned forward until her nipples grazed his chest. She stopped moving.

What was she staring at? Seconds ticked by and then he noticed it—her mouth.

The corners of her lips lifted in a smile reminiscent of a famous portrait of a woman, but for the life of him, he could not remember the name. When he blinked, her face changed again like a kaleidoscope. Were his eyes playing tricks on him in the dark? Numbness seized his brain as if intoxicated. A prickling sensation moved across the surface of his body.

He watched her lean to the side, lifting a leg to dislodge him from her body. Her movements were cautious and exaggerated, reminded him of a mime. He still had a full erection, which he took pride in until he realized he felt nothing. No arousal. No pain. No sensitivity at all. As she moved away from him, he swatted her arm, emitting a sound like a wounded animal mixed with static. She appeared unfazed by his weak attempt to grab her. With the flexibility of a Russian gymnast, she rolled to the opposite side of the bed and turned around. Her face appeared wooden, as if she were waiting for him to say something.

"I can't … breathe …" His chest rose and fell in rapid succession. "I can't … breathe …" The words carried terror to his own ears.

He had no strength to even move his pinky finger. All he managed was to tilt his head and glimpse her getting off the bed. Bare feet slapped the floor until she closed the door to the bathroom. The sound of running water caused him to swallow hard, and it hurt. His panting had dried up his throat.

As he stared into the dark, a memory sprung to mind. *Mona Lisa.*

Her smile reminded him of the Mona Lisa, only now he realized hers was not a smile at all, but a sneer.

A grainy, silent movie of the past week played back in his brain, flickering with black and white images. He gasped when her face appeared, speeding up his heart rate.

She was saying something to him, but he couldn't hear the words, couldn't read her lips.

The movie zoomed in for a close-up, her eyes dark and indecipherable, her lips curled upward. The film reel sputtered and freeze-framed. As the image of her faded to black, a subtle hell settled in his brain knowing he had misread her from the start.

TAKING CARE OF BUSINESS

Inside the bathroom, she stood in front of the mirror, toggled the light switch to its maximum brightness. Her skin appeared and felt normal, not flushed and clammy as she worried it might be. Her breathing was stable.

She twisted her hair and pinned it up. Work had to be done. Panic was not an option.

With her legs spread apart the width of her hips, she squatted over the plastic sheeting draped on the floor earlier in the day. Tools lined the wall, arranged as they would be for a surgeon's tray in an operating room. From left to right: neoprene gloves; surgical mask; sugar cube tongs; plastic bags; cotton balls; rubbing alcohol; and an auto-injector.

After donning the gloves and mask, she picked up the tongs and brought them to her groin. It was the only instrument taken from the villa, having already used and discarded her own pair of tweezers.

Mental note, buy extra pairs of tweezers.

Anchored firmly with her weight on her heels, she slipped one of the spoon-shaped ends of the tongs under the edge of the flexible ring covering her external genitalia.

She pulled it across to the opposite side and clamped the outer ring of the female condom shut. With a slow and steady hand, she held her breath and inched out the contraceptive from her body. Only after the closed end popped out, did she allow herself to exhale.

To minimize disturbing the contents inside the sheath, her painstaking motion continued until she sealed the condom and tongs in a plastic bag. At one point, she almost feared he may have had an orgasm, but in hindsight, her angst was unfounded. The amount of poison laced in the condom would have made ejaculation impossible.

An hour before he knocked on her door, she had already injected herself with a dose of atropine and pralidoxime chloride. The only side effect from the initial antidote was tightness where she had punctured her right leg. Because of it, she now chose the other leg. After swabbing an area on her upper left thigh, she jabbed a second dose of the antidote into the muscle. Counting fifteen seconds, she closed her eyes and held the auto-injector firmly against her skin.

Upon removing the needle, she grabbed a cotton ball and applied pressure to the injection site. Her heartbeat sped up, as she expected. It happened the first time as well, so she didn't panic.

Glancing at herself in the mirror again to ensure everything looked normal, she rose from her crouched position and stretched her legs. Everything was going as planned. After sealing items she had touched and setting them aside, she picked up a separate bag of tools prepared earlier in the day and opened the door.

It was time to attend to the body.

* * *

A sharp breath caught in her throat upon seeing he had moved from where she left him. It surprised her he had found the strength to do so. The contorted shape of his body suggested those final moments of lucidity must have been painful.

With the air conditioning set on high, she approached the edge of the bed and turned on the table lamp.

His face appeared frozen in a wide-eyed stare toward the bathroom door. Drool lined the corner of his mouth down to his chin like a snail's trail. One hand clutched the fitted sheet with such force, he pulled it off the mattress at the top corner of the bed. A leg bent awkwardly on top of the other, as if he had wanted to roll on his side. And that's where he remained, in mid-roll. It reminded her of an infant learning to flip on his stomach, but with neither the neck nor arm muscles to do so. The only part of him that appeared calm was his penis, resting against a wrinkled sac the size of two walnuts.

While stepping around to the other side of the bed, she flipped up the remaining three corners of the sheet. The clock showed 5:34 p.m., with sunset in a half hour. The room was cool and well lit.

Time to begin.

The mask made breathing difficult, was probably overkill given the poison only *warned* against inhaling the vapors. Fatal exposure occurred when absorbed through the skin anyway. Still, prudence won out, and she took the added precaution as she had done when she delivered the dose—administering three times the lethal amount for a man his size.

Braced against the bed, she took a firm hold of the fitted sheet and pulled the man toward her. It glided easily over a plastic covering she had layered atop the mattress. In addition to facilitating movement of the body, the sheeting served another purpose. It protected the mattress in case he had emptied his bowels.

She rolled the body toward her and re-positioned him flat on his back to examine him. A look of despair and fear stared back at her. Behind the mask, she exhaled a breathy sigh. How she wished things could have been different, but he left her no other option. With detached sensibility, she passed a rigid palm on top of his face and swiped his eyelids shut.

She pressed large cotton balls to a bottle of alcohol and cleaned his upper body from his mouth down to his shoulders. Along the way, she wiped his chest and hands too. It was doubtful the poison touched these areas, but she was not one to take any chances.

Aware it would require extra care, she saved his genitals for last. To her amazement, he was not completely flaccid. It was as if his penis had not received the signal from his brain of his demise, or he had expired at the height of arousal. Was it tragedy or comedy that his erection died a slow death, or that his little head did not listen to his big head, or …?

An overwhelming urge to giggle rippled through her stomach. How could she entertain such absurd thoughts at a time like this?

She needed to see a shrink.

Her humor quickly vanished when she grabbed a hold of his unusually, long foreskin. The lengthy layer of tissue encased his penis like a hoodie. When she tried pushing it back, her efforts proved unsuccessful. A flush crept up her neck from this unexpected roadblock. To sterilize the area, she had to retract the skin.

Why did he have to be uncircumcised?

The clock showed she had no more than ten minutes to clean his penis before the final stage.

Given the tight schedule, using force would be her only option to get underneath the foreskin.

She inserted the tips of her index fingers into the opening and firmly pulled in opposing directions. Along with this motion, she tried inching inside to stretch out the membrane. No success. He was extremely narrow. She decided on a change of tactic by yanking the foreskin away from the body. This motion stretched the skin where it connected at his groin, loosened the opening somewhat. *Good.* To speed things up, she repeated the tugging action fast and furious, inserted her thumbs instead. Back and forth. Back and forth. She jerked the skin so quickly her hands became a blur. It didn't take long until the opening expanded enough for the foreskin to fold over the head of the penis.

A sigh of relief escaped her lips.

Instead of a cotton ball to wipe this area, she used a facial cleansing wipe wrapped around her middle finger. She dipped it in alcohol to the knuckle and crammed it underneath the foreskin, scraping the underside as far up as she could go. The skin was still tight, but once she made it around once, it became more elastic.

Scrape and wipe. Up and around the shaft she went, repeating the process twice more with a fresh cloth each time.

From her bag of tools, she grabbed a packet of swabs similar to Q-tips. A patch of foam instead of a cotton tuft sat at the end of each plastic stick. These were especially helpful for applying eye make-up as they did not shed fibers like cotton swabs did. After wetting the foamy end with alcohol, she grasped the penis and pinched the head until the hole opened wide. She pushed the stick inside until it hit resistance. Slowly, she moved the swab in a clockwise direction, swirling it toward her as she cleaned the inside wall of his shaft.

Upon withdrawing the stick, an opaque, runny substance covered the foamy end.

Semen? Urine?

It didn't matter as no residue remained after she swabbed him several more times. With the remainder of the wipes, she scrubbed down the external parts around his genitalia.

A quick glance at the time revealed sunset was happening in less than two minutes. From the floor, she picked up his boxer briefs and slipped them on him.

Time to get him out of bed.

With strong determination, she swathed the body in the bed sheet for transfer to an oversized chair. Once she leveraged his body against hers, his heavy frame was easier to move than she expected. When his behind slid in the seat, torque and balance determined the rest. Pulling the chair away from the bed, she held his legs until his feet hit the floor. With his arms hugging the armrests, he almost appeared as if he were sleeping.

The time read 6:04 p.m.

A quick peek through the jalousies revealed the sun setting. Darkness would fall in a couple of minutes as predicted. A golden orange atmosphere greeted her when she opened the double doors of her balcony. The beauty of the fiery orb lowering itself behind a crimson sky almost distracted her, but she reminded herself to stay focused awhile longer.

What a relief to catch a faint scent of the ocean, even through the obstruction of her mask. The humidity dampened her skin and reminded her of her nakedness, made her consider throwing something on before stepping outside, but there was no time.

When she approached the body, she checked to make sure he sat as snugly inside the seat as possible. Bracing a leg firmly behind him, she wrapped her right arm around the corpse's chest and tilted him backward. With the chair balanced on its hind legs, she grasped the back of the seat and began dragging the body toward the balcony. The hard, plastic feet of the chair rumbled each time they slipped between grooves of the clay tiles. Only her baby steps kept the sound to a minimum. Hunched forward, bearing the weight on her back, her legs stiffened with every step. Either symptoms of the antidote or fatigue had set in. Breathing became more difficult. She contemplated stopping, pulling off the mask …

Without warning, the body slumped to the side, tipped the chair awkwardly and lifted it off one of its legs. Her brain demanded she right the chair, but her instincts ruled. She thrust forward to grab the body before it fell to the floor. The corpse slid backward. The chair collided against her thigh. Her arm slammed behind her to break the fall.

"Shit!" she sputtered into the mask.

Teetered in a crab-like position, her twisted body shook with the weight on top of her. A pain shot up her shoulder with a weakness at her wrist, possibly sprained from the impact. Her knees trembled, but she refused to fall, knowing the corpse would slide on top of her if she did. With little more than sheer determination, she gritted her teeth and curled her chest toward her legs. Little by little, she shifted her center of gravity until she was able to replace her throbbing right hand with the other one on the floor. The chair stayed on top of her, balanced precariously, but not for long. Her knees started buckling from the weight.

Clutching the body with her injured arm, she summoned her screaming thighs to pull herself up. She inched along the floor raising the chair until she feared her spine would snap. When she could no longer hold on, she did the only thing she could before collapsing on the floor.

She thrust herself upward, risking further injury and a racket if the corpse fell to the ground. Almost as if in slow motion, the body pitched forward. The chair landed with a thud, rocked like a cradle, and then steadied itself on four legs. To her amazement, the body crumpled but remained in the seat.

The commotion resonated like an explosion in her head, though she suspected it only sounded that way to her. She stopped and listened for sounds outside her room, heard nothing but the thrashing of her heartbeat. Perspiration dampened her brow, and her body glistened from exertion.

She needed a minute, but a peek at the clock showed she didn't even have that. Her attention to detail had cost her time. Tightness around her jaw added to her discomfort as she picked herself up off the floor. When she rubbed her tender wrist, she feared she had sprained it. It throbbed so much she peeled off her gloves and exposed her clammy hands to the air. She flexed and shook out her fingers.

Even the thought that she could have broken a wrist narrowed her throat. It called attention to her inability to breathe properly. With panic setting in, she reached behind her and ripped off the mask as if ripping out a tumor. The air was moist, and she gulped greedy mouthfuls.

In eyeing the floor, she realized how close she had been to the balcony when the chair toppled. An uneven patch of tiles had caused the body to shift. In mapping out the remainder of the path, she detected no more obstacles and pulled the corpse the rest of the way without incident.

Once outside, she maneuvered the chair as if negotiating a three-point turn, re-positioning the body back and forth until it looked out toward the sea. With his arms draped atop the wrought iron barrier and his forehead rested against it as well, he appeared to be napping. The swirls of the crimson sky morphed into a deep purple.

Lifting the body to its feet, she peeled back the bed sheet and used the railing as her means of support. She hung the corpse at his waist over the balcony's edge.

High tide.

With muscles flexed, she held her breath and waited. When the tide rolled in, she hoisted the body over the railing. He dropped thirty feet into a thunderous fury. It swallowed him up so fast she didn't even see him before he disappeared underneath. It frightened her, almost as if she had fed the ocean something unnatural. Then in the distance, she thought she saw a leg or an arm reappear like parts of a disembodied mannequin.

Panic. Did it catch on a branch or a rope?

Her eyes darted across the ocean as she waited for the next wave. When the waters receded and left nothing but darkness, she blew out the air from her lungs in a sigh of relief. He was gone.

She gathered the bed linen and carried it to the bathroom, where she threw it in the tub. There, she collected the neatly-packaged bags and plastic sheeting, inserted them into a black garbage bag for storage until later. When she returned to the bedroom to check for other items, she saw cushions under the bed that belonged to the chair on the terrace. After placing them outside, she closed the French doors to the balcony.

The clock showed 6:28 p.m.

She was ahead of schedule by a couple of minutes, with enough time to take a breath. Moving in front of the window, she glanced in the direction of the Goldeneye resort. Tiny lights dotted the buildings along the shore—such a beautiful night. She stood a moment longer before closing the shutters.

Without further delay, she entered the bathroom and turned on the shower. Just before getting under the water, she heard a bell ring in the distance, triggering a Pavlovian reflex. Perfect timing. Until then, food was the last thing on her mind. Now, hunger pangs jabbed her side.

After adjusting the shower dial to the hottest setting she could stand, she squirted a generous amount of shampoo in her palm. Her hands massaged vigorously to work the lather into her scalp with her nails. Rinse and repeat, then she added a thick conditioner. With the scent of rosemary in her hair, she scrubbed her skin with a peppermint cleanser until her entire body tingled.

As spirited as she was with cleaning her hair and skin, her genitals received the opposite treatment. With a mild bar of soap, she washed herself as gently as if she were bathing an infant. Before spraying off the suds between her legs, she lowered the water temperature.

Upon exiting the shower, she flipped her hair forward

several times to shake it dry, then sprayed moisturizing oil on her arms and legs. Her body felt invigorated from the shower.

Back in her room, she eased into a little black dress, applied mascara and lipstick, then slipped into a pair of sling-back sandals. For her sore wrist, she encased it in a set of silver bracelets to hide any sign of bruising.

One more thing had to be done before dinner. She picked up the phone and pressed the number for housekeeping.

"Hello, Rita? I'm sorry to call at this late hour."

"Yes, how can I help ma'am?"

"I woke up from a nap earlier and found I've soiled the sheets. That time of the month, I'm afraid." She inspected her fingernails and cuticles. *Time for a manicure.*

"I understand," said the voice on the other end.

"I've soaked the linen in the tub along with a few towels. If you wash them immediately with bleach, they should not stain." She paused to shake out a kink in her hair. "I don't want such expensive sheets ruined."

"No problem, I will personally take care of it."

"I appreciate it, Rita. I'll leave something for you on the table, as this goes above and beyond."

"Yes, ma'am, thank you."

She set aside two 1,000 Jamaican Dollar bills. Before she left the room, she checked her reflection once more. Her favorite bottle of scent caught her eye—Poison. Picking up the aubergine-colored jar, she contemplated spraying herself with it, then changed her mind.

She rather liked the fresh note of rosemary in her hair.

SOMETHING'S COOKING

Violet watched the giant clock mounted above the stove, five more minutes. She closed her eyes and took in the aroma of garden tomatoes and basil from the sauce bubbling on the gas burner. Dipping a wooden spoon into the pot, she stirred the contents and caught another whiff. More pepper, it needed more pepper. Holding a grinder containing a mixture of black and red peppercorns, she ground another teaspoonful into the pot and continued stirring. Her eyes strayed to the clock again. Along with pasta and fresh-baked garlic bread, her popular deconstructed Caesar salad was also on the menu tonight. Anchovies and sautéed garlic made up the key ingredients to her unique version of an otherwise pedestrian dish. Nadine had taught her a few secrets over the years, and she enjoyed being more creative with food.

"You're not a cook, Violet," Nadine said. "You're a bona fide chef. So what if you haven't been to culinary school? You have a natural talent with food, and your cooking is one of the main attractions to Sunset."

The Pearsons had told her the same thing, and the kitchen was part of their first phase of renovation. A commercial-sized stainless steel fridge replaced a small one, and industrial strength machines took the place of household appliances. It was heaven for her to stay in the kitchen all day.

Violet always knew she had a talent with food, but to hear it from Nadine, someone who had written books on it … That gave her a feeling of pride like she never had before. No matter how many past guests complimented her cooking, she never believed they meant it. Of course they would say nice things to boost her ego, if they wanted their meals. She never took them seriously, but with Nadine, it was different.

Violet started believing it when Nadine sat down with her, and together, they listed all the dishes she had ever created. Upon seeing her huge repertoire, they flirted with the idea for a cookbook. Between her and Nadine, they compiled fifty of her favorite recipes for the book. The dishes comprised a mixture of traditional Jamaican fare like jerk chicken and oxtail. It also included her take on popular Western recipes she re-invented such as Shepherd's pie and lasagna. Anna, ever the savvy businesswoman, wanted to use the book as a promotional tool for Sunset Villa, a tribute to Violet, its chef of more than forty years.

The book would feature a picture of her on the cover, her recipes inside. It was a dream come true, not bad for a girl who grew up destitute on the streets of Montego Bay sixty-four years ago.

Her eyes darted to the clock again.

At 6:35 p.m., Harrison rang the dinner bell as the phone rang. She launched herself across the room to where the phone hung on the wall, grabbed the receiver and slapped it to her ear.

"Hello?"

"It's done," said a man's tight voice on the line.

Violet bowed her head closer to the phone. "Are you sure?"

"Yes … I'm sure."

She hovered on the line expecting him to say something else but heard only silence.

Shaken, but feeling a sense of relief, Violet hung up the phone quietly just as Harrison returned to the kitchen. She wiped her hands on her apron.

"The sauce smells delicious," he said. Opening the dishwasher, he loaded his cart with cutlery and plates. "I'll set the table first and come back to grate the cheese."

Violet slipped on oven mitts to hide her trembling hands. "No rush. We can do it before the guests sit down." She opened the oven door and pulled out a cookie sheet holding three French sticks covered in aluminum foil. After peeking underneath the wrapping of one, she slid the tray back in the oven.

"Needs more time?" Harrison asked.

"Yes." Violet turned up the oven.

When Harrison left the kitchen, she removed her mitts and hung them on a hook by the stove. Her mind was on the cookbook. A professional photo shoot was scheduled for April to take pictures of both her and the food she would prepare. She looked forward to resurrecting dishes like oxtail with broad beans, Jamaican saltfish fritters, and her own version of Caribbean Sofrito.

Violet had dreamt food for the past year, felt intoxicated by the prospect of her picture on a book cover. When the hurricane hit, she feared it had killed the project. What a relief it was to learn Ms. Nadine still wanted to do it.

Nothing was going to stand in her way of becoming a famous author. Tonight, she just bought herself a little added insurance.

VACATION CUT SHORT

Rob fixated on the note in front of him.

The neat lettering surprised him. Weren't doctors supposed to be messy writers?

He knew he had a problem, had known it for several years but refused to get help for it. The last thing he wanted to admit was that he had fainting spells.

Teenage girls fainted.

Old ladies fainted.

A six feet one, twenty-three year old man from the south did not faint. And yet, he did. Now he knew why. There was even an official name for it.

His mind wandered back to what happened earlier in the day, starting with the confusion that flooded his brain when he woke up this morning. He was in familiar surroundings, yet it did not feel the same. The room was warmer and brighter than usual. His first thought was he had missed breakfast.

When he lifted his arm and dropped it beside him, he wasn't on his side of the bed. He wasn't even lying completely on the bed.

What time was it?

Where was Jessica?

Then he remembered what happened—what he did ... and how it ended.

Panic set in like a poisonous gas. Undetectable at first, but then it began choking him. Rob bolted up in bed as if the sheets were on fire. He flung the blanket off him and gazed upon wine-colored splotches, saw his hand and fingers encrusted in blood.

The queasiness in his stomach, which he had mistaken for a hunger pang, exploded into revulsion. Like a frightened cat, he sprang out of bed toward the bathroom. Bile rose so quickly, he could not catch his breath fast enough. He threw himself in front of the toilet, gagging, clutching the seat, with no time to push it up. Gasping air in short, quick breaths, he retched and vomited. The force of the expulsion splashed liquid and globular pieces back at him. His disgust manifested as a loud groan while he blinked away droplets of sweat rolling over his eyes. Another contraction ratcheted up his abdomen. He hurled a second mouthful into the bowl. His gut gurgled, his heart beat like a jackhammer. The stench of stomach acid gripped his throat. Drool clung to his lower lip inches from the greenish-brown mess below him. He stayed in that position, afraid to move for fear of triggering another torturous convulsion.

He envisioned this as death.

No.

Death would be more merciful.

Minutes ticked by before he had the strength to open his eyes.

Raising his head out of the toilet, he slammed down the cover and flushed. As he collapsed on his backside and slid back against the wall, he silently prayed he had completely emptied his stomach. Exhaustion and relief set in while his breathing returned to normal. The dizziness subsided. He unrolled a wad of toilet paper and wiped around his mouth. Never in his life had he felt so vile. When he pushed himself up off the floor, the bandage on his arm caught his eye.

How did he not notice that earlier?

With eyes scrunched in trepidation, he depressed the wound with a finger. He winced from the soreness but was thankful no blood seeped through.

He turned on the tap and scoured his hands with soap, dared not look at the water as he scraped dried blood from his skin and nails. When he was certain he had scrubbed his hands clean, he held his head close to the faucet, gulping mouthfuls of ice-cold water. He splashed his face and behind his neck. Questions began cropping to mind as his senses awakened.

Did Jessica bandage him?

Where was she?

When he trudged out of the bathroom, he avoided looking at the bed. Instead, he moved to where the thermostat hung on the wall, cranked up the air conditioning and fan to their highest settings. The dank smell of the room mixed with his own body odor muddled him.

Crouching down, he scooped the blanket from the floor and shuffled toward the bed like a frightened matador. With eyes squinted, he flung the covering on the mattress to hide the blood. The light filtering into the room hinted at mid-morning. When he glimpsed the time, it confirmed his suspicion. Ten thirty-five—he had definitely missed breakfast.

The bag of broken glass next to the clock caught his eye. He recognized pieces from the rum bottle. A note was propped against it, held in place by his makeshift ashtray. Approaching the table tentatively, he snatched the piece of paper and read it—twice.

He began to shake. The fan could not circulate the stale air quickly enough to remove the stench in the room. With the back of his hand, he mopped the sweat falling like raindrops down his face.

Fuck, he was in trouble.

A loud knock on the door confirmed it.

It was Ben and Nolan. He had enjoyed a good rapport with Ben all week, but the big man's expression told him their bond was now broken. A lump formed in his throat as Ben glared at him with disgust, not saying a word.

Even though Jessica chose not to press charges against him, Nolan wanted him off the property within an hour. Rob had apologized, begged to stay, but Nolan shut him down. Something in the owner's face told him the situation was not negotiable.

After a quick shower, he packed his things. The villa was deserted as he left his room escorted by Freddy and Willy. Sam the driver met him at the lobby and took his luggage.

Rob left Sunset Villa with no sign of Jessica and no fanfare.

* * *

"Sir, do you want a drink?"

Rob did not move but continued to stare at the piece of paper in his hand.

"Sir?"

The woman seated at the window beside him nudged him with her elbow.

"Uh ... what did you say?" he asked.

The plump stewardess with the twisted nose repeated her question. Before he had a chance to answer, the woman next to him chirped, "I'll have tomato juice, please."

As the attendant poured the juice, a light turbulence jostled the cabin, causing her to spill some of the thick liquid on her cart. Rob grimaced and looked away. The economy aisle seat offered him little legroom in the small charter, a huge difference from the first class treatment he had received when he flew into Jamaica.

After the sour, crimson drink passed in front of him, Rob requested a beer.

"Budweiser okay?" said the attendant, looking her Roman nose down at him.

"Uh ... do you have Red Stripe?"

"No, sir."

"Fine then." He turned his head away from the woman's drink beside him.

Chubby squeezed her large middle around the cart and slid open a drawer, creating a clang of tiny bottles against cans. "That'll be seven dollars," she said in a shrill voice.

Rob winced. "Seven dollars?" He lifted his bottom as much as he could while wedged in the narrow seat. "It's not free?"

"No, sir, only the non-alcoholic drinks are free."

"Shit," he said, huffing and grunting. He searched in the back pocket, then the side pocket of his shorts. The effort of moving around in the cramped space caused him to sweat. Finally, he dug out a twenty that looked like it had gone through his laundry's spin cycle. He handed it to the attendant. "Can I get three beers? That's all I have."

She glimpsed the piece of pulp with contempt. "Sorry, I can only give you two at a time. I'll come back if you want another." Holding the bill like a dirty rag, she dropped it on top of her cart, not bothering to unfold it.

Rob thought to protest, but he wasn't in the mood. He felt out of his element. "Fine, whatever," he snapped, "and I don't need a cup. Just leave the cans."

Hook Nose leaned in front of him and pulled down his tray. She placed the beer on it.

As she straightened, Rob caught her making eye contact with the passenger next to him. A smug expression crossed her face while picking coins from her wallet for his change.

Women.

They could all go to hell as far as he was concerned.

Rob popped open the first can of beer and guzzled down half of it. The smell of precooked food and stagnant air filled the cabin as the plane crackled and hummed along.

He stared at the paper again and read the note for the umpteenth time.

Rob:
I know what you did.
I have evidence of Jessica's injuries, along with pictures of you.
By the way, you have a condition called *vasavagal syncope*.
You faint at the sight of blood.

In so few words, the writer both threatened and instilled fear in him. She didn't even do him the courtesy of signing her name, but he knew who wrote it. Dr. Kate Hampton used a sheet from her prescription pad.

MISSING

The women huddled at the bar before dinner. Jessica appeared radiant with her hair down, wearing a sleeveless black dress, a chiffon scarf wrapped loosely around her neck. Anna and Nadine spoke with her in quiet tones as Kate approached.

"Hi," Jessica said, a smile stretched across her face.

"Hi, everyone." Kate stopped short and gave a playful smirk when she saw what the other women were wearing. "The guys are going to think we co-ordinated our wardrobes."

"We do look fabulous in our little black dresses, don't we?" Anna said, striking a pose.

"Excuse me." Nadine wagged her head. "Mine isn't black, the girl at the store called it ebony moonlight."

The ladies laughed while Harrison offered a glass of red wine to Kate.

"While we're together, and before the guys get here …" Jessica cast her eyes toward Kate and then to Anna and Nadine, "I want to thank you for everything with Rob, for sending him home. I'm sure it took a bit of planning. Kate knows how distraught I was … I don't know what I would've done if he were still here."

Anna patted Jessica's arm. "Nolan and I don't tolerate violence of any kind here. When Kate told us what happened, we were ready to call the police."

The young woman touched her neck beneath her scarf. "I couldn't go through with that. I just wanted Rob out of my life. Now he is."

"You must be exhausted. We could have brought dinner to your room if you were too tired," Anna said.

Jessica tossed her hair back and shook her head. "Oh no, I slept most of the afternoon. It helped re-energize me. Now I'm starving!"

"Good, we're happy you're joining us." Nadine wrapped an arm around Jessica's waist.

"Thanks." Jessica leaned against the older woman. "I hope this did not inconvenience you and Nolan too much," she said to Anna. "I feel so embarrassed. Does everyone know what happened … with Rob, I mean?"

"Only that he's left. Nolan announced it at lunch, but of course, he did not elaborate, so don't worry, okay?" Anna's comforting voice showed her as the consummate host. "You have no reason to be embarrassed. It's our responsibility to look after the well-being of our guests, and we're grateful you're okay."

"Thanks to Kate," Jessica said.

"Glad I was here to help." Kate took a slow sip of her wine and glanced past Jessica's shoulder. "The men are here."

The women greeted them, and they sauntered to the

dining room, followed by Harrison who made his way to the kitchen. Greg and Tom were already seated.

Anna counted out the chairs around the table like counting kids in a kindergarten class. "Are we missing someone?"

"We're eleven now, right?" Nolan said.

"Yes, but ..." She looked around. Everyone took to their seats except for her.

One chair remained unclaimed.

"She's right," Jerry said, "where's Matthew?"

* * *

Dinner continued while Nolan and Jerry headed out in search of Matthew.

"Maybe he's taking his dinner in his room again tonight?" Jessica said.

"Well ... I guess we'll find out soon enough." Anna served herself a small helping of potatoes. "I think he would've told me, but then ... who knows?"

"I don't remember seeing him after lunch," Ben said.

"That was when I last saw him too." Adam poured gravy over his roasted beef tenderloin and scalloped potatoes. "He's missing a great meal, wherever he is."

"You spoke with him earlier, Kate. Did he say anything?" Anna asked, concern on her face.

"No, after lunch, I told him I'd be taking a dip prior to dinner if he wanted to meet me at the beach. He never showed up. I'm not sure he likes the ocean all that much."

"The man is a strange duck," Nadine said. "Maybe he decided to leave and didn't bother telling anyone. I wouldn't put it past him."

"Neither would I. Pass the vegetables please," Tom said.

Jessica moved the tray of tomatoes and green beans in Tom's direction. "I agree. He's a bizarre man, though he and Rob became friendly the last couple of days. Imagine that."

Silence fell across the table at the mention of Rob's name.

"Honestly, the two were a bit off to me." Adam leaned back and turned to Jessica beside him, running his fingers over his hair. "I don't mean to offend you. I know Rob is your boyfriend."

"*Was* my boyfriend," she said in a starched voice.

"Oh?" Adam tilted to one side. "I stand corrected then. I don't know why Rob is gone, and I don't care, but now Matthew is missing. Could there be a connection?"

"No, that much is certain," Anna said. She gave Jessica a reassuring nod.

Speculation and small talk circulated the table. Harrison cleared the dinner dishes as Nolan returned with Jerry and Daniel. Anna requested Harrison prepare three more dinner plates.

Nolan introduced the Englishman to the guests who had not met him.

"I was hoping to see you again, Kate. You look beautiful." Daniel's greeting accompanied a subtle glance normally shared between lovers.

"Thank you, nice to see you again, too." Kate blushed.

"Did you find anything?" Anna asked her husband.

"His things are still in his room, so he hasn't skipped out on us. Willy is checking the common areas. Daniel noticed a man down by the beach a half hour ago. It's possible he decided to go for a swim."

"Hmm … Kate says he doesn't like the ocean," Tom said.

Daniel glanced at her. "Is that so? Perhaps I was imagining things. My vision isn't what it used to be."

Kate locked eyes with Daniel. "I'm sure your vision is fine. Perhaps he did go for a swim. The man is … unpredictable." She offered a coy smile.

"So I've heard," he said, appearing calm. Daniel's face lit up as Harrison set a plate in front of him. "It would be dangerous to swim this time of night, too dark to see a thing."

"I agree." Kate's voice matched the seriousness of Daniel's tone. "And I don't think he's a strong swimmer."

"He's not," Adam injected, "he needed a noodle in the pool."

The OMG boys snickered.

"Kate, you went with him to James Bond Beach, right?" Tom asked.

"Yes."

"Could he have gone back there?"

"I suppose anything is possible … though somehow I doubt it."

Tom turned to Greg. "Why don't you and I head

over there? Is it possible he decided to eat at one of the restaurants?"

"Unlikely, since we all know how fussy he is with food. Can you imagine the poor waitress who has to take his order?" Adam said.

"No kidding." Greg scratched his head.

The group continued to bandy about possibilities.

Did he fall asleep while meditating in the Zen Garden?

Did he leave the property after lunch and get lost coming back?

Was this a ploy for more attention?

No one panicked. Harrison served chocolate cake with tea and coffee. He poured more wine. Lively chatter continued around the table until Willy approached, carrying a small bundle.

"I did not find him, Mr. Pearson, but I found this by the beach." Willy held up a man's shirt and shorts. Wrapped inside was a pair of flip-flops.

"Those definitely belong to Matthew," Tom said.

"You sure?" asked Anna.

"Yes, I recognize the sandals."

Greg nodded. "He's right. Those are OluKais, expensive, a Hawaiian brand."

Nolan's demeanor turned solemn. "Where did you find this, Willy?"

"By the large rock, the one underneath your room. I checked the snorkel equipment, and one set is missing. Maybe he went snorkeling?"

"Good thinking, that's a possibility … I suppose."

"I doubt that," Nadine said. "He knew about my run-in with a stingray."

Nolan tossed his napkin on the table and rose from his seat. "Prepare my boat, Willy."

"Are you sure, Nolan? It's so dark you can't see a thing out there," Jerry said.

"I know, but I need to do something."

Anna drifted over to her husband and draped a comforting arm around him. "All right, take out the boat. If you don't find him, we'll call the police. It's a bit early to file a missing person's report, but the sooner we do it, the better."

"I'll go with you," Jerry said, glancing at his tactical watch. "Ben, can we borrow your diving flashlight?"

"Sure, I'll get it for you." Ben left with Nolan and Jerry.

Anna sat down on Nolan's chair.

"Anything you want us to do, Anna?" Tom asked.

"Nothing, really, but thank you." She blew out a *there's not much we can do* sigh.

"I don't like the man," Greg said. He rose from his chair and patted Anna's shoulder. "I'll grab my binoculars for them too, but if this guy's been pulling a stunt … god help him."

Anna touched Greg's hand before he strode off. She did a tour of the faces around the table. "And then there were seven," she said with her chin resting on her hands. "I've never had to call the police here."

"I can help. I know the captain." Daniel took a last bite of his chocolate cake.

Anna reached over and tapped his arm. "Thank you."

"One thing is true," the Englishman said, "there's no shortage of excitement here at Sunset Villa. It's the place to be."

"It sure is." Jessica took a drink of her water. "Daniel, where is your house?"

"Not far. You can see it from the beach. It's the two-story building with the wrap-around veranda before the Goldeneye office."

"Daniel's a great neighbor. It's good to have friends here."

"You've been good to me too, and to the people who work here."

Anna appeared restless. "Let's hope things work out for everyone," she said in a soft-spoken voice, twisting the bangles around her small wrist.

No one questioned her vague statement.

DISPOSAL

With the moon and stars hidden behind clouds, the man crunched his way through the dark winding path covered in vines and dead branches. He had a small window of time before anyone would notice his absence. A few minutes later, he arrived at his destination, an area located on the periphery of the property. Old metal bed frames and mattresses formed one pile; broken chairs and discarded furniture formed another. Several burn barrels made up a third section. It was a dump, but a neat and tidy one used for compost and unwanted items awaiting disposal.

At the far end of the junk piles stood a lone building to where he proceeded. When he arrived, he pulled open the shed door and let it bang shut behind him. Three steps inside to the left, he swatted air until a string brushed against his fingers. With a gentle tug on the cord, he flooded the room with light from a bare ceiling bulb. After depositing the black garbage bag on the workbench, he donned a pair of rubber gloves.

"Be careful," the General had said. "We don't know the contents." That was the essence of the first phone call he made to apprise of what he had found.

Excited and frightened, he wondered what he might discover.

He twisted open the bag and carefully removed each item packaged in a meticulous manner. Aside from several sheets of folded plastic, everything else was contained in its own individual bag. He set aside the ones holding items he recognized—cotton balls, cotton swabs, gauze, rubbing alcohol. He replaced them in the large bag. What remained on the table were the unknown items.

In the first packet was a plastic container sans label about the size of a salt shaker. He pulled it out and removed the cap, sniffed it. The smell made him flinch, immediately alerting him to what had been inside. He quickly sealed the empty bottle.

Insecticide.

The resort had moved toward an organic means of pest control several years ago, eradicating the spraying of toxic chemicals altogether. The only remaining evidence of insecticide on the property was in an old sprayer. He couldn't even remember where it was, but recalled it was three-quarters full the last time he saw it. As its contents couldn't be used or disposed of, the best option was to keep it undisturbed. Toxic waste was difficult to get rid of properly.

In the second package, he recognized what appeared to be a condom but not like one he had ever seen. He eyed the sugar cube tongs and wondered about the connection. The final package contained two needles with the same name and description on both.

He turned on his cell phone and pressed a few numbers. "General?"

The man proceeded to rhyme off the items he found. With the pack of needles held up to the light, he squinted and spelled out the name on the label.

A couple of nods and *um-hmms* later, he ended the call. Time to get back before anyone missed him.

He moved quickly, returning all the articles to the black bag along with his gloves.

A giant dumpster sat adjacent to the trail on his way back to the villa. It was nearly full. He hurled the bag inside it.

By tomorrow noon, the garbage would be on its way to the landfill.

CALLING THE POLICE

Nolan and Jerry returned in the boat after almost an hour away—no sign of Matthew. Both men were wet as the result of a light rain that had started to fall. With Daniel's help, the owners contacted the police. It was close to eleven o'clock.

Everyone stayed up and gathered in the lounge awaiting news.

Nolan entered the room fifteen minutes later. "The police will send someone in the morning."

"I'm not surprised," Jerry said. "I didn't think they would come now."

"Who did you speak to?" Daniel asked.

Nolan stretched his arms above his head, a look of exhaustion on his face. "Inspector Johnson."

The Englishman nodded. "Ray, he's a good man."

"He didn't sound all that concerned, says they get these types of calls about tourists all the time." Nolan yawned. "And he said to say hello to you."

"Hmm … okay," Daniel said.

"He thinks Matthew's gone into town, met a woman and is having a great time. Maybe he'll sneak back into his room sometime during the night."

Nadine looked up from where she and Ben were playing Cribbage. "That's possible, if it were anyone else, but he doesn't strike me as the type. And what about the clothes Willy found?"

"I told him, but that could have been left there from another day, he said." Nolan shrugged. "I even suggested calling the Coast Guard, but he dismissed the idea."

"I suppose he's right." Anna leaned against her husband. "There's no point in them coming now."

"You've told them everything they need to know." Daniel crossed the room to where the Pearsons stood. "Things will be fine. Ray's been around a long time. If he said not to worry, I wouldn't lose sleep over it."

"Daniel, Matthew Kane has been nothing but trouble since the moment he arrived," Anna said out of earshot of the other guests. "He's put our business in jeopardy with a review he wrote in the summer."

"Yes, Greg and Jerry told me a few days ago when I came by."

"You came by?" Nolan asked. "Sorry I missed you."

"Yeah, we took a stroll in the Zen Garden. You may have been out. It was Wednesday."

Nolan tilted his head, scrunched his eyes. "Hmm ... yes, we were at the Falls that day."

Daniel exuded calm. "The police will come by and fill out an official report if your man is still missing. It sounds like this Matthew Kane had some issues."

Anna shook out the bangles on her wrist. "Yes, and we have no clue if he was going to write a retraction ... now he's disappeared."

"Darling …" Nolan hugged his wife close to him. "We don't know anything right now. Let's go to bed and figure this out tomorrow, okay?"

Anna rested her head on Nolan's shoulder. "You're right, I must sound callous, being worried about this place when the man is missing."

"Not at all." Daniel gave Anna's arm a squeeze.

"I don't wish him ill," she said.

"Of course not," Daniel said. The three exchanged a few more words before the couple bade everyone good night.

Ben and Nadine finished their board game and left shortly thereafter.

Adam sat with the OMG boys discussing strategy for their upcoming fundraising campaign, with Jessica an earnest listener in an adjacent chair. Jerry strummed his guitar. Kate curled up on the couch reading a book. The mood was quiet but not somber.

Daniel approached Kate. "Care to go for a walk?"

She set down her book and swung her legs off the couch. "Sure." Her delicate hand slipped into his.

"I hope you don't mind getting wet."

A pink glow covered her cheeks. "Not at all, I love walks in the rain." Kate bid good night to the thinning crowd.

The OMG boys said they were turning in too. Jerry packed up his guitar. Adam stayed behind with Jessica.

When Kate and Daniel descended the steps by the bar into the warm mist, Harrison nodded in their direction and flashed a gleaming smile.

DAY SEVEN
IN DEEP TROUBLE

The dance began the way it always did with a coyness that offered a hint of innuendo. Her subtle body language separated them from the crowd, made it obvious to anyone who saw them that she had eyes only for him.

The difference here was, there was no crowd.

It was just the two of them, under a hazy moon dancing on the beach. With one hand around his neck, and the other caressing his chest under his shirt, she stepped in harmony with him, moving to the rhythm of the ocean waves. To dance in the rain with this stranger seemed perfectly natural.

No man had ever conjured these feelings in her.

She felt like a goddess under the moonlight.

They were out in the rain for more than an hour. By the time they returned to the villa, the lights had dimmed, the bar closed. It was well past midnight. Daniel escorted her to the foot of the staircase leading to her bedroom. Her hair was wet, her dress damp. Vibrations from him warmed her body. And he was warm, in every sense of the word. Daniel embodied the languid rhythm of Jamaica, a man in no rush, at ease with a country he had known since he was a boy.

"Kate, I am … Words somehow seem inadequate." He gazed at her with sapphire eyes that shimmered in the dark.

"I know." There were breaks in their conversation during the evening but not one uncomfortable silence. She caressed his cheek, and her bangles clinked against each other as they settled down her arm.

He took her hand and held it against his heart. "That's all your doing, young lady. It's not beaten this quickly in a long time."

His gentle aura beckoned her closer. With his mouth starting at the heel of her palm, he brushed his lips across her hand to the tip of each finger. Such sensual pleasure caused her to tremble. She closed her eyes and soaked it in.

"Kate."

He spoke her name quietly.

"Kate."

His tone became more urgent.

"Kate."

Her eyes clicked open. Daniel's lips had not moved.

Who was calling her? That voice … that familiar penetrating voice. Her breathing sped up.

No.

She spun around and came face to face with her father.

Wearing his navy blue swim trunks decorated in palm trees, he stood with his arms folded across his bare chest. His scowl hit her like a punch to the head. What did she do wrong?

"Daddy? How did you get here?"

"Never mind how I got here." With his thumb and index finger, he tilted up her chin. She began shaking as she stared at the tall, scary man. She was five again, wearing her yellow one-piece bathing suit with the frilly pink skirt. Her father's eyes conveyed neither love nor affection.

"I didn't have to use my water wings," Kate said. "I put my head under water and counted ten seconds." She held up her palms as if to say *Look Daddy, no hands!*

"Not good enough, Kate. You're still in the shallow end."

"But ... I'm scared, Daddy. I'm—"

"Kate, you will sink or swim today. Do you hear me?"

His stern expression told her there was only one way to respond. "Yes, Daddy."

He grabbed her wrist and led her toward the pool.

Daniel. What happened to Daniel?

She turned back to apologize to him and say good-bye, but he had vanished.

Her father did not accommodate her shorter gait. His long legs took rapid strides. To keep up, she had to run. Goosebumps dotted her arms, still chubby with baby fat. She fought back tears. Daddy was not a patient man. It didn't matter that she dreaded the water. It didn't even matter that her mother had drowned in their pool a year ago.

"There is nothing to be afraid of. I know you can do

better."

She whimpered, "Yes, Daddy."

They stood at the edge of the deep end. With her head down, Kate hugged her father's thigh and stared at his large feet. He was a towering man with oversized extremities and a presence that frightened small children. Now that it was just the two of them, she never wanted to disappoint him. He always said he loved her more than life. She was his angel and his savior, and yet, he terrified her.

A cool breeze rippled the pool. The water sparkled like diamond slivers against the noonday sun. A mirage of checkered blue and white tiles lulled her into thinking the pool's floor was closer than it appeared. An image of her mother face down in the pool floated to the surface. She could not stop shivering.

Kate's father picked her up, and she immediately clutched his neck. "No, Daddy!" she said, wrapping her legs around him.

"Kate, it's time."

"I … I'm not ready." She pressed his cheeks between her little hands, batting her teddy bear eyes at him. "Tomorrow, okay, Daddy?"

"You've been saying that for a week, Kate."

"I know," she squeaked, "but I can't swim. I need more time."

"This is the only way you're going to learn. I can't coddle you forever."

Upon realizing he wasn't going to give in, frantic sobs shook her body. "I promise, tomorrow … I promise." She locked herself around his neck so hard, her fingernails dug into her own flesh.

"Empty promises are useless," he said, without any warmth. "How do you expect to get ahead in life?"

"Daddy … please …" She clung to him like a barnacle.

He ripped her away from him limb by limb, held her outstretched as if she were a baby who had soiled her diaper.

Kate wailed. "No, Daddy, please, I promise!" Dangling in the breeze and pitched forward, she violently kicked and pounded air.

"It's for your own good, Kate."

"No!" she screeched. "No!"

A gust of wind rushed by when her father hurled her away from him.

Time did not exist after that moment. She soared and watched her father standing still as she broke the glassy calm of the water. Her small body somersaulted several times before gravity pulled her under. She lost her bearings, then shot up over the water, gasping for air. Daddy yelled at her to kick. His words did not register. She sank again, panicked at not being able to touch bottom.

Kate tried holding her breath, flailed her arms to push herself above the surface. Water entered her nose. Her mouth sucked in more of it. When she coughed, it opened the floodgate to her lungs. She remembered counting to ten under water, but had not been able to hold her breath longer. A fear of suffocation kicked in.

The sun cast a bright light above her head. Air. She craved air, and the only way to get it was to rise to the top and reach for that sun. Something clicked, a crystal-clear moment that told her she did not want to die like her mother had died.

Even as her lungs burned, and she ran out of breath, Kate began kicking—hard. Her head cracked the surface. She gulped a huge breath, saw her father crouched at poolside yelling, "Yes, my girl! Kick! Come to Daddy!"

On the verge of exhaustion with eyes stinging from chlorine, her vision blurred through tears. Still, she powered herself toward the edge of the pool where her father kneeled. He extended his arm toward her. She was so close to him ... so close.

"You can do it, my girl. You can do it." With his large hand almost within her grasp, she heard him say, "Sink or swim, Kate, sink or swim."

She kicked and kicked, but he moved farther away from her, disappearing into a tunnel.

"Daddy ..." she croaked. "Daddy ..." He appeared in and out of focus. She could not reach him. He did not try harder to reach her.

With her lungs on fire and pain stabbing her muscles, hopelessness weighed her down like an anchor.

She glimpsed her father one last time before going into free fall.

Falling.

Falling ...

Kate jolted up in bed from the sound of a primal scream. Was it hers? The sound echoed in her ears. Pinpricks of sweat flared up her back. She sat gasping to catch her breath.

"Just a dream … just a dream …" Over and over, she repeated the words, hugged her knees to her chest and rocked back and forth. Thoughts of her mother, her father, herself as a child whirled in her head like a cyclone. Her conscious mind had compartmentalized these memories, burying them, she thought, forever. Her unconscious mind had dug them up.

After a few minutes, her breathing returned to normal, but memories of the dream lingered. She switched on the lamp and let the rush of light chase the remainder of the images away. The clock read quarter after four. Her bed was damp with perspiration. Her father had not appeared in her dreams in a long time, not like this. He felt so close, so real.

Kate sifted her brain to figure out why he would show up now.

She sprang out of bed and ran to the closet.

After taking a deep breath, she opened the door. A sense of dread descended on her when she realized nothing had changed. She had not dreamt this part. Her clothes hung neatly inside; her suitcase propped against the wall. Everything appeared normal, except for one thing.

An important item had disappeared when she returned to her room after her walk with Daniel—an item she needed to dispose of.

Someone knew what she had done.

"Help me, Daddy," she whispered, curling into a ball on the floor. "Help me."

FOUND

Kate tiptoed downstairs. It was not yet seven. No one was up except for Harrison who would have already prepared the coffee station in the dining room.

They were the two early risers, and today she had jumped in the pool even earlier than her usual time. It turned out to be a painful exercise. She was winded after twenty minutes. The remainder of the swim was agonizing.

Speculation of her father's appearance had interrupted her breathing between strokes. Ever since she was a child, her need to please her father had both haunted and compelled her toward accomplishment. The thought of disappointing him had kept her constantly mindful of what she needed to do. She rarely let her guard down. And yet, she did yesterday. It could become a costly mistake for her.

And then there was the ghostly flash of her mother, the woman who breathed life into her, only Kate could not even remember the last time she thought of her. To think she had forgotten her mom stabbed her like a knife through the heart.

Her mind was still addled with painful memories when

she turned a corner into the dining room, led by the smell of fresh brewed coffee.

"Good morning, Kate."

She jerked back like a threatened animal. "God, you startled me!"

"I'm sorry." He advanced toward her. "I didn't mean to scare you."

Kate stood wide-eyed, frozen in place. Her breath bottled up in her chest.

"How can I make it up to you?" Daniel said. He led her to the table and swung out a chair for her.

She took a few extra breaths. "A cup of coffee would be nice."

"At your service." He placed a mug under the spigot of the stainless steel coffee urn and depressed the handle. "Cream and sugar, or would you like Baileys instead?"

"No Baileys. Just cream is fine, thanks." Kate reached behind her neck and shook out her damp hair.

Daniel handed her the mug and pulled out a chair beside her. "You're up early."

"I was up two hours ago, had a swim. I couldn't sleep."

"Funny, neither could I." Daniel gave her a genuine smile.

Kate held the mug of coffee to her nose and inhaled deeply. "Umm ... so good."

"Nectar of the gods, I can't start my day without it."

Kate brought the cup of Blue Mountain coffee to her lips and took a sensuous mouthful, savoring the taste. "I had a nightmare. That's why I couldn't sleep." She found it funny she should disclose this to Daniel without his asking, though it seemed a natural thing for her to do. "What's your reason?"

"My mind was racing, and Nolan asked me to be here in case the police showed up early. Besides …" He stroked Kate lightly on the arm, "… I haven't been able to stop thinking of you."

A flutter in her belly accompanied a warmth on her face. "I had a lovely time last night."

"Me too, I hated to see it end." Daniel continued to trace figure eights on her skin.

"It's good you're here …" She shifted in her chair, "… to help with the police, I mean."

With his coffee in hand, he leaned back. "Tell me about your nightmare."

Daniel stared at her behind tendrils of steam that spiraled upward and disappeared into the air. His matter-of-fact approach disarmed her. Most of the time, she asked the questions. Rarely was she on the receiving end of them, but something about Daniel engendered trust in him.

"It was about my father, old stuff. I don't want to bore you." She set down her cup.

"Kate, there's nothing about you that would bore me. I want to know everything."

"Everything?" She tossed her head back and laughed. "Not much to tell, really."

"I highly doubt that, Kate." Daniel grabbed the seat of her chair and dragged her closer to him. He cupped her cheeks in his hands.

Before Daniel's lips grazed hers, she already felt a yearning bubbling inside her. They had kissed last night in the rain for the first time.

"There is only ever one *first* kiss," he had said. "Every other one will bear no distinction."

With that in mind, she surrendered as she had never done before. The kiss was exquisite—slow, deliberate, infused with a gentleness that left her on the precipice. Time lost all significance.

In the light of day, however, reality hit her. Her emotions for Daniel intersected with an enormous uncertainty. It shocked her to feel so strongly for a man in such a short time. His charm was like none she had ever encountered.

If she considered their first kiss unforgettable, this one was intense, more carnal. She wanted it to last. She wanted him, but he was not part of the plan.

He broke off the kiss before she did. "Kate."

Her eyes remained closed. The warm vibrations on her lips lingered.

"Kate."

"Yes?" He appeared out of focus for a second.

"You're safe with me."

She moved back from him, wrinkled her forehead. "What are you talking about?" Her hand grazed her collarbone.

Safe?

With his fingers threaded in her hair, he strayed his touch down her neck. "I know what you did, Kate."

"I have no idea what you're talking about," she said in a

whisper, not daring to meet the Englishman's eyes.

"Kate, I saw you." He held a finger under her chin. "I saw—"

"Daniel!" a male voice called out.

Kate jumped up in her seat like a jack-in-the-box. She scraped her chair away from Daniel's and brought the coffee to her lips.

"I'm glad you're here already," Nolan said, bounding toward them. He gave a fleeting smile in her direction. "Good morning, Kate."

"Good morning," she said, her heart pounding but grateful for the interruption.

If the owner was surprised to see her, he did not show it. Daniel stood to greet Nolan.

"We just received a phone call. The police are on their way over." Nolan crossed his arms under his pits and bounced on his toes. "They've recovered a body."

Kate's mug slipped from her grasp and shattered on the floor.

IDENTIFICATION

Two policemen from the Jamaican Constabulary Force arrived after eight o'clock. Along with Nolan and Daniel, Anna met them at the entrance as they drove up. Ray Johnson exited first, a hefty bald man with eyes set deep against caramel skin. Nolan had spoken to him the night before. Daniel immediately shook hands with him, and they referred to each other by their first names.

Anna wondered about the relationship between Daniel and Inspector Johnson. She recalled Nolan telling her the police sometimes consulted the Englishman for his experience as an ex-military man. Whatever his connection, she felt a deep sense of relief having Daniel here.

Johnson's partner got out from the driver's side after turning off the ignition. He removed his hat and tossed it on his seat before stepping around the car. Greyhound-thin with an Afro, he wore a mustache that looked like a throwback to another decade. He introduced himself as Inspector Hewitt.

The breakfast bell rang as they stood in the driveway. She had instructed Harrison to apprise the guests that she and Nolan would not be joining them this morning.

"Is that for us?" Inspector Hewitt said, his tone dripping with sarcasm. He was at least twenty years younger than Johnson. His tiny wide-set eyes reminded Anna of a shark.

"No," Nolan said, "it's the meal bell. I can have Harrison bring you a coffee if you like."

Johnson shot a chilly stare at his partner. "Maybe a bit later," he said.

His quiet confidence showed Anna he had more influence and experience than his earnest partner.

"A body was found early this morning by two fishermen out for their daily catch."

"Where did they find it, Ray?" asked Daniel.

"Around the Cayman Trough."

Anna knew their shoreline bordered the edge of the Trough. Beyond their boundaries, the walls plunged 25,000 feet and extended more than four miles long, an area well known by deep-sea fishermen for its marlin and tuna.

"He reeled in the body?" asked Nolan.

"Yes, talk about luck," said the younger inspector. "I don't think he expected to catch such a big fish." He chuckled and stared at his partner who remained stone-faced.

"Luck, indeed," Anna said, blowing out a breath of disbelief.

"Was he wearing snorkel gear?" Nolan looked to Inspector Johnson.

Hewitt flipped open his notepad. "No mention of

snorkel gear. He was unclothed … no wait …" He scanned a few more pages. "The only garment on him was a pair of boxer shorts. Why do you ask?"

"We're missing a set of snorkel gear, wondered if there was a connection."

Anna noticed how Hewitt cast his suspicious shark eyes upon her husband. She wiped the sweat from her brow. Her temperature suddenly notched up, and she steadied herself with a hand on Nolan's elbow.

"Are you all right, honey?" Nolan touched his palm to her cheek. "You're burning up."

Anna wrapped her arms around herself. "I'm just anxious. Do we know if this body is Matthew Kane?"

Inspector Johnson gave a quick nod to his partner who reached into the back seat of the car and produced a manila envelope. "Why don't you tell me? Normally, we would still be searching for next of kin, but since you called this in yesterday …" He pulled out papers and passed them to Nolan. "The morgue sent us these digital pictures. Is it your guest?"

Anna glanced the first photo and clasped a hand to her mouth. The printout showed the head and shoulders of a man. His grim face appeared like a carved mask. His lips flattened in an expressionless line sketched out by an unnatural bluish tinge. A dark shadow along one side of his jaw hinted at bruising. "Oh god, …" she groaned and sensed the tiny hairs on the back of her neck rising.

Nolan rifled through the images. He returned the papers to the inspector with his lips puckered like he had sucked a lemon. "Yes … yes, that's him. That's our guest, Matthew Kane."

"Are you sure?" asked Hewitt.

"Positive."

"Oh my god …" Anna said, "oh my god …"

Nolan wrapped an arm around her. She rested her body against his.

Daniel pulled the two policemen aside. "Give them a minute, will you?"

"Sure," said Johnson. The three drifted a few feet away. Daniel spoke quietly with the older Inspector, while Hewitt bent his head and twirled his eighties' mustache.

"Nolan …" Anna pressed her fists to her lips, "what are we going to do?"

"Sweetheart, don't panic. The police are here to confirm identity. We haven't done anything wrong."

"But … are we responsible?" She felt sobs rising up her chest. "What does this mean for us … for this place?"

"Anna …" Nolan stroked her hair, "we are not responsible. Why don't you let me take care of it? Daniel and I can talk to the police and clear this up."

Anna blinked rapidly, hesitated. "No, no … I'm not letting you go through this alone."

Nolan held her and looked into her eyes. "You don't need to do this."

Her neck muscles tightened at Nolan's words. She understood he was trying not to worry her, but he was wrong. She *did* need to do this, especially since it was her idea to invite Matthew Kane back to the villa. Anna took hold of her husband's hand. "We're in this together, and I'm going to be fine," she said, steeling herself for whatever came next.

With her husband by her side, she approached the men. "My apologies," Anna said. "The pictures shocked me ... I'm all right now."

"Perfectly understandable, Anna," Daniel said in a reassuring voice. "The police want to see Mr. Kane's room."

"Yes," said Johnson. "We need his passport and a few personal effects. Do you know if he has family or friends in Jamaica?"

"No," Nolan said, "not that I'm aware. He was here on business."

"What kind of business?"

"He was a travel writer for an American magazine."

"I see," the husky inspector withdrew a notepad from his pants pocket and scribbled a few words. "How many guests do you have staying here?"

"Ten ... well nine now. One of them left," Anna said.

Inspector Hewitt tucked in his chin as if somebody punched him. "One of them left? When?"

"Yesterday morning. He flew back to the States, but Matthew Kane was still here at the time."

"How do you know?" Hewitt fixed her with an icy stare.

"Because we had lunch with him," Anna said, her voice seething.

Johnson stepped in front of Hewitt. "Do you know who was last to see him?"

Nolan shook his head and looked at Anna. She did the same. "We're not sure," he said. "We spoke of it yesterday over dinner with our guests when he went missing, but no one remembered seeing him after lunch."

"All right then." Johnson removed a handkerchief from his pocket and wiped his head as if buffing a bowling ball. "We'll need to question the guests and your staff."

Anna stood in silent resentment. She had expected the police but had hoped they would not need to question the guests.

"Is that really necessary?" Nolan crossed his arms in front of his chest. "As you can appreciate, this is terribly disruptive. These people are here on vacation."

"I understand," Johnson said, returning his notepad to his pocket, "and we will try our best to do this quickly. Any other information you can provide about Mr. Kane would be helpful."

Nolan gave a hesitant nod. He cast a concerned look at Anna. She returned a slanted smile and dipped her head ever so slightly. It was a look she knew only her husband would understand—a *I'm fine, don't worry about me* look.

She had to be strong. This was no time for a breakdown and not at all the way she expected events to unfold.

"Let's go see Mr. Kane's room," Inspector Johnson said. "We'll work out an interrogation schedule."

Anna motioned them to proceed toward Matthew's room, located in the secondary section of the villa. "Whatever you can do to make it as non-invasive as possible would be appreciated," she said to the older inspector.

"Of course," he said. "I don't like this anymore than you

do. The sooner we figure this out, the better."

"Is there a reason to think this is more than a drowning?" Daniel asked.

"We can't disclose—" Hewitt began.

"No reason," Inspector Johnson cut off his partner. "We're here to rule out all suspicion." He eyed Hewitt with a stern look, continued in a calm voice. "There's a protocol with foreigners, and we want to make sure to follow it, normal procedure." With a sympathetic shrug toward Anna and Nolan, he said, "I hope you understand."

Anna nodded mechanically. "Of course."

Hewitt gave a brisk crack of his knuckles. "Yes, we're just doing our jobs."

INTERROGATION

The two women stood leaning against the wall opposite the kitchen. Kate waited for her interview with the police by chatting with Anna.

"I made a special request for Johnson to talk to Jessica," Anna said. "I had to tell him the story of her boyfriend and why he left. The poor girl has been through enough." She let out a heavy sigh and stared at the floor. "I wish they didn't have to question her. Jessica had nothing to do with Matthew Kane."

"I know," Kate said, reaching over to stroke Anna's arm, "hopefully it won't be a long discussion. I'm sure the police just need to say they talked to everyone."

"You're right, and Jessica is amazing." Anna's shoulders drooped. "She's been through a lot this week, what with her boyfriend, a dead guest, and now a police interrogation. She probably wishes she never won the trip here."

Kate observed Anna's dejected posture. "Don't say that. She's stronger for this experience, believe me."

"Oh …" Anna teared up.

"What is it? Tell me." Kate angled her head to glimpse Anna's eyes.

"Kate, this is a nightmare. We invited Matthew Kane here. Now he's dead." She raised a hand and covered her mouth.

"Matthew wasn't all there, we both know that. I'm sure that's what everyone will tell the police. You're not accountable for his drowning."

"Yes, but … I was hoping he'd write a better review for us, now that will never happen." Anna pinched her lips together. "I feel horrible for even thinking about it."

"Anna …" Kate tried to stifle the tension building inside her head. "Matthew wasn't going to write a better review."

"What?" Her lashes shot up in a hard unblinking stare. "How do you know?"

Kate pressed hard on her temples. "He told me."

Fury replaced surprise on the genteel woman's face. "The son of a bitch."

The expletive did not surprise Kate. "Yes, he was."

"What did he say? That's if you're not betraying any confidence." A mixture of irritability and contempt oozed from Anna.

"Of course not, hard to betray a dead man." The pounding in Kate's head subsided. She exhaled a long breath. "He wrote a new review."

"You saw it?"

"Yes." Kate tried to exude a serene exterior despite the lingering pain. "He let me read the draft a couple of days ago, a vitriolic two-star review no better than the first one he wrote."

"Did he already send it to the magazine?" Anna blinked

rapidly, hunched forward.

"No."

Anna looked off into the distance before she met Kate's eyes again. "You didn't tell me." A sense of defeat replaced her anger.

"There was no point." Kate spoke in a consoling but direct voice. "He said he had a reputation to uphold, couldn't appear as if he'd changed his mind about the place only six months later." Her fingers drifted to her throat. "That's when I realized truth was just a convenient form of fiction for him."

Anna's eyes morphed into tiny slits. "Bastard. If that's the case, then he never intended to pen a better review, did he?"

"No, I don't think he did." Kate touched Anna's shoulder. "I held out hope I could persuade him to write something less harsh, but then …" She puckered her lips and shook her head. "Fate intervened, didn't it?"

"He was a deceptive man, Kate. It's hard to believe anything he said was true." Anna wiped her wet cheek. "How do you think the magazine will deal with his death?"

Kate hugged her arms around her stomach and sighed. "Hard to say, I think he fabricated his influence with the magazine too. I'm not convinced they regarded him so highly."

Anna slumped with a look of resignation. "Well, we both know he had a twisted sense of reality."

"No, it was worse than that. He enjoyed stringing people along. He strung me along. Imagine how floored I was when I read his review." Kate shifted her weight and planted her legs wide. "He thought so highly of his observations but never considered the consequences of his words. Beneath his public façade as a journalist lurked a sociopathic hatemonger." Heat radiated through her body burning the tips of her ears. "And he had the audacity to be surprised when I wasn't happy with what he wrote." She expelled a staccato of *tut-tuts*. "The reason was because it was lies. Nothing but lies. Despite it, he had no remorse." She felt Anna lay a tentative hand on her arm. "Matthew's lies exposed him for the small-minded, little man he really was, someone who took advantage of others, someone who—"

She stopped when Anna clutched her wrist. Kate saw the woman staring at her, open-mouthed and speechless, as if shock had stilled her tongue. Oh god, she thought. She had gone completely overboard. Was she even talking about Matthew Kane anymore?

"I'm sorry, Anna, I'm not sure what came over me." With a swift shake of her head, she tried to regain her composure.

"Kate, it's me who should apologize to you. I'm so sorry this holiday has turned into such a debacle." Anna gripped her arm. "Matthew Kane is dead. If I felt bad earlier, I certainly don't now. Am I a horrible person?"

"No, you're being honest, Anna. No one is going to judge you." Kate pointed a finger at herself. "Least of all me." She tried her best to remove the angry edge from her tone.

Anna bit her bottom lip and released. "Thank you for that."

"Some people don't deserve sympathy … even when dead." Kate massaged her temples. "I hope the police determine it was an accident. I'm sure they want this wrapped up as quickly as possible." She breathed a sigh of relief as the pressure in her head subsided.

"I hope you're right. It is the tourist industry, something this country survives on." Anna glimpsed her watch. "It should be your turn soon."

"I'm not worried." Kate rocked back on her heels.

"Matthew Kane was pretty well known, though. It's bound to make the news." Anna's energy returned to her voice.

"Yes, but that's for the magazine to worry about. They're the ones who sent him on this assignment. I'm sure they don't need the negative publicity either."

"Hmm … I suppose you're right."

Kate took a deep breath and rubbed her collarbone as the door to the villa's office opened. She saw Jerry step out. He shook hands with a thirty-something man, and they appeared to exchange friendly words. Jerry winked at her and Anna as he paraded by.

"Dr. Hampton?" said the man standing by the office.

Anna's facial muscles tensed. "Shit, that's Hewitt," she whispered.

Kate gave a half shrug and scrunched her lips. It didn't matter who questioned her. It wouldn't be the first time she had to talk to the police.

* * *

The small, private room housed computer equipment, a fax machine, telephone, and a large desk. A map of the world spread across one wall, and photographs of the resort taken by Anna lined the other walls. A picture window offered a scenic view of the path to the Zen Garden. Tiny pink blooms of a clay potted bougainvillea sat in the corner.

"Dr. Hampton, please have a seat." Inspector Hewitt motioned to one of two wooden fold-up chairs in the middle of the room. File folder in hand, he examined its contents like a physician reading a chart. "What kind of doctor are you?" He sat down across from her, their knees almost touching until he inched his chair back.

"A psychiatrist."

"I see." He clicked his ballpoint pen and scribbled on a sheet of paper, then slid the folder on the desk beside him. "And you're here from New York, correct, Doctor?"

"Yes, and please call me Kate."

"Well …" He hemmed. "That's not normal procedure."

"Oh please," she coaxed, "only my patients call me Doctor." She observed his Adam's apple bob up and down.

"All right … Kate, it is then."

She flicked her hair away from her face. "And what is your name?"

"It's … umm …" Clearing his throat, he pressed against his chest as if to expel something, "… Martin."

Kate noticed his nervous energy. Anna had described him as over eager, which was true, but there was something else. No wedding band. If he came off aggressive as Anna had said, it was probably to compensate for insecurity around his more experienced partner. Martin—the three words she chose to describe him were: *methodic, apprehensive, and reticent*.

"I haven't met a lot of psychiatrists, but I've met many doctors. They usually prefer being addressed with the title."

She tilted her head back and laughed. "It must be a formality left over by the British."

"Perhaps."

"Americans can be like that, but I'm not." She swung her right leg over her left knee and adjusted the soft hem of her skirt.

"I see." He picked up his file folder again and held it on his lap. "So … Kate … I believe the owner has told you Mr. Kane was found dead early this morning."

"Yes, so tragic."

"We're trying to establish a timeline for when it happened. Anything you can tell us to help our investigation would be appreciated."

"Of course, whatever I can do." She noticed his small button eyes deeply set into his skull, and his mocha skin that appeared smooth and flawless. If it were not for his cheesy mustache, she might even have considered him a handsome man.

"Good, when was the last time you saw Mr. Kane?"

"At lunch yesterday. I spoke with him around noon, invited him for an evening swim, but he never showed up."

"Invited him for a swim?" He thrust out his chest, clicked his pen twice. "Were you and he …?"

"What?" She raised an eyebrow.

"A couple … were you …?"

"If you're asking if we were intimate, then the answer is no." She licked her lips. "Mr. Kane was alone here, as am I. It made sense that we might socialize a little."

"Did you spend much time with him?"

"No. It's a small group, as you know. We were bound to bump into one another since we eat together. A few days ago, I took him to James Bond Beach, but that was it. Aside from meals and watching the band play after dinner, we didn't have much to do with each other. He wasn't an easy man."

"For any particular reason?"

She crisscrossed her legs in the opposite direction, noticed the inspector followed her movement with his eyes. "Mr. Kane was an insecure man. He over-compensated for it by being brutish and arrogant, not qualities which endeared him to the people here."

"Understandable." He looked inside the folder. "It says here he wrote for a travel magazine. Were you aware of that?"

"Yes, hard not to. He mentioned it at every opportunity, considered himself important in that regard."

Inspector Hewitt nodded, clicked his pen, and wrote in his folder.

"Martin, may I be honest? The last thing I want to do is waste your time."

"By all means."

"I felt sorry for him. He had a lot of issues, which manifested in odd behaviors."

"Such as?" He straightened up in his chair.

"The most peculiar allergies to food and the environment I've ever come across. Almost every meal had to be altered to suit him. The owners tried to accommodate his every request, yet he was never happy."

"Were these legitimate problems he had?"

"Sure they were—to him." She leaned back in her chair. "In my evaluation, he fabricated many of his symptoms to garner attention. He was not of sound mind."

"I see." Hewitt bent his head down and scribbled. When he paused, she shifted and re-crossed her legs, bumping his knee with her foot in the process. This time the inspector's approving gaze appeared less than discreet.

"My apologies." Kate brushed her hand slowly up her calf. "These wooden chairs are not very comfortable. Will we be much longer?" She caught his laser eyes wandering up her legs.

"No, just a few more personal questions … about Mr. Kane, I mean." He closed the folder but hung on to his pen. "You've been helpful, Kate, and I appreciate it."

"Not at all."

"Did Mr. Kane talk about any family?"

"He was an only child, his father is still alive, though I think he's in a nursing home."

"That's good to know." Clicking his pen again, he opened the folder and jotted a note.

"He didn't discuss his personal life with me. I don't think Matthew Kane had many interests outside of work."

"You found all this out despite not being with him much."

Kate offered a wide smile. "A hazard of the profession, I'm afraid. I can't turn off my analytical brain even while on vacation. People fascinate me."

Hewitt pushed out a long breath. "Were you able to diagnose Mr. Kane with a known condition?"

"No, I didn't spend enough time with him alone to do that, but his behavior in the group revealed a lot."

"Like what?"

"A grossly inflated ego," she said without hesitation.

"He thought a lot of himself, did he?"

"Yes, he could not grasp that others existed beyond his own needs, which meant he wasn't responsible for his actions. The rules of normal behavior and courtesy did not apply to him. It's as if he considered himself superior to everyone else."

"I can see why that might rub people the wrong way."

Kate nodded.

"One final question."

"Shoot." A boisterous laugh spilled out of her. "Sorry, I didn't mean to say that to a man who's carrying a gun."

Inspector Hewitt's face stretched wide with a grin, exposing small Chiclets-like teeth. "Is it possible he was depressed?"

Kate took a deep breath. "He was not a happy man, that much I know." She uncrossed her legs, planting both feet on the floor. "Can you imagine coming to a beautiful country like yours and not having a good time? He seemed to always be working indoors."

Hewitt's muscles tightened around his jaw. "In your opinion, then …" Click. Click. He inched forward in his chair. "Could he have been suicidal?"

A pregnant pause filled the room. She pitched forward and reduced the distance between them, connected with the inspector's crow-like eyes. "Yes, it's possible."

He lowered his head. When he glanced at her again, the tension around his brow softened. "I will certainly take your words into consideration, Kate. Thank you, you've been more than helpful."

She stood up and made her way to the door. He strolled alongside her. "If I have any more questions, do you mind if I contact you?"

She turned to the Inspector. "Not at all. I'll be here for another couple of days. I will drop off a business card to the owners for you."

"That'd be great. I don't want to keep you from the rest of your day." He wrapped his palm around the doorknob. "It's a hot one. A swim is probably in order."

Kate bowed her head politely as he opened the door for her. "That's a good idea." She extended her hand and felt he held it a bit longer than he needed to. "Thank you Martin for all you do. I have great respect for law enforcement."

Adam was leaning on the wall when she walked out of the office. He mimicked a Groucho Marx eyebrow lift in her direction. She shook her head in amusement when she passed him. Adam was a smug bastard, but she liked him. He would certainly not mince words about Matthew to Inspector Hewitt.

"Mr. Naderi," Martin called out.

By creating a scene of an unhappy man who was not well-liked, she had accomplished what she wanted with her interrogation. Inspector Hewitt was able to visualize Matthew's desperation and connected the dots himself. He had suggested suicide. She never uttered the word.

Ahead in the dining room, Daniel sat with his back toward her, speaking to the other inspector.

Kate made a sharp turn and headed in the opposite direction for the beach.

COOKED

Anna requested Violet prepare chicken wraps for lunch. Though the police presence excited the guests and created a buzz, she tried to control her own emotions. Mealtimes anchored the day, and she wanted to return to the routine as soon as possible.

Interrogation of the guests and staff ended at half past twelve. Anna wanted lunch served immediately afterward, concluding everyone would be hungry by then.

Just as she was about to proceed to the dining area, Violet approached her with a worried face.

"Mrs. Pearson, may I speak with you? I have a personal matter to discuss."

"Violet, can we talk after lunch?"

"No, ma'am, this cannot wait. I must speak with you and Mr. Pearson."

Anna knew Violet to always be smiling and good-humored. It was unusual of her to make such a request, so she asked to meet with her in the office. As she and Nolan waited, she wondered what else could go wrong.

Violet entered the office a few minutes later with Earl, their lunch server.

Why was Earl with Violet? Anna wondered. She tilted her head at her husband, who returned a confused shrug.

"Please sit," he said, offering his chair to Earl. Nolan chose to stand.

"Mr. and Mrs. Pearson, I have a confession to make." Violet sat across from Anna blinking as if she had sand in her eyes.

Anna had never seen the large woman so distraught. Earl's sheepish expression and slouched posture also worried her. "Violet, is everything all right?" she asked. "Does this have to do with the police investigation of Mr. Kane's death?"

The woman nodded. "Yes … no …" She hesitated. "Not really, but …"

Earl piped up, his arms flailing. His normal relaxed demeanor gave way to hysteria. "It's all my fault! I'm so sorry Mr. and Mrs. Pearson. The police questioned me and I panicked."

Anna felt Nolan's touch on her shoulder. "Earl, calm down, and tell us what happened," he said.

The young man took several exaggerated, deep breaths. "Inspector Johnson asked me where I was last evening. I told him I was out taking a swim. He kept asking me if I saw Mr. Kane on the beach …" He wrung his hands together. "I kept saying no, no, I was out fishing, then he said fishing? Fishing so late at night? I was so nervous … I—"

"Earl, let me speak," Violet said. "It's my fault, you were doing it to help me."

"What's going on?" Anna said in a sharp tone.

"Mrs. Pearson." Violet flashed a glimpse at Nolan. "Mr. Pearson … it's not Earl's fault. I don't want him to get in trouble."

"Just tell us what happened," Nolan said.

Violet looked to Earl. "We guessed the police would tell you anyway, so we wanted to do it first."

"Tell us what?" Anna asked, her patience dissipating by the second.

"It started because I was so upset when the stingray attacked Ms. Nadine several days ago, so I … I …" Her words trailed off as if she had run out of breath.

"What, Violet?" Anna grabbed her arm and shook it, a little harder than she intended. "Tell us!"

"We killed the stingray. I asked Earl to do it. He knows these waters better than anyone. That's why he was in the ocean Saturday night when Mr. Kane went missing."

"What?" Nolan leaned forward. "Why?"

Violet dabbed her face with a handkerchief she pulled from her apron pocket. "It worried me that Ms. Nadine might not come back after her attack. I know she hasn't been in the water since. I wanted to do something to help."

Anna laid a hand on Violet's knee. "Oh my …" She shook her head, "… you scared the hell out of me. Why would you hide this from us? Why?" She observed Violet's lower lip trembling.

"I knew you would be angry if we killed the stingray on purpose."

Anna looked up at Nolan, who let out a heavy breath,

then he said to Violet, "We're not too happy about it. Willy and Freddy chased the stingray with the boat to scare it from these waters. They're not normally dangerous unless provoked anyway." He turned his attention to Earl. "We certainly don't want to get in the habit of killing anything for no reason. The marine life is part of why people come here."

Violet began tearing more heavily. Anna sensed she might break into sobs. She put a firm hand on the small of her husband's back. "Violet, you should have come to us with your plan. We would have told you Nadine does not scare easily. It was her own fault for staying in the water so late, but she'll go back in the ocean when she's ready."

"I know it was stupid. We intended to pull up the stingray on shore today or tomorrow … pretend it had washed up dead. Earl was going to say he discovered it."

"Wait a minute, are you saying you still have the stingray?" Nolan asked.

Earl darted a gaze to Violet, who nodded at him. "Yes, I tied it behind the cove on the other side of the beach."

Silence ensued as if each of them had lapsed into a moment of grief.

"Violet, what were you thinking?" Anna finally said.

"I wanted the guests to feel safe in the ocean again. I was afraid if …" Her wavering voice appeared to dry up in her throat. Earl looked pitiful as he rubbed her arm in a lame attempt to comfort her.

Anna caught her husband's eye and lifted her chin, not uttering a word.

"Earl, come with me." Nolan gestured for the man to follow him. "You and I will get lunch ready. I want to know exactly what you said to the police."

Earl stood up reluctantly. He patted Violet's shoulder as he slinked by her.

After the men left the room, Anna took a calming breath. Her initial fear that Violet had anything to do with Matthew's death melted away. "What were you afraid of?"

The Jamaican woman bowed her head. "It's selfish of me. I feel so foolish now."

Anna touched Violet's hand. "You can tell me."

She kept her head down. "I'm not sure you would understand."

"Try me," Anna said, in a voice that she hoped conveyed the empathy of a friend, not just an employer.

Violet quaked with repressed sobs. "I was afraid if Ms. Nadine never came back, I would have no chance to be an author. I wasn't thinking straight." Retrieving her handkerchief again, she blew her nose and wiped her face. "Mrs. Pearson?"

"Yes." Anna observed Violet choking back tears.

"Have you ever wanted something so much you were willing to kill for it? I asked Earl to kill the stingray because it seemed like the only solution. I never meant to cause you and Mr. Pearson any trouble." Her body shook as she clutched Anna's arms. "Please forgive me … please forgive Earl …" Violet crumpled forward and wept.

Anna held the woman and let her cry. As Violet's sobs quieted to a whimper, she struggled to curb her own emotions. Violet had found power in destroying what she perceived standing between her and what she wanted. Anna understood her desire and the rage that ensued from the powerlessness to act. She had struggled with her own feelings of helplessness while trying to accommodate Matthew Kane.

Anna lifted Violet's head off her shoulders and gazed into her blood-shot eyes. "There is nothing to forgive," she said, "nothing at all."

LEVITY AND FICTION

Nolan appeared ruffled, not his usual even-tempered self when he took his seat. He apologized for the late lunch, and that they would have to start without Anna.

"Is she all right?" Kate slanted her head toward him.

"Yes," he said, "but this has been one hell of a day. I need a drink."

Nolan's statement, expressed with uncharacteristic levity lightened the mood. Chatter resumed as Earl set lunch on the table and made his way back to the kitchen without a word.

Daniel, who was staying for lunch, popped open a Red Stripe. "Is this good for you Nolan, or would you prefer something stronger?"

"No, that's fine." Nolan accepted the beer and immediately took a pull from it.

"Don't worry," Adam said. "The police are just following procedure. You reported him missing right away, which sped up the process, that's all, otherwise they'd still be trying to make an identification."

"He's absolutely right," the Englishman said. "Now that they have Mr. Kane's passport, they'll turn it over to the

U.S. Embassy in Kingston who will contact his next of kin." After grabbing a platter of wraps, he looked to Kate beside him, offering to serve her.

She nodded. "Just one, thank you."

Daniel brushed her arm as he slid a sandwich on her plate with tongs, then took two for himself. "Unless there is any foul play suspected, your involvement will be minimal after this. Jamaican law requires a post-mortem and a coroner's inquest when a foreigner dies. It's the inquest that can take a while."

"I don't want this dragged out," Nolan said, shaking his head.

"It shouldn't if it's ruled an accidental death. The inquest is just a formality for the coroner to sign off on the death certificate." Daniel took a bite of his wrap. "Medieval English laws."

"Well, Jamaica is still governed by many of those laws." Nolan appeared pensive. "And you know the English like their rules and regulations. No offense, of course."

"None taken." Daniel smirked. "And you're right, we do like our rules, but we've been known to break a few now and then. For what it's worth, I've asked Ray to expedite this to the best of his ability.

Nolan blew out a breath of relief. "So good to have you here Daniel, I owe you." He took a swig of his beer. "One thing in our favor is since we're so remote, we shouldn't be bothered by any press." He picked at his sweet potato fries. "We hope not, anyway."

"I told Inspector Hewitt that Kane was a loose cannon.

It's anyone's guess why he took a swim late at night," Greg said. "He was not a logical man."

Adam snorted. "That brings to mind a quote from Dale Carnegie. 'People are not creatures of logic, but creatures of emotion.' I don't tend to believe everything he wrote, but I've never met a man fueled by less logic than Matthew."

Jessica bobbed her head with enthusiasm. "He would've done well to read Carnegie's *How to Win Friends and Influence People*."

Adam supported her statement with an impressed arch of his brow in her direction.

"Hi everyone, sorry I'm late." Anna approached the table wearing a sweet smile.

Nadine immediately prepared lunch for her. When she picked up a second wrap, Anna waved a hand on top of her plate.

"You need to eat, you missed breakfast," the older woman said.

"I'm fine. One is enough. I'll take a few of the fries though."

"We were just talking about our police interviews," Jessica said.

"How did yours go?"

"Fine, it didn't last long. I told Inspector Johnson that Matthew gave me the creeps. The few times I tried to talk to him, our conversations went nowhere. He always referred back to himself or his work or his allergies." She shrugged and took a drink. "I didn't spend much time with him anyway."

"Good. I'm glad it wasn't too difficult." Anna sighed.

"Not at all." Jessica gave an animated nod. "It was kind of exciting."

Nolan made eye contact with his wife from the opposite end of the table. "Are you all right, honey?"

She smiled and mouthed *yes* before picking up her sandwich for a bite. "Oh, by the way, Willy stopped me on the way here. He found the missing set of snorkel gear under the stairs."

Nolan turned up both palms and shrugged. "Makes sense, considering Matthew wasn't wearing it when they found his body."

"I think Willy just wanted to help, that's all." She moved her attention away from her husband. "I hope the wraps are good."

"They're great," Ben said, "like everything else Violet makes. Love the fries too."

Nolan wiped his mouth with a napkin. "I want to thank all of you for putting up with today. This was not planned for your holiday, obviously." He sat back in his chair. "Anna and I will make sure to compensate you for the inconvenience."

"Not a chance," Adam said. "This is the most memorable vacation I've had in a long time, and I go away at least three to four times a year. You don't owe me anything."

"Same goes for me," chimed Jerry, followed by unanimous agreement from the table.

"And to show you how much I love this place, I'm referring it to my contacts when I return home." Adam withdrew his cell phone from his shirt pocket, clicked a few buttons. "One of my companies needs a venue for a conference coming up next month, third week. Can I have my assistant call you?"

Anna gave him a firm nod. "Yes, we have preferred rates for corporate bookings too. Let's talk after lunch, okay?"

"We really appreciate the support," said Nolan. "Anna and I want to say that we are devastated by what has happened to Mr. Kane. For those who may not know, we invited him here. No matter what we thought of the man, we never wanted this."

"Of course not," Kate said, "but you're not responsible for his death."

Daniel poured himself another beer. "I agree with Kate. He was a grown man. It would have been no different had he gone on an excursion and gotten himself killed. Life is full of risks."

For the benefit of Jessica who looked perplexed, Nolan elaborated on the circumstances of how Matthew came to be at the villa. "We're not sure how his death will affect Sunset's future bookings." He lamented.

"I'm a businessman, Nolan, as are you," Adam said. "I know a great place when I see it. This incident won't deter me from coming here." He stopped to take a drink of water. "It's not as if Kane was poisoned by your staff or broke his neck on your property. If anything, the cachet of the place just went up." He motioned with his thumb in the air and pushed it higher. "Way up."

Greg leaned in from across the table. "How do you

figure?"

"Well, Goldeneye had Ian Fleming, a writer of spy thrillers, right?"

"Yes …"

"Sunset Villa has its own real-life thriller, a true tale of a man who wrote a dishonest review. He gets invited back by the owners to make amends, but he has a chip on his shoulder. He is an insecure little man with no power in his life, no success with women, possessed by imaginary problems of his own making."

"Oh Adam … you're too much." Anna shook her head. She and Kate gave each other a knowing glance, both trying to conceal their smiles.

"Thank you, it gets better," he continued. "One night, after almost a week with people who don't pay attention to his drivel, his delusions overpower him. The voices in his head tell him he can do anything he wants, so he decides to take on his biggest fear here."

"What's that?" Jessica asked, breathy with excitement.

"The ocean, of course. That's even though he's a lousy swimmer, and a stingray was spotted nearby only nights earlier. He steps into the ocean almost as if in a trance, and guess what? The ocean swallows him up. She's not one to forgive those who spread false rumors or talk unkindly of the beauty here."

"You should write fiction," Jerry said, "though I admit there is an odd sense of justice to your story."

"Justice, that's a good spin, or call it retribution, revenge, whatever you like. What you market is never as important as *how* you market it."

"So market the mystery of the place?" Nadine asked.

"Yes, along with everything else that makes it great—the food, the terrific staff, the intimacy, the history. It's unfortunate Matthew Kane died, but he was not a sympathetic character. In fiction, the readers would have voted him off the island."

Nadine nodded. "I agree, we did not like him at all. Ben's blood pressure has yo-yoed this week from listening to his nonsense. We brought prescription drugs for his condition, but hoped he wouldn't need to take it." Ben put a comforting hand on his wife's arm.

"Are you okay now?" Anna turned to Ben with concern on her face.

"I'm fine," he said. "My doctor discovered a case of arrhythmia, an irregular heartbeat when I had my physical last year. It's not life threatening, but he recommended I take beta blockers with me in case."

"Beta blockers? That is fucking priceless! Excuse my French." Adam laughed aloud. "Matthew was a beta amongst men."

Nadine giggled. "True, and speaking of fiction, his writing was vile, and he had the nerve to call himself a journalist." She huffed a look of disgust. "He wouldn't know a fact if it slapped him upside the head."

"Exactly, the man had so little power," Adam said. "I would have helped him if he was serious about changing his life, but he wasn't."

"Why do say that?" Kate asked.

Adam wiped his mouth with a napkin. "Early on, he told me he went into my website. What he didn't tell me until I discovered it a couple of days ago was he signed up for my newsletter. It's for men only, advice on how to get women, money, and power."

"He input his e-mail to your site?" Greg asked.

"Yes, but he used an alternate address, which any amateur could have deciphered. It was an anagram of his name." Adam addressed Kate. "I think he was using my methods to make time with you. Not sure if you noticed, but I certainly did."

Kate's cheeks flared with a rosy hue. "Really?" she said. "I would have never guessed it."

SECRETS

Kate stood on the second floor veranda of Daniel's home, a stunning eighteenth-century plantation property. Shrouded by a red sky, the open sea reminded her of a painting by Monet, which captured a fading sunset not unlike this one. Beautiful place you have here," she said. "I love the Georgian architecture."

From inside the house, Daniel responded, "Thanks. You can't beat the view at this time of day."

It was one of Kate's favorite times too, the setting sun a spotlight lowering its beam across the ocean's brilliance. With her forearms folded, Kate leaned on the veranda to observe the tropical greenery darken patch by patch. Below, the waves rushed in and swept the sand into the ocean, depositing a fresh, smooth blanket in its place.

And so it would continue—the repetitive motion, like the circle of life, like a spinning Dhamma wheel, never-ending.

A gust of wind whipped up Kate's hair into a bedhead mess. She brushed strands away from her face and tucked it behind her ears. A cool snap this evening prompted her to wear a black chiffon scarf. She knotted the flowing fabric more tightly around her neck.

"Your drink, Kate."

From over her shoulder, she glimpsed Daniel approaching her. He handed her a half-full tumbler of amber liquid.

"Are you trying to get me drunk, Englishman?"

"Never," he said, clinking his gin and tonic to her glass, "I would sooner have you sober any day."

She sipped a small mouthful, savored the heat as it slid down her throat. Kate wasn't sure what warmed her cheeks more, the potency of the whisky or Daniel's words. "My god, that is so smooth."

"Lagavulin sixteen year old."

After another swallow, she said, "Thank you for inviting me for dinner."

"I made my best dish," he said with a chuckle, "baked fried chicken."

"Baked *and* fried?" Even as she tried to stifle laughter, her body shook.

"As I'm sure you watch what you eat, I'm baking instead of frying, but it'll taste fried."

She smiled her approval. "Thanks for considering my figure, so kind of you." Her insides felt cozy and tingled all over. "I'm not one for dieting, though. Food is one of life's pleasures. I don't deprive myself of it."

"Good." Daniel took a step closer to her. "What else don't you deprive yourself of?"

"What else?" His proximity felt like sunlight on her skin. "Oh … travel. I love seeing the world, and when I find places I really like, I make a point to return to them." Her fingers skittered over Daniel's chest as she looked in his eyes. "I'm one of those people who enjoys reading a book more than once. When something is good the first time … it can only get better. Right?"

Kate had prepared herself for tonight. She was playing with fire when she accepted Daniel's dinner invitation, and she knew it. Their conversations, filled with innuendo on both their parts did little to mask their desire for one another. Like a moth to a flame, she could not resist him.

"Kate …"

"Yes?" All her tension melted away like sitting in a warm bath.

"I need to say something to you before I change my mind," he said.

She waited for the words of endearment, but what she really wanted was for him to kiss her. Dizzy anticipation filled the air. She tilted her face to his.

"Why did you do it, Kate?" he asked.

It took her a second to comprehend his question, then she backed away from him. "What are you talking about?"

"Kate …" He removed the tumbler from her hand and set it on a nearby table. "I saw what you did the night Matthew Kane went missing." He held her face in his hands. "I know you killed him."

Daniel's voice took on a note of confession that sent her mind into high alert. She could not pretend any longer. Kate cupped her hands over Daniel's and slid them down to her heart. There, she held them, her head bowed, breathing fast, thinking faster. When the garbage bag disappeared from her closet, she realized it was only a matter of time before she discovered who took it.

Her father had invaded her dream for a reason, to warn her there was danger nearby. That danger was in the form of a British ex-military man, a General no less.

How would she handle him?

Kate spoke quietly while trying to herd her rambling thoughts. "You came into my room and removed the bag from my closet. Didn't you?" With his face now hidden in shadow, she tried searching his expression for a clue. The playfulness between them had vanished.

Daniel shook his head and whispered, "No, darling … a friend did that."

With closed eyes and rage bubbling inside her, her father's chastising voice erupted in her head, admonishing her for letting her guard down. Kate wanted to scream. Who else knew about this? A sudden pain jabbed the sides of her head. She released Daniel's hands and pressed fingers to her temples to still the pain. Her breathing sped up.

"Kate? Are you all right?"

Daniel's words registered in her ears, but he faded from sight. Instead, flashing lights and bright, wavy lines pin-wheeled inside her eyelids. A whirling sensation increased the pressure inside her head. She took one step and stumbled against the man in front of her.

Daniel swung her off her feet into his arms. "I'm taking you inside."

"No, no ..." Her raspy voice sounded far away.

"You don't have a choice in the matter."

She made a weak attempt to struggle against him, but his grip was unrelenting. Flopped like a rag dog, she watched the purple sky float by with each step he lifted and dropped to the ground. The rhythm and sway of his strides moved in tandem with her heartbeat. *Step, beat, step, beat* ... Without warning, her scarf caught a gust of wind and billowed out like a sail. Daniel immediately clutched her closer and grabbed the delicate fabric before it strangled her. He quickened his pace until they were inside the house.

After pushing aside a wall of cushions, he laid her down on a long plush couch. When her head hit the pillow, she tried getting up, but her rubbery limbs would not support her.

"Lie on your side," Daniel said. "And don't move, young lady. That's an order." He strayed away from sight.

The pain in her head dissipated, but her sense of helplessness did not. Somewhere deep in her brain, she heard her father yelling "Run, Kate, run!" Her muscles tensed, ready to spring off the chair any second.

Daniel returned and sat at the edge of the couch. After propping her head up, he brought a glass of water to her lips. "Come on, Kate," he coaxed, "take a sip."

Still shaky, she had no strength to protest. The ice-cold water soothed her parched throat. "More please," she said in a weak voice.

Daniel tipped the remainder of the water between her

lips with the tenderness of a mother feeding a child. She took greedy gulps. The liquid pearled into droplets down her chin, but she didn't care.

She pushed herself into a sitting position and dipped her head to regain equilibrium. "You sure know how to show a girl a good time," she said, lifting her face to him.

He caressed her cheek and studied her with his hypnotic eyes. "Fainting is my specialty, Kate."

"I didn't faint. I was testing your reflexes."

"And … how were they?"

She lowered her chin and forced herself not to smile. "Not bad."

"How's this for reflexes then?" He leaned in close and kissed her, a tender, unhurried brush of his lips against hers.

Every nerve in her body felt Daniel's lips. He didn't rush the kiss as if it were merely a step toward something else. He savored it, and Kate savored him. When her breath caught in her throat and left her wanting more, he released himself from her. She felt the fog lifting. "Daniel, I—"

"Kate, you're safe with me."

Her defenses crept up again. "You said that earlier today. Why should I believe you?"

Daniel scooped up her hands in his, held them tightly on his lap. "Because there is something special between us, Kate, and I know you feel it too."

Her heart thumped in her chest. She fought against her father's warnings in her head to flee. "You're asking me for a lot based on some feelings."

He kissed her fingers with lips she craved on other parts of her body. "Trust me to keep your secrets, Kate."

She stiffened. "And what do I get in return?"

Daniel kept his voice calm and even. "Tell me why you killed Matthew Kane … and I'll tell you something to ease your mind." She saw him take in a breath and slowly release it. "Unburden yourself to me, Kate. I give you my word I won't let anything bad happen to you."

She tried to pull away, but he would not let go of her. Instead, he insinuated himself closer, his body a hot, moist sauna against her. "Daniel, I'm not sure if I can …" As she struggled to hold on to defiance, a grip tightened around her throat.

He squeezed her hands against his chest. "Secrets eventually erode the soul, Kate."

Daniel's words hit her like an insult. She scrutinized his face trying to find one reason not to confide in him. Her eyes burned with unshed tears. He touched his brow to hers and pulled her close. Kate could not remember the last time she felt safe like this.

Not since she was a child, had she allowed herself to cry in someone else's presence.

* * *

"You are a dangerous woman," Daniel said as they sat down to eat outside underneath the stars—the meal of baked chicken that tasted fried.

She smiled the gentlest, shyest of smiles. "Why do you

say that?"

"You killed a man because he wrote a scathing review."

"It would appear that way, though I wouldn't call myself dangerous."

"How would you describe yourself then?" Daniel popped open a bottle of red wine.

Kate bowed her head. "I prefer to think of myself as fiercely loyal. I don't like to be betrayed."

Daniel raised an eyebrow. "Your candor is …"

"What?" She noted his upturned lips.

"I could've used you in my brigade."

Silence. And then she threw her head back and laughed, an uninhibited release that started deep in her chest. Daniel laughed too with a hint of dubious admiration across his face. Theirs was an easiness she had never felt, reserved for people who had known each other much longer, attainable only by a lucky few. That's what she thought anyway, until now.

How was it possible to flirt and weave dry humor into the most wicked of conversations? And to do it with a man she had just met? It belied all logic.

Kate slid her glass toward Daniel. "And since we're sharing secrets. Who removed the bag of evidence from my room?"

He poured her wine. "That would be Harrison. When you closed up your windows, I guessed you would attend dinner with no time to get rid of any evidence. That's when I called Harrison to search your room."

She arched a brow, both impressed and relieved by his

response. She had inquired about the missing bag with housekeeping, but to no avail. Pursuing it further seemed counterproductive and might raise suspicion. "I have the greatest respect for Harrison, and of all the people who work at Sunset, I'm happy it was him." She strayed her eyes from Daniel for an instant. "Does he know …?"

"You mean does he know what you did?"

She nodded.

"The answer is I think he suspects, but I would not worry. Even with all my years in the military, I've met few men as discreet and in control as Harrison. He is loyal to the bone." Daniel filled his own glass. "You mentioned fierce loyalties. I understand that well, and so does Harrison. I trust him—with my life, but … that's another story."

"I'd love to hear it." She reached out a hand across the table and Daniel took it. "Perhaps it's time you unburdened as well."

He linked his fingers with hers. "The truth is I've not felt a need to tell anyone … not until I met you, but …"

"But what?" She frowned.

"Let's save that for another time, so we can make sure to *have* another time." He picked up his glass and toasted her. "To more of you, Kate."

The outer corners of Daniel's eyes wrinkled as he smiled at her, devastating what little calm reserve she had left. With the glass tipped to her lips, she strived to mask her desire.

"Your method of killing, Kate … most unusual." He served her two pieces of chicken.

"Smells delicious." She held the plate to her nose before setting it down on the table. "What do you mean by unusual? I poisoned him."

"Yes, but auto-injectors, Kate? That's serious business. I only know of them because the military uses atropine and pralidoxime chloride in case of nerve agent poisoning."

"I'm aware of that." She looked away for a moment. "I suppose I came prepared though I never thought I would need to use it. I almost couldn't find any pesticides, had to dig around for it."

Daniel nodded. "Yes, Sunset is going green. It's a good thing." Sitting back in his seat, he gave her a serious look. "You took a huge risk Kate, if I'm correct in my thinking of what you did."

Was it judgment she heard? She searched for it on Daniel's face but did not see it. "I know, but I did not want to leave any evidence, no puncture marks, nothing that might be uncovered in an autopsy, although …" She cut slowly into a piece of chicken breast. "I expected his body to sink and stay in the ocean, at least for some time. It shocked me when he was found so quickly."

"It was a cool evening." Daniel smiled. "The colder water temperature may have added buoyancy to the body."

"Just my luck," she said, depositing a piece of chicken in her mouth. "This is delicious. This could rival one of Violet's recipes." When Daniel wiped his mouth and did not say a word, she put down her knife and fork. "I never wanted this," she said. "Matthew Kane confided in me he liked Sunset Villa very much, yet he never intended to give it a fair review. He lied. I don't like liars." Her voice sounded detached, even to herself. "Yes, I lured him with the oldest trick in the book. I appealed to his male ego, but my body …" She paused to search for the right words, "… my body was merely a vehicle for the weapon. It meant nothing."

"I believe you," Daniel said without hesitation.

Kate lowered her eyes, struck by a fleeting memory that niggled at her. She massaged her temples.

"Are you all right?"

Tension flowed from her head down to her neck. She nodded at Daniel and tried relaxing. "I just had a passing thought … couldn't hold on to it though." She pinched the back of her neck. "What I did with Matthew Kane was completely dispassionate." The elusive thought came and went again. She resolved to let it go. "Sometimes I feel like the cobbler's son. I assess others so easily, but …"

Daniel rose from his seat and walked to her. "If you're implying you lack insight into yourself, I disagree." He crouched by her chair. "We all have reasons to compartmentalize unpleasantness, to justify our actions for the sake of others who might not approve. In the end, we do what we want anyway."

Her head dropped against Daniel's as he trailed his fingers down the sides of her calves.

"You sir, would have made a good shrink."

"I have no interest in listening to anyone else's story." He fixed his hypnotic eyes to hers. "You're the only person I want to know more about, Kate, and I'm fascinated."

The night was cool and misty by the time they carried their dinner plates inside. A drop in temperature prickled her skin. When she grabbed her scarf from the couch, Daniel stood behind her as if to help her with it. She was mistaken. He let the cloth fall between them, warming her with his body instead. With her back pressed against him, he caressed down her arms, supporting her head with his broad chest.

She curled up her shoulders and heard him breathe in the scent of her hair. It was a deep breath, which he held for a long time, then exhaled as a slow, warm current across her neck. Tipping her head back, she listened to his throbbing heartbeat. Warmth radiated up her spine when she curved her buttocks into him. He kissed a trail from behind her ear, down the slope of her neck, and lower. It tickled her to the point where she could hardly stand it.

Cocooned in his arms, Kate went limp as Daniel turned her head to the side, his lips urgently searching hers.

DAY EIGHT
KARMA

Kate carefully folded her delicate dresses and laid them on top of her clothes in her suitcase. Only a few clothing items and her toiletries remained to be packed.

Clad in scarlet undergarments and silver bangles, she pranced across the cold tiles of her room, opening and closing dresser drawers to ensure she did not leave anything behind.

Tonight was her final evening here, and despite an upheaval of emotions over the past week, something had shifted. She felt lighter.

Kate slid a three-quarter length red dress off its hanger to wear for tonight's dinner. While slipping into it, a faint masculine scent floated by her nostrils, a hint of black pepper and cedar. Daniel's cologne. Armani?

On the floor of the closet, she spied her scarf, which must have fallen while she was packing. She cradled the slippery fabric in her hands and inhaled it. The smell recalled Daniel's mischievous eyes, a boyish smile, and a touch that made her heart soar. He had unraveled the scarf from around her neck last night.

Last night …

A knock on the door pulled Kate from her daydream. "I'll be right there," she said, reluctant to let her thoughts fade just yet. She contemplated wearing the scarf again but tucked it in the pocket of her suitcase instead. The scent of Daniel would only distract her.

As she scurried past the dresser, she glimpsed her flushed cheeks in the mirror before opening the door.

"Kate, I'm so glad I caught you."

"Anna, come in. Is everything okay?"

"Yes, I have good news … no wait, let me rephrase," she said, breathless. "I have great news."

"What is it?" Kate observed Anna floating into the room. They both took a seat.

"Nolan just got off the phone with the police. The autopsy turned up nothing, no physical injuries, no evidence of a heart attack." Her eyes glinted excitement. "They're ruling Matthew's drowning as death by misadventure. They've cleared us of any wrongdoing."

"Oh …" Kate covered her mouth and realized her hand trembling. "That's fantastic news." She leaned in and hugged Anna.

"I really didn't expect this so soon." Gazing heavenward, she clasped her palms together as if in prayer. "I wanted to share the news with you before Nolan tells everyone at dinner."

"Thank you, you must be so relieved." Kate flopped

back in the chair, breathing a little easier for herself too. "What a week."

"No kidding." Anna's bottom lip thrust forward and pushed a loud breath up her face. "Oh, one more piece of news, you'll appreciate this."

"What is it?"

"As a courtesy, we called the editor of *Travel in Style* yesterday, to tell him what happened, offer our condolences, so to speak."

"Yes?" Kate wrinkled her forehead.

"I received a call back from the editor of their online division." Anna paused as if to remember something. "Carlton was her name. Apparently, Matthew was on his way out."

Kate tugged on an earlobe. "She told you that?"

"Yes." Anna shifted in her seat. "New management wasn't impressed with his negativity, intimated it wasn't good for business any more. His bad reviews were popular with a shrinking segment of readers and turning off advertisers." She let out a sigh. "Do you think he suspected they were going to get rid of him?"

"Hard to say, maybe he did ..." Kate pursed her lips. "Maybe that pushed him over the edge.

"A cry for help?"

"Desperation, depression, I guess we'll never know what was going on in his head at the time."

"The editor said she butted heads with Matthew too." Anna twisted her mouth as if to say: *Who didn't Matthew butt heads with?* "We had a good talk. She even apologized for his initial review, said they're lining up new reviewers. One will evaluate us again this summer. And the best part is …"

Kate canted her head.

"I asked her to issue a retraction in the meantime, and she was completely on board." A giggle escaped Anna's lips along with a little hip wiggle in her seat.

Kate made a fist and punched the air with it. "Good. People will forget Matthew Kane's bad review in no time."

"Well, Adam has already booked two conferences with us. That man operates so many businesses. I'm sure he will refer more clients our way."

"He will." Kate nodded with enthusiasm. "He's blustery, but he's a man of his word."

"Agree. Carlton and the magazine will arrange for Matthew's body to be flown back." Anna's words hitched in her throat. "His father is in a nursing home, not really in any condition to take care of things."

"Hmm …" Kate sat in a moment of quiet reflection. Her voice softened, tinted with tenderness. "I hope you don't think you are at all responsible for Matthew Kane's death—because you're not." She touched a hand to Anna's arm. "I want to share something my father taught me a long time ago." She took an extra breath and hesitated. "And I don't quote my father often, but he's been on my mind this trip."

"What is it?" Anna looked at Kate as if she were about to divulge the secret to immortality.

"He said that in this life, we create our own karma."

Bewilderment shaded Anna's face. "Do you really think it was Matthew's karma to die here?"

"Yes, I do, just as it was your karma to own Sunset Villa … and to continue owning it." A comfortable warmth swept up Kate's back.

Anna stared at her with a blank face, then she bit her lower lip and released. "I'm going to hell for not feeling worse about this."

Kate reached out and patted Anna's shoulder. "No you're not. Think of it this way. Someone must have been looking out for you and Nolan … and for this place." Her eyelids clicked once, twice, and lightness filled her chest. "In the end, everything worked out for the best. That's all that matters."

THE GENERAL

A ruckus of croaks and hoots fell between a symphony and a cacophony this time of night, the result of tree frogs and lizards, persisting until birdsong at dawn.

Kate strolled with Daniel along the beach, her hand nestled comfortably in his. They kicked up sand like toy soldiers and stopped to listen to the whoosh of the ocean. A tang of salt water and burning firewood drifted past her nostrils. The horizon offered a picture perfect scene as moody and atmospheric as an Edward Hopper painting brought to life.

A sense of melancholy overcame Kate at having to return home tomorrow. In previous trips, it was because she would miss the resort. This time, she would miss Daniel more. Much more.

She had not planned for him, or for the labyrinth of feelings he stirred up in her. Daniel was complicated and simple, mysterious and open, like no one she had ever met. For most of her life, she had slotted people into categories or ticked off boxes in her head. With Daniel, she found this impossible to do. She could not define him with a just a few words. He was a complex jigsaw puzzle, the type you assembled over days, maybe weeks, and yet ... all the pieces effortlessly fell into place with her.

They stepped inland as the Caribbean swelled into crests of white foam, licking at their feet before flowing out to sea again.

Daniel turned to her, dropped the sandals he was holding as if to mark the spot. He traced her jaw from ear to chin, then lightly trailed down the curve of her neck to her shoulder.

Kate stared into Daniel's eyes, aware an emotional storm was threatening to overcome her. "The last couple of days with you, ..." she said.

"Yes?"

"They've been really special." She rubbed against him like an affectionate cat waiting to be petted. "*You've* been really special. This time with you has meant a lot to me."

Daniel held her face and brushed his lips to hers. She surrendered to the sweet taste of his breath, slid her hands under the back of his shirt and pressed her body to his. Their passion increased until he pulled her down on the sand. Entangled side-by-side, Kate writhed against his touch, her head cradled in the crook of his arm. Not even the cool, gritty surface could diminish her desire.

Daniel twisted her hair, nibbling the seashell curves of her ear. "Stay with me Kate," he said.

Wave upon wave washed up to pull sand from beneath them, as if beckoning them toward the sea. With her head buried in his neck, she shivered, swimming in emotions. "I wish I could," she said, unable to fathom how this man had stolen a piece of her heart, and how her feelings had veered from admiration to affection to something unknown to her in such a short time.

She heard him exhale a heavy breath before he helped her up.

They headed back toward the villa as the next crescendo of waves rolled in. Kate leaned her head on Daniel. No words were exchanged, but their kisses along the way spoke loudly of his feelings for her. With Daniel, it was not the dialogue that bonded them, but the spaces between the words. Those silences declared their affinity for one another, conveyed their shared loneliness. In the most basic terms, he got her, and no one in her life had ever got her.

When they approached Sunset, Daniel stopped short, pulled her close to him. "I'm not coming in, Kate. It will only make it harder to let you go."

She touched the pad of her index finger to the cleft of his chin. "I like this," she said, moving her tip lightly inside the groove. "There isn't anything I don't like about you, Daniel. I can't say that about anyone else." She lowered her gaze to the floor.

"The feeling's mutual, Kate, you know that." With his eyes on hers, he lifted her chin. "Not making love to you …" He sighed. "It's been the most excruciating agony I've ever experienced."

Her own yearning sat as a knot in her belly. "And for me too."

"You've pushed my willpower to a whole new limit,

young lady."

She ran her hand up his chest, absorbed the memory of his heart pulsing against her palm. "I took a risk with my body, but I won't allow you to do the same, not until I'm certain everything is fine."

"You are being overly cautious." His fingers strayed down the side of her neck. "I don't like it, but I understand."

His hug united their bodies. It left no question as to how he felt about her. Daniel had made her safe as he had promised. That was even before he revealed he had used his influence to close out Matthew Kane's case, and to do it quickly. It showed her what he was willing to do for her, and what he was capable of. Beneath the mask of an upstanding decorated General, hid the face of a shadow man with demons of his own. For the first time in her life, Kate felt at home in a man's arms.

Just when she thought her emotions would spill over, Daniel pulled back. He kissed her forehead down to her nose, and lifted her chin for a final kiss on her lips.

"Good-bye, Kate," he said, looking at her with eyes that reflected midnight blue. "Don't be a stranger."

She confirmed with a smile and a nod, then held her breath as she watched him walk away. Only after she could no longer make out his silhouette in the darkness did she push out the air from her lungs.

She would miss him. Their Machiavellian natures and their secrets bonded them. As she had suspected from the first time she laid eyes on him, their attraction to each other transcended the physical. Though she didn't quite understand it, Daniel had filled an empty space inside her she never even knew existed.

As she entered the villa and headed to her room, an overwhelming sadness inched up her throat.

DAY NINE
GOOD-BYE

Due to the early scheduling of her return flight, Kate said her good-byes to everyone after dinner the night before. She had left her suitcase outside the bedroom before falling asleep for one of the staff to carry down. By six, she ambled toward the dining room to grab a coffee before the car arrived to pick her up.

While filling her mug at the coffee station, something shiny inside the bowl of sugar cubes caught her eye—a brand new pair of tongs. A smile formed as she poured cream in her cup. To her knowledge, no one had noticed a small spoon had taken the place of the tongs the last couple of days.

Who replaced it? she wondered.

From the far corner of the main floor, the banging of cupboard doors clanged against an orchestra of metal utensils and rattling dishware. Only one other person got up this early.

Kate meandered through the lounge, until she stood

at the entranceway of the kitchen sipping her coffee. Harrison was bent forward, emptying the dishwasher. He looked up at her as she took a seat on the stool next to the stove.

"Miss Kate." A row of dazzling teeth greeted her.

"Good morning, Harrison."

"Good morning." He stacked dinner plates on the counter. "You're leaving us today."

"I'm afraid so, always sad to leave." She finished her coffee and set the mug on the stove.

"Sad to see you go, Miss Kate." He closed the door to the dishwasher.

Kate stood up, pulled out an envelope from her bag. "This is for you, Harrison, with my sincerest thanks for your wonderful service."

While accepting the gift, he bowed his head. "Thank you, Miss Kate. You are always so kind to me." He slipped the envelope in his shirt pocket.

"And you, sir, are a prince amongst men." She stepped forward to say good-bye.

Harrison held her hand and leaned in for an embrace. It was the first time he had ever hugged her. When they released one another, Harrison's eyes gleamed against his shiny face. "Everything is going to be fine at Sunset again, Miss Kate."

Warmth radiated throughout her body. "I think you're right, Harrison." She gave him a satisfied smile. "In fact … I know you are."

EPILOGUE

The electronic gates opened after Kate spoke to the concierge through the intercom. She drove through the property along the curving driveway past the stone courtyard, twenty minutes early for her nine o'clock appointment. From her rear-view mirror, she watched the gates swing shut, the security cameras swivel back in place.

She shuddered. A luxurious mansion in New Canaan, Connecticut greeted her, so why did she feel as if she were entering a prison?

With more than a month of winter left, it surprised her to see elegant perennial borders contrasting spring wildflowers. Trees and flowering shrubs blended with an impressive array of foliage. Gardeners must have tended the grounds year round.

Confiding in Daniel had turned out to be easy but not simple. She had unburdened herself, in a way she imagined a good Catholic would unburden to a priest at confession. But for her, it was not without a cost. Three Hail Marys would not make her forget. While scraping beneath the surface of *what* she had done to *why* she had done it, she disturbed deeper layers of her unconscious.

Slowly, these buried memories had shuttled into her conscious mind with little warning. In the past, she had been frantic to repress them as quickly as possible. The difference now was: she wanted to know. The process of addressing old memories would hurt, and it would not be easy. Returning here was the first step.

Upon spying the house, she slowed her speed.

Before she approached the columned portico of the grand entranceway, the front door opened. A middle-aged man walked toward her as she parked in front of the house. Resisting the urge to let herself out, she waited for him to come around her side of the car.

Formalities. It was all about formalities here.

"Miss Hampton," he said, bowing at the waist as he opened the door for her. "Good to see you."

"Hello, James, how are you?" She stepped out of the car and laid a gloved hand on his arm.

"Older, as you can see." The Asian man closed the car door, offered a shy smile. "We haven't seen you in a while."

"I've been busy." Kate nodded. "Time flies, doesn't it?"

"Yes, it does."

He led her into the house where she wiped her dry boots several times on the Oriental entrance rug. The snow had melted by the time she returned home from Jamaica, but the cold temperatures persisted throughout the East Coast. She removed her scarf and winter coat, which James promptly hung up in the walk-in hall closet. They proceeded through the two-story grand foyer. A faint aroma of almonds wafted by her nostrils. As she drifted past the curved staircase leading upstairs, she noticed the shiny wood steps, which appeared recently stained. Kate had slept in a room up there once, almost two years ago after a snowstorm forced her to stay overnight. It was the last time she was here.

"You are joining us for lunch, I hope," James said, guiding her forward with a wave of his hand.

"No, I don't intend to stay that long." Sliding off her leather gloves, she placed them in her purse.

"Oh?" He tipped his head, frowned at her. "Your father, he's—"

"That's all right, James." She walked with a slow, steady gait, talking as if they were old friends. "I'll tell him."

"Umm ... all right."

They strolled by several rooms, all with their doors closed. "I know you like the library, Miss Hampton." He moved a few steps ahead of her. "I'll take you there."

"Thank you, James, for remembering."

On her previous visit, she had remarked the library was her favorite room. It was the only one in which she felt comfortable. All the other rooms lacked warmth, reminded her of an exhibit cordoned off at a museum. *Look but don't touch.* Furnished with too many elaborate pieces for her liking, the house screamed of opulence and eccentricity. There was nowhere to look where something would not catch her eye—a painting, a sculpture, an expensive collectible, no spaces in between all the *stuff,* nowhere to breathe. In contrast, books in dark mahogany shelves filled the library, which for Kate, gave the room life.

James opened the doors to the room located at the far end of the floor. From what she recalled, the library was added as part of a new wing during one of the home's many renovations. "Miss Hampton, please make yourself at home. As you can see, I started the fire. I hope you're warm enough."

"It's perfect." She placed her purse by the arm of one of the chairs.

"May I get you a coffee until your father comes?"

"No thank you. I've had my two for the day."

"Yes, ma'am." He turned to go, then stopped, stared at her with slow-blinking eyes.

"Was there something else, James?"

"No, just that …"

"What is it?"

"Your father will be happy to see you, Miss Hampton."

She sighed, expected her father would be anything but. "Thank you, James."

He left her in the room with the eighteen-foot vaulted ceilings, surrounded by three walls of more than 10,000 books. Kate took small steps along the shelves, reading the titles at eye level. The wood crackled in the stone fireplace and took the chill out of the air. The dark atmosphere in the library created an illusion of nighttime.

Even as a child, she remembered her father had an extensive collection of art books. He had added much more to it since then, particularly because of his love for

Eastern art. Half a wall was stacked with books on Asian ceramics, paintings, and furniture. His expensive taste and knowledge informed his choice of furnishings and art throughout the house. Another large section contained historical books. Her father was aware of almost every major event that changed the world, could converse about philosophy, politics, mythology, and science, moving from one subject to another seamlessly. The only genre he rarely read was fiction, though she had heard him recite more useless trivia from Shakespeare than some literary scholars she knew. His brain held boundless capacity for minutiae.

Kate glanced at her watch—three minutes to nine. It was just like her father to be punctual, never late, and certainly, never early.

She made her way to the fireplace, situated between the two lone chairs in the room, which were surprisingly not of Asian influence. The oversized wing back chairs made of well-worn brown leather sat cozy and unpretentious. They faced each other next to a twin set of teak bamboo floor lamps, probably imported and expensive. Each lamp provided a soft, comfortable light.

Kate remained standing. She turned to face the far wall of the room, counting down the seconds in her head until her father's approaching footsteps. He was right on cue.

"Hello, Kate."

Blinking once, she turned around. A shock of salt-and-pepper hair greeted her. The man appeared tanned, healthy, and nowhere near his age of sixty-two. "Hello,

Father." She took a few steps toward him.

He bent toward her, hands on her shoulders, kissing both her cheeks. When he stepped back, he looked at her with what appeared like admiration. "You've been away, Kate?"

"Yes, I returned from Jamaica not long ago."

"Nice tan ... how long has it been since I saw you?"

"One year, ten months, five days ..." She made her way to the chair with her purse on it and sat down, "but I'm sure you knew that, Father."

He sat his tall, lean frame in the opposite chair, his lips puckered in a scrutinizing expression. "Really, Kate, must you be like that?"

"Like what?"

"Like calling me Father, for instance."

"Would you prefer John?"

Vacant eyes stared back at her. "No," he said.

"Then Father it is."

At that moment, James entered the room carrying coffee and tea on a silver platter. He set down the tray on the Noguchi table in between them. A plate of petite madeleines rested on napkins next to the silverware. Fresh out of the oven, the shiny morsels hinted of lemon zest and almonds. "Kate, please have something, may I pour you a cup of tea?"

She admired the plate of little oval cakes lightly dusted in powdered sugar. "All right, James, I'll have tea."

His face brightened as if she had said he won the State lottery.

"I know you love madeleines." He offered the tea to her. "I baked them just for you."

She gave him a big smile. "Thank, you, James. I thought I detected a sweet scent when I came in." After a sip of tea, she replaced the cup on the saucer.

"My pleasure." James gave a quick glance to her father who shook his head. "I'll leave you two then." After he exited the room, James pulled the French doors shut.

Kate slid her cup and saucer on the table. She unfolded a linen napkin over her lap and placed one of the shell-shaped cakes on a dessert plate. All the while, she was aware her father was staring at her, yet said nothing. It was his way of rattling her, but she would not have it.

She picked up the warm cake and took a bite. "Delicious."

"Glad you like it, since James went to the trouble of making it."

"He's a lovely man." James was not only the housekeeper and chef. He was also a part-time business partner and full-time confidant to her father. She took another cake for her plate. "Did you know that Marcel Proust used madeleines in his book, *In Search of Lost Time*?"

"No, I did not." He bent forward and poured himself a cup of coffee.

"Proust was trying to contrast different types of memory."

Her father dropped five sugar cubes into his cup with a pair of silver tongs.

"Yes," she continued, unconcerned by his disinterested

look as he stirred his coffee. "In his book, voluntary memory is considered flawed because it relies on our ability to consciously remember things. It can result in prejudicial, inaccurate memories since they're affected by external events." To punctuate her thought, she plopped another piece of the dense sponge cake in her mouth.

"Ergo …" He glared at her as if she were a child taking too long to make a point. "Involuntary memory is better?"

"Not better. More accurate." Kate set her plate on her lap. "There is a famous passage in Proust's book, where the narrator is emotionally overcome. Upon reflection, he realizes his feelings stem from tasting crumbs of a madeleine in his tea. The origin of the memory is revealed as an experience he had when his aunt fed him madeleine as a child." She contemplated taking another cake, decided against it. "These types of episodes, triggered by the senses, can conjure important memories of the past." Kate folded her napkin and placed it on her plate, returning both to the tray.

"Now that I know more about Proust and madeleines than I care to, why are you really here, Kate?" Her father's voice held no humor.

She took a deep breath. No amount of intellectual small talk could hide the fact that her father still intimidated her. No matter how she broached the subject, he was not going to like it. "I learned something important recently."

"What's that?" He took a sip of coffee, peered at her over the rim of his cup.

"That secrets are a heavy burden, and you and I have

been carrying them for years."

He lowered his cup on to the saucer with a pinched face. "What are you babbling about, Kate?"

"I know what you did."

"What do you think you know?"

"I trusted you." Her pulse sped up. "You threw me in a pool when I was five, do you remember?"

He narrowed his eyes, replaced his coffee cup on the table. "I was teaching you to swim."

"I would have drowned if Simon had not shown up." Heat flushed her body. "He's the one who saved me."

"Is that what this is all about?" Nostrils flaring, he shook his head. "God sakes, Kate. You've been angry with me for years, and I've had no idea why. Yes, I was a strict father, but look at how you turned out. You're a successful doctor on the board of numerous hospitals and associations. If it wasn't for me pushing you—"

"Don't …" A lump inserted itself into Kate's throat. "Don't you dare make yourself out to be the model parent, because you are the furthest thing from it." She picked up her tea and gulped down the remainder. "This is not about being thrown in the pool."

"Then get to the point." His scowl marked the end of his patience.

It was now or never. She had rehearsed the line dozens of times, but no amount of preparation could make this moment easier for her. Without a hint of emotion, she said, "You killed my mother." Kate observed her father stiffen in his chair.

"What is this?" A visible vein at the side of his temple throbbed. "All that Proust mumbo jumbo was leading to this?"

"No, that was purely coincidental." She fought to maintain calm.

"Kate, your mother drowned. You were four years old at the time, too young to remember what happened."

"I know she drowned." Her insides churned as her father fixed her with his gaze. Kate put on her best poker face. "I found her floating in the pool, remember?"

For a second, his eyes shifted from her. "If you know that Kate, why are you suddenly confused?"

His stony, imperceptible glimpse away from her was all the confirmation she needed. "I'm not confused, Father." The fragmented memories of finding her mother surfaced after she returned from Jamaica. The traumatic episode had her in pain for almost an hour until she was able to lock the images away. Only … she refused to throw the key in the ocean as she had taught herself to do. This time, she wanted residual thoughts to linger, to remember what she had always suspected. "I was never able to reconcile my memories properly, and now I understand why." Kate licked her lips. "Just because Mom drowned does not mean you didn't kill her."

Her father gave a disgusted snort, threw up his arms. "This is psycho-babble horseshit."

Lifting her chin, she notched up her courage meter. "Is it?"

"This is the reason for your visit?" He spoke through

clenched teeth. "To accuse me of killing your mother, with no proof but some old memories that don't fit right in your head? Kate, you're a shrink, but you're in desperate need of one yourself."

Spittle flew in her direction. Her father's ire only fueled hers. "Do you know I don't even remember mourning Mom? It was as if she never existed, and you were never around." Her voice deepened. "You never kept her memory alive."

"So this is punishment, right?" He jolted up in his seat. "You accuse me of something this vile to get back at me? The reason I wasn't around was because I was too busy making a living. My brother and his wife took good care of you."

"Really?" Kate braced herself against the chair.

"They did the best they could, considering they had three kids of their own."

Her bottom lip jutted out as her breathing intensified. "Your brother was a deceptive, abusive coward who terrorized his family."

"So you say. Karen never saw Matthew that way." He looked down his nose at her.

Kate pinned her eyes to her father. "That's because she drank too much and self-medicated. Did you really expect her to rat out her husband? Your darling little brother?"

"Kate, this is all old news. It's history, damn it! I've moved on. You've moved on. Why the hell are you bringing this up now?" He smudged his fingers along the heavy glass tabletop as if to rub out a stain. "My brother's dead and buried. Can't you leave him in peace?"

"I'm not sorry he's dead." Her words fell out of her mouth like ice cubes.

"Kate …" His mouth tightened. "When did you become so cold?"

"I had a good teacher." She sat in silence glaring at her father, suddenly feeling fragile. It was as though the roaring fire had sucked the breath out of her.

"And for the record, Kate …" He slanted his body away from her. "Don't paint yourself as a deprived child, because you weren't."

"Just deprived of my mother," she said, resuming her icy tone. "Aside from that, life was peachy."

From the side of his mouth, he huffed. "You're impossible to talk to."

With a bloodless hand pressed to her breastbone, Kate strived to calm her breathing. "Like you, I buried Mom a long time ago. And she has stayed locked up in my mind for all these years, but I always suspected something horrible happened to her." An image of her mother floating in the pool flashed by her eyes. Kate struggled to maintain her external cool.

Her father shook his head, heaved out a sigh that signaled for Kate, his revulsion. "What do you want from me Kate, to confess to something I didn't do?" He glowered at her. "Would that make you feel better?"

"I don't need you to confess. I'm not here to absolve you."

"Then why are you here?"

"To let you know that you don't get away with it. You don't get away with a clear conscience." She sank into the chair. "We don't have the typical father-daughter relationship, so let's stop pretending that we do."

Her words flickered like flames and disappeared into the air. She turned to stare at the blaze, felt its dry heat tighten and burn her throat. Amongst the ghosts of dead writers, the silence between them struck her as almost poetic.

"Kate …" her father said, his voice steady, "your mother suffered depression, anxiety, and a host of other conditions we didn't even have names for back then. Despite all that, I loved her."

She shot him a hateful glance. "How magnanimous of you to love her with all her problems."

"Listen to me, Kate!" he shouted, thrusting forward in his seat. "You may not want to believe it, but your mother was not well. I've never wanted to tell you this, but …"

Her tone hardened. "Say it, Father."

"All right." A pained expression crossed his face. "Your mother, she … she took her own life. Do I blame myself for not being there? Of course I do." He blew out a loud breath. "Unfortunately, it was only a matter of time. Your mother was not a happy woman."

Kate stared at him, waited, then applauded in a deliberately, slow and false manner. "Bravo, Father. You do know how to draw sympathy. You should become an actor."

He flapped his hands in the air. "This is getting us

nowhere. You've obviously made up your mind."

"I have …" She paused for effect. "And I have proof."

The skin around his mouth stretched taut, baring his teeth like a mad dog. "Proof. What kind of proof?"

"It's not important," she said, followed by a sweeping, exaggerated gesture of her arms. "You are the great John Hampton. Man of the World. Philanthropist. Respected business magnate. But from this day forward, I know what you did. And you can't change that."

From across the table, the man who gave her life stared blankly at her. Her father juggled difficult situations. He didn't get to where he was without being a shrewd negotiator with words, but Kate detected resignation in him, maybe even fear.

He raked his fingers through his hair. "You are my daughter, Kate, and I love you despite what you think of me. In time, you will realize how wrong you are."

She picked up her purse and stood up. "This is goodbye, Father. We have nothing more to say to one another."

He pushed himself up slowly, as if contemplating what else he could say. "You're being overly dramatic, Kate. It doesn't suit you."

By the time she made her way to the door, she wanted to run out. Instead, she turned to face the man who stood within reach of her, refusing to give him the satisfaction of belittling her. "You killed my mother, and for that, I will never forgive you." Thickness coated her throat. "You won't be seeing me again."

Her father stared back at her with cold eyes that gave

away nothing. "You'll be back, Kate."

She opened the door and stomped out like a runway model, focusing on the echo of her boots hitting the hard wood floors. The extravagant surroundings faded into a peripheral blur as tears welled up behind her eyelids.

At her back, her father shouted, "My blood runs in your veins, Kate Hampton!"

She stopped, closed her eyes, and swallowed hard.

"You will be back, Kate," she heard him say. "You will be back."

With tears dampening her cheeks, she lifted her chin and kept on walking.

Dr. Kate Hampton returns in

A FRAGILE TRUCE

READ AN EXCERPT

She mouthed something inaudible under her breath, then raised her head. "Dr. Hampton?"

"Yes, I'm listening, please continue."

"Sorry, I'm on edge today."

"I sense that. Has something happened?"

"Oh, you know." The pretty blond woman's head swung back and forth like a tennis ball. "The same old pattern with me, another one bites the dust."

"David?"

"Yes, can you believe it?" She collapsed in her seat and threw her head back.

"Take your time. Tell me what happened."

"Who the fuck knows? He was crazy about me only a couple of weeks ago, and now he's gone." Her eyes brimmed with tears. "I promised myself I wouldn't cry for him, now I'm crying. God, I hate myself for being so weak!"

The doctor uncrossed her legs. She pushed the box of tissue forward on the table between them.

Her patient pulled out two tissues and dabbed her eyes.

"Tell me why you think he left." As Kate listened to the predictable story, her mind wandered back to when she acquired Sheila as her patient from a fellow psychiatrist.

"You're better suited to treat her," Jack had said. "She needs a strong woman's voice."

"What's her story? I'm booked up as it is."

He pulled out a chart. "Twenty eight year old fashion designer, unmarried, low self-esteem." He scanned quickly moving his head side to side as he read. "First of three suicide attempts a year ago, last one two weeks ago, precipitated by a relationship breakup, sounds like a Cluster C personality disorder."

"Who has she been seeing?"

"No one."

"What?" She gave him a *Whatcha talking about Willis?* look.

He nodded. "She's refused all counseling, until now."

"What changed her mind?"

He mumbled his way down the chart. "Hmm … She's not working again, and the parents are footing the bill. The referral came through their family doctor. My guess is the parents are cutting her out of the will unless she gets some head-shrinking."

Kate wrinkled her nose. "You can be so crass, Jack."

"You love me, Kate." A broad grin crossed his face. "So, you'll take her?"

Kate grabbed the file folder from him. That was six months ago. Today, it would appear, Sheila's relationship failure count increased by another one.

"… I was falling in love with him, Dr. Hampton, doing everything I thought he wanted, and then … he ended it, just like that, wouldn't even accept my calls." Sheila squeezed her eyes shut, dislodging more tears. "He was only using me."

Snapping back to the present, revelatory words connected to Kate's ears. The clock discreetly placed behind her patient informed she had thirty minutes left. It was time to draw Sheila out of her self-pity and shift her into a position of power.

"You just said something extremely important, Sheila."

Sheila's posture stiffened. "I did?"

"Yes." Kate offered a warm smile, speaking in a slow, dulcet tone. "You said David was only using you. This is the first time you've attributed fault to someone other than yourself."

"I …" She covered her mouth with her hands like a surprised child. "Really? Is that a good thing?" Sheila's eyes darted left and right. "How … how is it good?"

"By all accounts, David showed interest in you, right?"

"Yes."

"You chose him based on what he wanted you to see. He deceived you."

She lifted her shoulder blades and let them drop with a heavy breath. "But why do I keep making these wrong choices?" Unshed tears formed in the red corners of her eyes.

Kate had carefully layered the foundation for Sheila's treatment, her main concern initially to alter the cycle of self-destructive behavior. Prescribing the right antidepressant was also important. When they first met, Sheila's delicate psyche was in no position to dissect her failed relationships, let alone her own culpability in attracting the wrong type of men. Now, she exhibited rational thought, or at the very least, asked questions that made sense.

"When you started going out with David, I asked how he made you feel. Do you recall that?"

"Vaguely... I'm not sure ..."

"Let me ask you now. Do you remember how you felt in the beginning?"

Sheila furrowed her brow, tapped hard on her forehead with her index finger. "I was ... yes, crazy happy, so flattered by all his attention. He made me feel desirable and special." Her eyes twinkled. "He was romantic, sent flowers, showered me with gifts. He was so generous."

"Was he generous in the bedroom?"

"Yes ..." Confusion flushed Sheila's face. "He was a wonderful lover, of course he was."

"Are you sure?" Kate knew it was a tough question, but she needed to push through.

"Yes ... What are you saying, doctor?"

"You were with him for four months. The first month was intense from what you told me, but then something changed, didn't it?" From their early sessions, Kate had deduced David possessed low impulse control. He was hypersexual, common for social predators who derived excitement from the chase. "I'm referring to when he asked you to dress provocatively in public." She tilted her head. "You were not comfortable with that, were you?"

"No ... yes ..." Sheila rubbed her nose. "I mean, I was flattered at first, and I wanted to please him, but then ... he asked me to wear less and less. He started comparing me to other women, belittled me in front of others."

Kate had suspected David of dangling his heart under false pretenses from the start. Her patient had described him as loving and attentive, but his actions showed him as a manipulator, slowly weaning Sheila of her autonomy. When she later revealed she couldn't do what he wanted, he punished her with emotional withdrawal. Sheila always blamed herself when this happened. Today was the first time she voiced a negative word about David. "It's been sometime since David has pleased you, hasn't it?"

Sheila folded her arms across her chest. "What do you mean?"

"Sexually, have your needs been fulfilled?"

Sheila's face turned ashen, and she lowered her chin. "Uh ..."

"You can be honest with me. That's what I'm here for." When her patient looked at her with wide eyes, Kate observed the fog of uncertainty lifting. "He treated you like a sex object. Only you didn't want that, did you?"

Tears rolled down Sheila's face. "No ... I truly believed David loved me. I always attract the guys who come on hot and heavy but then end it for no reason ... at least not for any reason I can see." She blew her nose quietly.

Kate glanced at the clock. "Sheila, realizing that you're attracted to the same type of man is an important step. You're becoming stronger each time you come here."

"I hope so, Dr. Hampton."

Kate shifted in her chair and leaned forward. "Let's stop here, Sheila. It's been an emotional session, but you've made good progress today."

Some of the tension ebbed from Sheila's face. She took her time gathering her belongings, wrapped a scarf around her neck and draped a trench coat over her arm.

"Hard to believe it's still so cold," she said while getting up.

Kate rose from her seat and accompanied Sheila to the door. "Winter is taking its sweet time making an exit."

"Dr. Hampton?"

"Yes?"

"I never thought I could say this after another breakup, but … I'm relieved. I feel like my head is not so foggy anymore."

Kate stopped in her tracks and offered a comforting nod. "I'm happy to hear that. I really am."

"Now if I can just avoid all the charming men who come my way, I'll be all right." Sheila expelled a nervous laugh.

Kate opened the door. "You're going to be fine. See you next week."

After her patient left the office, Kate loosened the hair from her bun and shook it out until it cascaded below her shoulders. The sound of a siren squealed by twelve floors below her Manhattan office. She stared out the window and decided to exchange her heels for boots. Temperatures were expected to rise over the next few days. Still, it was odd to see snow in April.

She was pleased with her patient's progress. The men Sheila had a history of attracting were indeed charming but dangerous. In time, Kate would reveal the profile of these charmers to her. Sheila would eventually realize David did her a huge favor by abandoning her. Not all women were so lucky to escape. For now, it reassured her that a cancer had removed itself from her patient's life.

A quick glance at her schedule showed she had more than enough time to get back from the post office before her next appointment. She pulled on her coat and checked her purse for the mail notice she received yesterday. The card indicated a delivery but didn't specify the details.

When she thought of who the sender might be, her spirit soared with excitement, only … no one would know it to look at her. The ability to mask her feelings was a skill she had mastered.

It made her an extraordinary psychiatrist. It made her an even more elusive psychopath.

ABOUT THE AUTHOR

Eden Baylee left a twenty-year banking career to become a full-time writer. She incorporates many of her favorite things into her writing such as: travel; humor; music; poetry; art; and much more.

Stranger at Sunset is her first novel, on the heels of several books of erotic anthologies and short stories. She writes in multiple genres.

An introvert by nature and an extrovert by design, Eden is most comfortable at home with her laptop surrounded by books. She is an online Scrabble junkie and a social media enthusiast, but she really needs to get out more often!

To stay apprised of Eden's book-related news, connect to her via her website at www.edenbayleebooks.com.

Made in the USA
Middletown, DE
26 September 2017